CONFESSIONS OF AN ALLEGED GOOD GIRL

Also by Joya Goffney

Excuse Me While I Ugly Cry

CONFESSIONS
OF AN
ALLEGED
GOOD GIRL

JOYA GOFFNEY

An Imprint of HarperCollinsPublishers

To all the alleged good girls.
And all the bad girls too.

1

It never fails. Daddy always finds a way to make morning service extend well into the afternoon, even after he promised he'd keep it short. Today, during his sermon, he took twenty minutes to really drive home the point that Jesus helps those who help themselves. Like, he repeated that sentence over and over, broken up by heavy gasps, performative joy, and call-and-response praise from the congregation.

And it's not just him either. Bertha, our choir director, and Miss Annabelle, our lead singer, are in on it. I swear, they try to turn every Sunday into an episode of *Sunday Best*. Not every song should be ten minutes long, and I promise you, they shouldn't all end in an elaborate praise break.

But that's partly Dom's fault. With him on the drums and his best friend, Terrence, on the bass, together they're always egging on the congregation, summoning the Holy Ghost, trying to get Sistah Betsy to jump up and down in the aisle—but really they're just trying to get her wig to fall off again. I've told Dom I'm sure she's found better ways to secure that thing on her head after how embarrassed she was that magnificent Sunday. But he thinks there's still hope.

Daddy has already "opened the doors of the church," we've already done the last offering and final announcements, but for some reason Daddy's trying to start his sermon back up. I don't have time for this. At this rate, I won't get to straighten my hair before Dom picks me up for our date tonight. Today is our two-year anniversary. I stressed that to Daddy before we left the house this morning. I said, "Daddy, tonight is important. We have to get out on time. *Please.*" But he kept saying, "You can't rush praise, Mo-Mo, but for you, I'll try my best."

Really, Daddy? Is this your best?

"It don't matter who," Daddy shouts into the microphone, closing out the service with his familiar chant. Thank *God*, we're almost out of here.

"It don't matter what!" He's got a big smile on his face, sweat dotting his forehead. This is his favorite part of the week, his favorite part of the day, his favorite part of everything. He loves being in this church more than he loves working on the deck in our backyard, and he loves doing that a *whole* lot.

I know that being pastor of this church is his greatest joy, but I don't get it. Just, like, *how?* Doesn't this get old? It's the same thing every single Sunday, ever since he was a kid. But somehow, when he was a young, poor boy in the eighties, he came to this ancient building, with its stained-glass windows, haunting

Jesus paintings, and funeral flowers, and was like, *Yeah, I like this a lot.* How can someone that young appreciate the rules and the politics and the *"shhh, pay attention"* and the *"you better close your eyes when you pray"* that comprises every Black Baptist church in the South? How does anyone of any age fall in love with that?

But it's his—the church and the congregation and the title—handed down to him after Pastor B. D. Jackson died. I was only five then, but at the time, the congregation was unsure about Daddy. Since he was so young, they worried he would be flaky. At least, that's what he tells me, because all I've ever seen is their adoration for him. They worship the ground Pastor T walks on, while I do everything I can just to keep my eyes open every Sunday.

I love my daddy, but I hate church.

The only good thing about coming to this place, sitting on the front pew beside my no-nonsense tyrant of a mother, is Dom. His drums are set up below the pulpit, so he's literally sitting in front of me at all times. He's the reason I can't ever keep my eyes on my Bible.

As the congregation shouts back, "Yeah," Dom joins in with a kick to his bass drum and a few taps on his cymbal, then his eyes lift slowly to mine.

Dominic Hudson is my daddy's protégé. He's really good at performing in church. But he's also really good at sports, so *everyone* in town knows who he is. And despite the fact that he's more involved in church than me, the pastor's daughter, he doesn't have that unbreakable reputation of being a Christian kid. Probably because he's a lot different when we're not in church, and when adults aren't around to hear him cuss.

Dom's my dream boy. He's gorgeous, popular, sweet, and really into me. When he holds my gaze, nothing else matters. My daddy's voice and the accompanying praise fade out. My heart lurches, beating faster than his kick drum. I'm so lucky to have him. That's what everyone says. I'm so lucky to have captured *The* Dominic Hudson's heart. And they're right. He treats me like my daddy treats my mom. Like a queen. Like a gem. Like *his*.

Dom smirks at me and nudges his head over to Deacon Hanson, whose eyes are closed and whose face is pointed up to the ceiling, as if he's wrapping himself in God's word. Dom rolls his eyes to the back of his head and moves his mouth up and down like a fish. He's so goofy, and he knows exactly how to make me laugh.

But then, amidst my snickering, my mother snaps her fingers in front of my face.

My stomach clenches, and the butterflies inside go *poof.* Looking at her is like looking at Medusa. Her dark, narrowed eyes and flaring nostrils turn me to stone. That's the second time she's caught us playing around today. She leans into my ear. "Don't make me get onto you again, Monique, or I promise you won't be going *anywhere* tonight."

She straightens her back and crosses her legs at the ankle, pasting a pretty church smile back on her face. It's not like my mom is ever a sweet person, but in church, she's extra, *extra* callous. She won't have me embarrassing her in front of all these people.

Ever so perfect and elegant, my mother is exactly who you picture when you think of *Southern Black Women*. She carries herself like a queen, and in this tiny town with only about ten percent Black people, we kind of are royalty. My daddy is the pastor of the only Black church in town; he's a mentor to all the Black athletes and friends with all the coaches. Everybody knows him, and everybody knows my mother—pastor's wife, first-grade teacher, three-time first-place winner of the Annual Fall Festival Pie Baking Contest with her famous sweet potato pie.

While I'm just their daughter. Which means people at school tend to be careful around me. They tend to watch their language, neglect to invite me to parties because they know I won't be allowed to go anyway, and act like I'm some Goody Two-shoes snitch, even though I've never snitched on anyone in my life. I wish I was afforded the same benefit of the doubt that they give Dom—even though he's practically the pastor's son, he's still *cool*.

"Amen," Daddy says, calming the congregation, wiping his brow with his handkerchief. "Praise God. Now, as you know, every first Sunday I like to have our closing prayer led by one of the youthssss," he hisses, amplifying my anxiety, because then Mom lays her hand on my back and starts pushing me forward.

No. I will not get up in front of all these people and pray.

With literally every Black kid who goes to my school watching? Nope. Not only will that be terrible for my already ingrained reputation as a church girl, but I'm also just really bad at it. Daddy says praying is as simple as having a conversation with God, but it's obvious that there's a cadence to it.

"Anybody?" Daddy asks, looking around the church.

"Go," Mom says, pushing harder, but I don't move. And I know there's a chance she'll forbid me from going out with Dom tonight if I don't get up there, but there's an even bigger chance she'll disown me if I go up there and choke. She needs to ask herself, what's more embarrassing—me not volunteering, or me choking in front of all these people?

Before she can drag me up by my hair, Sasha Howser, Terrence's little sister, stands and goes to the front—saving me and burying me at the same time, because she's always the example Mom uses when critiquing my behavior. *Why can't you do this like Sasha or do that like Sasha?* Now I'll never live this down.

I've never seen someone so young be so committed to Christ. And I, honestly, have never hated anyone more than I hate her. She's always got her nose tucked in her Bible, always has her fingers clasped tight during prayer.

"Come on up, Sasha. Give her a hand, church," Daddy says, making his way to the edge of the pulpit to hand her the microphone. The congregation claps for her and praises her for her initiative. Mom reluctantly removes her hand from my back to join in on the praise.

Sasha walks up in her modest bag of a dress with a smile

pasted on her pretty face. Microphone in hand, she says, "Thank you, Pastor T. Everyone, please bow your heads and join me in prayer."

I bow my head, but I don't join her in prayer. I'm fuming. This might actually be worse than me going up there and choking. I just know all the way home Mom is going to go on and on about how Sasha is so much better than me.

"Father God, we come to you, humble and grateful for another day to give you the glory. You didn't have to spare us, but you did, Lord. Touched us early this morning, filling us with the breath of life."

"Yes, Lord," my mom whispers beside me.

I've got my head bowed and my hands clasped in my lap, like a good pastor's daughter, but then I feel a vibration on the pew. My open eyes widen and still, my gaze freezing within the cracks of my knuckles. It's not my phone—I know that immediately. It's Reggie's.

I almost forgot that he was sitting next to me. He's been unusually quiet and well-behaved, up until now. I watch out of the corner of my eye as he reaches into his pocket and pulls out his phone. The screen says "Laser" as it buzzes in his hand. I can feel my mom's nerves getting worked up, feel her body getting stiffer with every second that he doesn't decline the call.

Then, oh my God, while Sasha prays into the microphone, and as the congregation throws in "Yes, Lord" and "Amen" and "Thank you, Jesus," Reggie *answers his phone.*

"Yo, Laser." Then he laughs.

My mom scrambles, pushing against my shoulder as she reaches across me.

"Nah, man, I'm gonna have to call you—"

Mom snatches the phone right out of his hand, scowling at him in utter disbelief.

My body burns with embarrassment. And I'm not exactly sure what I'm embarrassed about. That everyone is looking at us? Yeah, but also how my mom has no shame in disciplining a child who isn't even hers. I know that while he's at church, Reggie is our responsibility—we're his ride here and back—but still.

He looks at my mom, aghast at her audacity, then he looks down at me, like I have the power to do anything about it. I don't. So I slowly duck my eyes back down to my lap, clasp my hands a little tighter, and mentally thank God for what just happened. Nothing I've done today compares to what Reggie just did. Mom won't even remember having to get onto me and Dom. She won't remember that it should have been me up there praying, instead of Sasha, because *Reggie answered his phone in the middle of church.*

He's not from here. And he, apparently, hasn't gotten his fill of my mom's vengeful glares, because every Sunday he makes a scene. Last Sunday, he was caught singing, "My God is awful," instead of the classic, "My God is awesome." The Sunday before that he actually tried stealing from the offering bowl, which is kind of ironic, because stealing is the whole reason he's here— in our town and in our church.

From what I've heard, Reggie used to live in Huntsville, just one town over, but he allegedly got expelled for breaking into his school and stealing a bunch of dumb stuff, like those crappy TVs that teachers wheel in when they don't feel like teaching. You would think he'd have learned his lesson. But lessons slide off this boy like bald tires on black ice. Nothing fazes him. Especially not Daddy praying for him at every family dinner, forcing him to be here every Sunday, or making him do volunteer work around the church, as if just being in this building will change his heart. He's only been here a month and he's already made a terrible name for himself. I'm convinced that God has given up on Reggie, and I'm starting to think my daddy should too.

Sasha closes out her prayer and Reggie exclaims, "Amen," louder than anyone.

My mom drops his phone in her purse and whispers, "See me after church."

He smiles back at her sweetly. "Sure thing."

I don't think he understands what he's getting himself into with my mom. She doesn't hold herself back for anybody, and she definitely doesn't stand for being disrespected by a child—especially not troublemakers like Reginald Turner. She's had more than twenty years of experience with kids like him in her classroom. She didn't get her reputation as the most respected teacher in the district by letting kids walk all over her.

After service, Mom holds him hostage in the back seat of our Cadillac while she and Daddy make their rounds, consulting with everyone in the congregation. And when they get stuck in a day-long conversation with Deacon Hanson about how he's still waiting on his disability check, Dom pulls me around the side of the church.

Pinkies linked, I check over my shoulder at the crowd in the grass lot, then back to his low fade and the chain around his neck. I notice a red gift bag dangling from his free hand and bite the corner of my lip. He got me a gift? Glimpsing the size of the bag, I think it must be jewelry. Maybe a ring—a place-holder until we're old enough to be married, like my parents.

They were together at seventeen, just like us. After high school, they went to the same college, graduated four years later, got married, and conceived my sister. They did every-thing right. That's all everyone (especially my parents) has ever wanted for me and Dom—for us to do everything right.

He presses my back against the big oak tree behind the build-ing, our feet caught in the grooves of the roots, then we turn invisible. We've got spots like this all over town, spots where we can kiss without anyone (Mom) calling us inappropriate, "trying to be grown," or demons of lust. But Dom's kisses liq-uefy me. I *am* a demon of lust. I am raging hormones cloaked in a church dress.

"I got something for you," he says against my mouth. My eyes flutter open as he pulls back, blinking at me with his heavy brown eyes, the color of iced tea in the sun. My heart drums against my chest when he holds up the little red bag. "I couldn't decide if I should give it to you now or tonight. But I figured I'd give it to you now, so you can wear it for our date."

My eyes bulge. It's *definitely* jewelry.

It's one thing to wear Dom's letterman jacket—to have its sleeves swallow my arms whole, to have his last name, *Hudson*, printed on my back as I stroll down the hallway. But a ring? That would make me more than just his high school girlfriend. It would make me his future.

I take the bag with a stupid grin on my face. "I thought we said we weren't doing gifts."

He shrugs. "Couldn't resist."

There's a single piece of red tissue paper stuffed inside. After I pull it out, my fingers land on something softer and much more delicate than the tiny felt box I expected. I hold my expression steady as I pull out a clump of red lace. "Is this . . . lingerie?" I ask, horrified and disappointed and confused, but still smiling.

"Yeah. We were gonna try again tonight, right?"

My lips still. *Were* we? I was really hoping tonight would be unencumbered with struggle. I drop my gaze to his black dress shoes tangled in the tree roots, sorting through the sudden anxiety clogging my throat.

"Mo, it's our two-year anniversary." His tone hardens. "I think it's about time we get this figured out, once and for all."

"I know," I say, nodding but not making eye contact. When I look back up, his expression is toeing the line between frustration and anger.

"You *want* to have sex, right?" he asks.

I think so. I mean, yeah. I do. I really do. But for some reason, for me, just wanting to isn't enough. I nod and force a smile, though, because I don't want him to stop believing in me. "I'll wear it for you," I say.

"Yeah?" His eyes light back up, and he kisses me fast. "I can't wait to see you in it. And you know what?"

"What?" I ask, trying to feign enthusiasm.

"I've got another idea for how to make it work this time." I ask him what it is, but he just snuggles his face into my neck. "I'll tell you later." I giggle at his tickles, then find his chin and pull his lips back to mine. We kiss through the chattering and the laughing at the front of the church. We kiss through my fear and my apprehension. We kiss like a married couple.

My daddy says kids like us should keep our tongues in our mouths. He says kisses on the lips shouldn't last any longer than a couple of seconds. Anything longer is a precursor for activities that we've got no business partaking in—until we're married. But Dom and I are in love. He's the only boy I've set my eyes on for the past ten years, and eventually we *will* get married. So, what's the use in waiting? If we end up in the same place as my parents, who cares about all the stuff in the middle?

Dom slides his lips over my neck, slides his hands down my backside, filling up his palms and squeezing. I tilt my neck to the right so he can kiss me lower. Then, as his lips near the neckline of my dress, I hear "Monique?" behind us.

My eyes pop open to find Reggie standing a few feet back, watching us go way too far on church grounds. I rush to lift Dom's hands off my butt. "Yeah?" I squeak.

"Sorry to interrupt, but your dad told me to come get you."

I nod at him, my cheeks on fire. "Okay. I'm on my way."

He takes one last look at us tangled up together. Then he spins on his heel and heads back to the front. God only knows how long he'd been standing there, or how much he saw.

Dom slides his hands over my backside again. "I love your dad, but I don't understand why he's trying so hard to help that kid. He's a lost cause."

"Daddy doesn't think there's anything wrong with Reggie."

Dom pushes off the tree and grabs my hand, leading me around the side of the church. "Oh, there's definitely something wrong with Reggie. I mean, who answers their phone during church?"

When we get to the front, my parents are beside the Cadillac. The second my daddy sees Dom, his smile grows too big for his face. That's how he always reacts when he sees Dom. Daddy grabs him by the back of his neck and pulls him into his chest. "Good job up there, boy."

"Thanks, Pastor T." Dom laughs sheepishly, pulling out of my daddy's embrace. "But Pastor, I was wondering, am I still good to take Mo out tonight? It's our anniversary."

Daddy looks at me, like he's thinking about it. "I don't know."

I tilt my head impatiently. "Daddy." We talked about this at length before church. He knows how much I've been looking forward to tonight.

"I'm serious, baby. Your auntie and uncle are coming over for dinner. Maybe you two should join us, instead of going out."

"Daddy, no."

"And there's that movie you've been wanting to watch. What's it called?" he asks me. "That's right. *Terrible Twos*."

"Daddy, that's you! You've been pushing that movie on me for weeks!"

He laughs, pinching my cheek. "I'm just messing with y'all." Then he opens the passenger-side door and reaches for Mom's hand. "Of course y'all can go out. What's on the agenda for tonight?"

The tiny gift bag in my hand suddenly weighs a ton.

Dom says, "Probably go to dinner in Spring—somewhere we've never been before. That's almost to Houston, so we might be a li'l late getting back." He's trying to tack on time in case our *once and for all* takes longer than planned.

Daddy tilts his head. "Are you asking for an extension on her curfew?" He smiles.

"Daddy, it's our anniversary," I say.

And just when it looks like he's about to agree, Mom comes in and sucks the fun out of everything—as usual. "Monique's curfew is ten p.m. Absolutely no exceptions, Dom."

Dom and I both look at Daddy, waiting for him to override her decision, but she keeps going. "And you *need* to stop all that playing in church. Stop distracting my daughter, or else *this*"—she waves her finger between me and Dom—"is over."

There it is—the ultimatum. Dom nods. "Yes, ma'am. I understand. I'll have her back by ten o'clock sharp."

Dom knows my parents as well as he knows his own dad. And with my mom, he knows exactly the point to stop pushing. He's spent enough time with her to know she doesn't bluff.

Daddy leads her into the passenger seat, closes her door, and walks around the front. "See ya at the house later on, son."

"Yes, sir."

Reggie's already buckled in on the other side when I climb into the back seat. Dom bends down and whispers in my ear, "I'll pick you up at six. Don't forget to wear that for me tonight." Then he kisses my cheek. "See y'all," he says before shutting my door.

I stay facing forward, not watching him grow smaller in my window, not looking down at the burning-hot contraband in my lap, ignoring his words ringing in my ears: *once and for all.*

2

The car ride home is awkward.

I'm staring out my window at the pine trees lining the road, while freaking out about the fact that Reggie caught Dom and me making out behind the church—what we must have looked like from his perspective, what he must think of us, what he must think of *me*.

I'm not the kind of girl who gets caught making out with boys behind buildings—at least, I don't want anyone to think I am. As much as I want to shed this church-girl image, I don't want to replace it with *that* one.

Reggie doesn't say a word about it, though. He doesn't really get a chance, what with my mom chewing his head off about answering his phone during service. He's staring out his window. I don't even know if he's listening to her.

She asks him, "Will your mother be home when we get there?"

Two whole seconds go by without an answer. I check his side of the car, and yep, he's wearing AirPods in his ears.

I stare at him, aghast. Doesn't he get enough of being in trouble? How is he so unafraid of punishment?

Maybe I should warn him. Maybe I should reach over and tap him on the shoulder, be like, *dude, take those out,* but I don't think of it fast enough. Mom checks over her shoulder, and her mouth plops open. "Reggie!" she snaps.

He slowly turns to face her with a conniving smile. "Yes?"

"Give them to me," she growls, holding out her hand.

"I mean, I'm not even listening to anything."

So, he was blatantly ignoring her?

"Give them to me," she says again.

"I'm almost home anyway."

She raises her voice, her left eye twitching. "Give them to me!"

It drops my stomach. Reggie licks his lips and swallows hard. He takes them out of his ears and hands them over. Mom drops the AirPods in her purse alongside his phone. And now the car is silent, except for the light rumble of our tires on the road, the light shush of air blowing through the vents, the light whisper of gospel on the speakers.

Mom says, while facing the windshield, "While you were ignoring me, I asked if your mother is home right now."

"I don't know," he says. "How about you give me my phone and I'll give her a call?"

Mom looks at him over her shoulder, wordlessly, and waits.

He stares back, testing her with cold, hard eyes. He has no idea who he's messing with.

Finally, he breaks and says, "She's working today," and turns back to his window.

"Is that right? Last time I talked to her, she told me she doesn't work Sundays."

"Hmm, that's weird." He looks at her with a furrowed brow. "She's never home on Sundays, so . . . Do you think she's . . . No, she couldn't be." He looks at me with mock thoughtfulness. "Could she be leading a double life? Maybe she's secretly a mule for the cartel, and at this very moment she's smuggling drugs over the border. That'd be pretty crazy, though, because all my mom talks about is *promise me you won't do drugs*, and here she is, smuggling. How hypocritical."

My mom looks at him with parted lips. She has no idea what to say to him, and it's . . . hilarious. It's *hysterical*. I don't think I've ever seen her so speechless. I laugh. I can't help it. Everything he just said is the most ridiculous nonsense I've ever heard, and his fearlessness is even more ridiculous.

He looks at me, surprised to hear me laughing. Then he smiles. And I don't think I've ever seen him smile before—at least, not genuinely. I know how unhappy he must be living in this tiny town and going to our church every Sunday and sitting through unsolicited car lectures from my mom. So, it's weirdly satisfying that I'm able to make him grin.

But then I catch myself, because I know I'm not supposed to find his disobedience amusing.

"What's so funny, Monique?" Mom asks, turning around in her seat.

I cannot afford to get on her bad side right now. I have to keep the focus on Reggie and his unruliness. "Nothing," I say.

She scrutinizes me a second longer. Then, thankfully, she turns back to Reggie. "Everything's a joke, huh, Reggie? Everything is funny?"

He shrugs. "It really depends on your perspective."

I cover my nose and mouth, hiding my enjoyment of this.

"Were you laughing when you were in the back of that squad car?"

The smile slips off my face at the same time that the smile slips off his.

"And I bet you won't be laughing when you end up in juvie. Start your life this way, laughing in the face of authority, and you'll spend your whole life in and out of the system. I've seen it time and time again with my students. You're only sixteen years old. You still have time to make something out of yourself, but you want to laugh. Try laughing when the only place you can call home is prison."

I can see the fury stacking in his jaw. I can see her words poking at his composure, and I'm not sure what will happen if he loses it. Nothing good, because if he goes up against my mom, he *will* lose. He hasn't had enough experience with her to know how badly this will end.

And maybe I should say something, save him from himself, but the worse he behaves, the better my chances are of never hearing a word about *my* behavior.

"You know what?" Reggie says with a furious smile.

Don't do it.

"You don't have a clue—"

No, I can't just sit here. I can't let him do this to himself, so I cut in. "Mom, did you hear the way Sasha prayed during service today? Can you say pretentious?" Then I laugh.

My mother stops and slowly switches her attention to me, brows furrowed. It's like I threw gasoline on the flames. "Excuse me?" She gets so triggered. "Sasha did an amazing job. When your father asks for a youth leader to lead us in prayer, *you* should be the first one up, instead of flirting with Dominic for the entire service. I shouldn't even let you go out with him tonight!"

I bite my lip, bracing myself.

Then Reggie looks my way. I can feel his head turn, feel him staring at my cheek. I hesitate to meet his gaze, but when I do, I can see in his eyes that he knows what I did for him. Within our gaze, there's understanding. Because he caught me and Dom making out behind the church, but he would never say anything about it to my parents. He's sorry that I have to live with this woman, while I'm sorry he has to deal with her at all.

It feels like it's us against the parentals, like we're a team. And it's really comforting right now, because I haven't felt this kind of camaraderie since my sister left. A quick little smile lifts one side of his lips as he ducks his eyes away and back to his window.

Second time that I've been able to make him smile.

"You don't see Sasha wrapped up in some boy. She always pays attention, she always sings along to every song, she never forgets her Bible at home. Did you know she's planning to start a Christian club at your school?" Then Mom looks back at me, snarling. "A stranger might think *she* was the pastor's daughter."

My eyebrows twitch. Don't take anything she says personally, I remind myself. Nothing she says counts. But it's difficult to defend against comparisons to Sasha, because Sasha is everything I should be. She's an amazing singer. She's amazing at praying. She's genuinely enthusiastic about church. I can't make myself care like that. I barely even know if I believe in any of it. But Sasha? Sasha takes church with her everywhere.

"B," Daddy says, grabbing Mom's hand and holding it on the console. "Volunteering in church and doing this and that doesn't make Sasha any better than my little girl. God knows Mo-Mo's heart." He looks back at me with a comforting smile. My muscles relax as I sink into his warmth. That's why I love him. My daddy might be a pastor, but he's not cold and unforgiving. Not like my mother. He says, "And I'm proud to have Dom in this family as well." He kisses the back of Mom's hand. "I don't trust anyone else with my little girl. He's the perfect gentleman."

I smile at hearing my daddy stick up for me and Dom, but at the same time Reggie snorts his disbelief. I cut my gaze over to his side of the car to find him smirking at me with a cocked eyebrow. He mouths the question, *The perfect gentleman?* Then to demonstrate the irony, he wraps his hands around an invisible body, closes his eyes, and starts miming my make-out session with Dom. My eyes round as I check to see if my parents are watching him. Daddy's still listing all the reasons Dom is a perfect match for me. Mom's just listening.

"Stop!" I hiss at Reggie.

He puts his hands down, slips his tongue back in his mouth, and opens his eyes. Then he looks at me with a subtle, playful smile. This is a first for us. Usually, on the rides home from church, we keep quiet and keep our eyes on the trees flashing past our windows. We never smile at each other, and we for sure never *tease* each other.

The sun flashes across his face, and for the first time since I met him a month ago, I notice the freckles sprinkled across his nose and realize that I've never seen a Cupid's bow as deep as the one parting his top lip. For a second, I allow my stomach to fill with butterflies.

Reggie is supposed to be the bad boy—the mysterious, hardened criminal that my daddy is trying his best to reform, because that's another one of his hobbies. He takes bad boys and makes them good. He did it for Dom way back when we were kids. He did it for Tyreke and the Johnson brothers, and he'll do it for Reggie too.

I've gone this whole month under the impression that Reggie didn't know how to smile. I've gone this whole month thinking he was cold and hard like peppermint candy, but his smile makes me think otherwise. His smile is much warmer than I expected. Makes me want to smile too. And I do. . . .

But not for long.

When my daddy glances in the rearview mirror and says, "You know, Reggie, you and Dom could probably be really good friends, if you tried talking to each other," I quickly turn out of his hazel eyes and back to my window. I haven't felt these kinds of butterflies in years—at least, not for anyone besides Dom. That realization is unsettling.

Reggie doesn't respond to my daddy, and no one says anything else until we pull up to Reggie's ancient blue house, falling apart in the middle of the woods. Mom hands him back his phone and AirPods, and he hurries to open his door. "Thanks, Mr. T."

"Pastor T," my mom corrects him. It's either Pastor T or Mr. Tinsley. *Never* Mr. T.

"We'll talk later, son," Daddy says. "Tell your mom we said hi."

"Tell your mom that we will be calling her," Mom adds.

I hide my eye roll.

Reggie gets out, but he falters, holding one hand on the edge of the door and the other on top of the car. When I catch his hesitation, the pointedness of his inspection of me makes the hair on my arms stand at attention. He looks like he has words for me. But he doesn't say them. He closes the door, and Mom starts bad-mouthing him as soon as he's out of the car.

As Daddy turns around in his driveway, I watch his lanky body kick up rocks. Until he glances over his shoulder at the car. At *me*. He catches my eye, and I jerk away, my heart racing faster than it should.

I wonder what that was. That look. What did it mean? What were the words on his tongue? Why do I care so much?

No, I don't. I don't care.

All I care about is my date in a few hours. All I care about is Dom.

3

My big sister taught me how to do makeup when I was twelve and way too young to be wearing makeup, according to our mother. Mom would always blow a gasket when Myracle made up my face like an Instagram model's, but My-My was just trying to practice—she hated wearing makeup on her own face. She just liked doing it.

I wonder if, wherever she is now, she's still doing other people's makeup. If she's making a career out of that. I know how much she cherished her precious creativity—so much so that she'd throw away our relationship for it. Surely, she's still pursuing a career in art.

With one eye closed, leaning over the sink in what used to be our shared bathroom, I apply my eyeliner as carefully as I can—my hand has never been as steady as Myracle's. But then a head pops around the corner, appearing next to my reflection and scaring the bejesus out of me.

"Aunt Dee, could you not?" I grumble, putting down my eyeliner and reaching for my makeup remover. Now there's a little heartbeat in what was supposed to be a flat line above my lashes.

"What are you doing?" she asks, leaning against the doorframe, watching me remove the liner from my eye.

"My makeup." *Clearly.*

"For what? It's just us at dinner tonight."

I take a deep breath and try laying the liner again. "Dom and I have a date."

She jerks her head back with an amused smile. "You two go on dates? Aren't you, like, twelve?"

"I'm seventeen." And I still can't for the life of me get my liner to match on both eyes. "Today's our two-year anniversary," I say, reaching for the remover again.

"You really suck at this." She grabs my shoulders and steers me to the toilet lid, where I sit with a sigh that sinks my shoulders. "Two years, huh?" she asks, while removing my shoddy work. "Wow. I can't believe you put up with that egghead for that long." I frown, and she laughs. "No, but seriously, you and Dom are a lot like your mom and dad were back in high school."

My face settles and questions swirl around in my head. "That's what Daddy says, but I don't think I'm anything like Mom." And Dom may seem like a perfectly innocent boy, but he's nothing like my daddy. She doesn't know what we have planned for tonight—or the fact that tonight isn't our first time trying to have sex. My parents, on the other hand, waited until marriage.

"Your mom is kind of a hard-ass now—only because working with kids and having to demand respect every day forced her to be—but she used to be . . . cool."

"Cool?" I laugh. "Not as cool as you." Because where my mom is the epitome of elegance and class, Aunt Dee is the definition of *cool*. I mean, out of the blue, she chopped off all her hair and dyed it purple. She has tattoos up her arms and wears a different pair of trendy glasses every time I see her and clothes so tight they look painted on. I've always kind of wished *she* was my mom instead of her big sister, but I don't know, Aunt Dee is also kind of a mess. She doesn't act like a mom, or even an aunt, for that matter. She acts like my sister.

"Oh, Bianca was much cooler than me. I used to hide out in the library. Your mom was the cheerleader type."

"Yeah, but that doesn't mean she was cool. She was just popular. I mean, she's popular now, but she's still not cool."

Aunt Dee grabs the eyeliner off my sink and rests her hand on my cheek. "Well, *I* thought she was cool. At least, before she got with your dad."

"Why do you hate my dad so much?"

"I don't hate your dad. I just don't think he's—"

"Cool?" I ask.

"Yeah," she whispers. "He's not cool enough for your mom."

"I think you've got it all wrong." *And all kinds of backward.* If either of my parents is "cool," it's my daddy.

She starts on my mascara, not arguing. "So, what are you wearing for your little date?"

I wave my hand over my long blue T-shirt dress and white sneakers. I can't see her expression, but I can hear the disgust cracking across her face. "Are you fucking kidding me?"

"You can't cuss in here," I hiss.

"And you can't leave the house wearing *that*. Oh my God, did Myracle teach you nothing?"

My sister was also really into fashion—another reason Aunt Dee reminds me a lot of her. But the way Aunt Dee casually mentions her catches me off guard. My parents and I never talk about Myracle, like *ever*. It's almost as if she was never a part of our family. Hearing her name come so easily out of Aunt Dee's mouth is unsettling, but also a little refreshing. I have to admit, I miss Myracle. A lot more these days, since I have no one to talk to about this sex thing. I know if Myracle was here, she'd have a solution drawn out in seconds.

I open my eyes as Aunt Dee runs across the hall to my bedroom. "Where are your real clothes?" she shouts.

"Those *are* my real clothes."

She tsk-tsks. "That's shameful."

"What's shameful?" my mom asks, suddenly appearing in the doorway.

"This child's closet. You've gotta do better, Bianca."

"I buy my daughter appropriate clothes for her age. She

doesn't need to be showing her body. She needs to be focused on her schoolwork and God."

I think I hear Aunt Dee laugh. "Tell your teenage self that."

Mom looks at me, checking to see if I heard that. When I raise my brows at her, she hurriedly turns back to her sister. "Dee-Dee, come out of there. You're supposed to be helping me cook, remember?"

"Yeah, yeah, yeah." Aunt Dee comes out of my room holding a black maxi dress that I forgot I owned. It's just as long as the one I'm currently wearing, but it has slits that go all the way up my thighs. Mom didn't know about those when she bought it, and I was sure to not let her find out until after the expiration of the thirty-day return window. I love this dress so much, but I still haven't found a way to get away with wearing it.

"Absolutely not," Mom says.

"Oh my God, B, she's seventeen. And this is Mo we're talking about. She and that eggheaded boy don't do anything but hold hands."

I keep my expression steady. If only she knew.

"That dress is too revealing, Dee-Dee."

"Let's go." Aunt Dee grabs my mom's arm and hooks her own through it. "The food will burn."

That's the thing about Aunt Dee—she's the only person who can talk to Mom that way. I don't know why, but Mom is always a softer version of herself when her little sister's around. That's why I *love* when Aunt Dee is here. I get away with so much, like eating ice cream before dinner and watching R-rated movies and listening to non-gospel music.

Aunt Dee and Mom go back to the kitchen. Daddy and Uncle Raven are outside looking at Daddy's handiwork on the deck out back. I come out of the bathroom wearing the dress with a pair of black sandals and my hair in pigtail buns. Aunt Dee smiles, while my mom sighs, frustrated. "Dee-Dee."

"You look beautiful!" Aunt Dee exclaims.

I can tell Mom wants to tell me to go change by the way she's looking at me all uncomfortable, but then the doorbell rings. I keep watching her, though, waiting for her to finally demand that I find something else to wear, and Aunt Dee waits too. She stands beside me looking at my mom like she's *her* mom too. Maybe that's why she feels more like my sister than my aunt.

She and my mom are ten years apart, and their mom (my grandma) was pretty absent when they were growing up. Mom took care of Aunt Dee. Protected her. Supported her emotionally. And when Aunt Dee was in college, she wasn't welcome back home during her summer breaks, because Grandma didn't approve of the way Aunt Dee was choosing to live her life, so Aunt Dee stayed with Mom and Daddy.

Aunt Dee has never really gotten along with Daddy. She's always said that he was the straitjacket that choked out Mom's *cool*. The only times that I ever get a peek at Mom's so-called cool is when Aunt Dee is around and Daddy's not. It's like a glimpse into what it was like when they were growing up together.

Like now—just when I think she's going to demand that I

go change, Mom's eyes soften. She says, "You better go, before your daddy sees you."

Wait, seriously?

Aunt Dee hisses "Yes!" as my eyebrows shoot up. Then she's pushing me to the door before Mom can change her mind.

Dom stands on the steps outside. When he sees me, his lips part. I'm always so covered up—not as much as Sasha, but still, he's never seen me like this. "Hey, Mo," he says, breathless, pulling a flattered smile to my lips, but then he realizes that Aunt Dee is standing behind me. He straightens his face. "Hey, Aunt Dee!"

"That's Mrs. McDowell to you."

"Sorry," he says with a polite smile. "Hey, Miss McDowell."

"*Mrs.*," she corrects him again, pushing me out the door. "Go on, get out of here."

"Back by ten," Mom shouts after us. "Not a second later!"

"Yes, ma'am, Momma T," Dom calls back, grabbing my hand. He leads me down the driveway to his truck. My heart races faster with every step we get farther from my house and closer to our "date."

I didn't prepare for this. I've been getting primped up, trying to figure out how to put on the lingerie, trying to figure out a restaurant to lie about going to, but I haven't for a second thought about the sex.

He opens the passenger-side door of his rickety old Chevy, and when I don't immediately step inside, he asks, "Are you ready?"

No.

But I nod with a glassy smile. "Yep." He helps me climb inside, and I'm sweating in places that I really wish I wasn't. Then I watch as he skips around the front, excited out of his mind.

I'm wearing my favorite dress. My hair is perfectly pinned up. My makeup is flawless. But none of that matters where we're going, because as soon as we get there, Dom will take my dress off and reveal the red lingerie underneath. My head will be pinned to the bench seat of his truck, mussing up my laid edges. My makeup will be smeared by sweat and Dom's lips.

I think a part of me wanted Mom to cancel this date, because as much as I want to have sex with Dom, I'm scared of disappointing him again. And maybe that's why I stepped in when Reggie was about to blow up—maybe it had nothing to do with saving Reggie and everything to do with avoiding what comes next.

4

New Waverly is one of those towns you fly through on that long drive from Dallas to Houston. Once you hit New Waverly, about an hour later, you'll finally be in H-Town.

And on your way through, you might say, "*New* Waverly? Well, where's Old Waverly?" And you might be joking, but . . .

Old Waverly is east of the tracks. It's one of those unincorporated communities that you only know about by living there. That's where Dom lives, in a house probably as old as the unincorporated community itself, cow pastures surrounding him on all sides.

And five miles up the road from his house, there's an unmarked dirt road, so thin and bumpy that at some points it starts to feel like a trail rather than a road. After about a mile or two, it opens up to a creek with a gravel bank where people probably fish, but *we've* never seen them. The creek is one of the places where we turn invisible. It's the only place we feel safe enough to take our clothes off.

It's been two months since Dom and I last tried to have sex. The last time was after our junior prom, this past April. The memory burns so bright, I could swear it was last weekend.

I cried—not because of the pain. I had every intention of pushing through the pain, but when it didn't happen that way, my spirit broke in two. I was tired of trying and failing. I was tired of disappointing Dom. I was tired of not knowing what we were doing wrong. So, I cried hard and loud, and Dom had never seen me that way. He gathered me against his chest and told me it was okay. But I knew he was just as frustrated as me.

"Huh, Mo?" Dom asks.

"What?" I turn away from my window. The sun is sleeping now, and in its absence, we're left with pink and orange streaks in the sky.

Dom examines the panic in my eyes. "Are you okay?" He's driving ten miles per hour up the dirt road—anything faster might knock off a wheel.

I nod with a tight smile. "I'm fine."

But he knows me. He knows exactly what's on my mind, and he knows that I'm not okay. "Did you see Deacon Hanson waving his cane in the air today?" he asks.

My lips curl up on their own, and I laugh despite everything I'm feeling. I can't resist, and he *knows* that. I love trash-talking people from church. "I can't believe he didn't fall," I say, excited.

"Mo-Mo, I told you ain't nothing wrong with that man. He

just wants everybody to feel sorry for him so nobody can say shit when he don't put money in the offering bowl."

"No, Dom," I say, "he's still waiting on his disability check to come in."

Dom throws his head back, laughing. "That nigga on some bullshit every Sunday, I swear!"

My eyes bulge. It's still weird hearing Dom cuss. Any time we're around his dad or my parents or definitely anybody from church, he's *The* Perfect Golden Boy. But when it's only us, he lets it all fly. I just wish I had the nerve.

"And I swear he sang for ten hours straight," I say.

Dom bursts out in a negro spiritual. "Wade in the water!"

I join in, "Wade!"

We stop, keeling over laughing. I can't do this with anybody else. Pastor T's daughter, Monique Tinsley, and her perfect boyfriend, Dominic Hudson, are to be respectful and wholesome at all times. *Psh.* This is the only time we can complain.

"That nigga went on and on. The only person who could keep up with his ass was Sasha."

I squeal, "Did you see her today?"

"*Everybody* saw her! She might actually be an eighty-year-old woman trapped in a sixteen-year-old's body."

I can't breathe for laughing. "She dresses exactly like my grandma!"

"With them thick-ass turtlenecks," he adds, smiling at me. "It's a hundred and ten degrees outside! Girl, why you wearing all them clothes?"

"You know, her grandma died last year. Maybe she thinks dressing like her will bring her back."

"Mo-Mo!" Dom turns to me, surprised. My eyes widen and I instantly feel awful, disgusting, monstrous. But then Dom busts out laughing. "I swear, nobody knows how savage you are. You got everybody thinkin' you sweet or something."

I bite the corner of my lip, remembering the praise my mom rained down on Sasha in contrast with the disgusted look she gave me. It's clear she'd like to switch daughters with Mrs. Howser. That's fine. I'd rather be Mrs. Howser's daughter anyway.

"The way she was thanking God," Dom continues, "makes me think she finally got some."

"Dom!"

"Maybe somebody took one for the team, because I wouldn't touch that girl with a ten-foot pole. Probably got some spikes or a claw down there."

"You're crazy."

"Nah, but for real, you know who I bet would do her?" He looks at me with an impish grin on his face. "Reggie."

"Eww. Stop, Dom."

"I'm serious! We should set them up. Sasha can cool him down, and he can warm her up a little." I give him a look, and he laughs. "You know I'm right."

"I don't know that." I turn back to my window, remembering the look Reggie gave me when we dropped him off today. He looked like he *saw* me . . . for the very first time.

And, honestly, it felt like I saw him too. I noticed things about him, like how in the sunlight, his hazel eyes look more green than brown, and his sandy brown curls look blond, and how his lips match his skin tone. But I felt like I shouldn't notice those things about a boy who isn't Dom, so I turned away fast.

Somehow, though, that image is still burned into my brain.

After another five minutes of bumping along the trail, Dom parks on the white gravel before the creek. *Our creek.* Then he turns to me, but I don't turn back. My blood pressure is sky-high. It's time for the *once and for all* part.

"Mo-Mo," Dom croons in my ear, having taken off his seat belt and closed the distance between us on the tweed bench seat. His breath is hot and damp. It turns my stomach. "Mo-Mo," he whispers again.

My eyes are glued to the reflections of the trees in the water, but then I rip them away and peek at Dom. He's close, watching me. I'm slightly backing away, until I see the tiny gift bag in his lap, gold with white paper stuffed inside. "Another one?" I ask.

He grins. "Of course. You think all I got you was . . . lingerie?"

Well. Yeah. All I got him was my vow to try again. We agreed months ago that we weren't doing gifts. That our being together was the best gift we could give each other. Now I look like a chump.

He hands me the bag, and I have no idea what to expect. First lingerie, now what? Condoms? He watches as I hesitantly pull the paper out of the bag. But then my stomach flips at the sight of a white felt box. He *did* get me jewelry! I open it, excited. It's a very simple silver necklace with a heart-shaped charm—*simply breathtaking*, because it means so much when a boy gives a girl a piece of jewelry.

He grabs it, then motions for me to turn around. As he's putting it around my neck, he says, "Mo-Mo, it doesn't even feel like we've been together for two years. I fall in love with you more and more every day." He clasps the back, then I face him again, my eyes all gooey.

"I love you too," I say, throwing my arms around his neck. "So much."

My anxiety melts away. The weight of the necklace on my collarbone makes me want to crawl into his lap—makes me want to crawl all over him.

We're supposed to be out of town right now, eating a fancy dinner somewhere we've never been before. But we're here at the creek that it seems only we know exists, parked in his idling truck right by the water, fogging up the windows. I'm straddling his lap, fingers interlocked behind his neck. He's kissing me slowly, his lips barely touching mine, melting me piece by piece.

It's dark outside now. My lips are swollen and tingling, and my eyes are gently closed, until he reaches over to the glove compartment. "Ready?" he asks. The condom wrapper glimmers in the dark of the truck cabin. I nod, holding my breath.

He helps me out of my dress, then he marvels at the red lace against my skin. "Damn, Mo." He rips his own shirt off and gets right down to brass tacks. "So, I researched this thing called Lamaze breathing." After he lifts me off his lap, he unbuttons his jeans. "It's a technique that pregnant women use to give birth." I give him a weird look, and he laughs. "I know you're not pushing a baby out or nothing, but it's kind of the same idea, just the opposite direction." He shrugs, like he's embarrassed.

"That makes sense."

His eyes light up again. "You think so?"

"Definitely."

"If it works for childbirth, surely . . ."

Surely. I wish I could be that optimistic, but last time was our twenty-eighth attempt over the past two years. Failure after failure after failure. So much so that when he kisses me here at *our creek*, sure, I get turned on, but I also get a little triggered. I'm so terrified of what will come next.

As he delicately removes the lace from my skin, he introduces me to the mechanics of Lamaze breathing. It's kind of cute to watch how focused and excited he gets, but it's mostly just sad. Because no matter how hard he tries, his research always turns out to be a waste.

I don't want to think negatively, though. More than anything, I don't want to disappoint him again. I swear, right here and right now, twenty-nine will be my last attempt at giving him my virginity.

5

Thirty's not a bad number to be "my last." Right? It's an even number, a multiple of ten. It *sounds* better than twenty-nine. But I guess nothing sounds better than one and done.

Dom and I follow our waitress to a booth against the window. Only two other people occupy the dining room, and we're all spread out, so we have plenty of privacy. But no one is talking, especially not us.

He always brings me here afterward, like some sort of consolation prize for attempting to give him my virginity. It's like the Sprite chaser you drink after a nasty shot of medicine, or like watching a cartoon after a horror movie so the scary stuff isn't the last thing you see before bed—but I'm starting to feel like IHOP is the horror part of our movie, instead of the attempted sex we just had. It's getting to the point that the food tastes like failure, and this secluded booth feels like punishment.

His face is hidden by his menu. I glance down at mine, but

I already know that I'm getting an omelet. And I bet you a hundred bucks he'll get a burger. I don't even know why he's looking at the menu. Probably so he doesn't have to look at me.

"I was thinking—" I say at the same time that he says, "I think I might get breakfast food this time."

He looks up from his menu. "What'd you say?" His eyes look at me like he's just remembering that I'm here.

I keep my voice low. "Dom, I'm sorry."

He rubs his lips together, laying his menu down on the table, like he's getting ready to read me instead.

"I was thinking that maybe next time I can try getting drunk. Maybe then I won't feel—"

"Monique." He uses my whole name. He never uses my whole name. "You don't even drink."

"I know, but—"

"And you shouldn't have to get drunk to have sex with me." He looks back down at his menu. It sounds like he's emphasizing the *me* in his statement, like he's what's the matter with my body.

I whisper, "I've never been more attracted to a guy than I'm attracted to you. You know how turned on I get." So turned on, in fact, that we hardly need lube.

He says, "But, clearly, that's not all that matters."

The waitress bounces over to our table. "Are we ready to order, folks?" She smells like she rolled in on a cloud of cigarette smoke.

"Yeah, we're ready," Dom says, uselessly moving his eyes

back to his menu. "I'll have the Mega Monster Cheeseburger." Like always. I order my omelet, and the waitress takes our menus, leaving us with a lack of distractions and a mountain of tension.

Dom lowers his voice. "Sometimes I feel like I'm the only one who wants this to work. I'm always the one who initiates sex. I'm always the one coming up with new ideas. I'm always the one who's pushing—like, physically pushing."

"Okay, Dom." I reach for him, placing my hands atop his. "You want me on top? We can try that again next time—"

"I just don't get it." He moves his hands from beneath mine. "Are you scared about your parents finding out?"

I will my eyes to sit still. I don't want him to see my answer sitting right there in my pupils—*yes*. I'm afraid that what happened to my big sister will happen to me—that my parents will take all my pictures off the living room wall, from the day I was born to my most recent picture as a junior, and then they'll stack me up and put me away, as if I never existed. I'm afraid to lose them.

But also, *no*, because I think I'm more afraid of losing Dom.

He says, "I know we had that bogus promise ring ceremony your dad made us do at church. . . . Do you actually want to wait until marriage?"

"No! I don't want to wait."

"Okay, so . . ." He looks at me like he's all out of answers, all out of theories and techniques to try. Like I'm hopelessly dysfunctional.

I don't know what's wrong with me. It seems like everyone is having sex, so why can't I? My sister told me about her first time, how it hurt at first, but that it got better after a while. If I could just swallow the pain, we could finally get to the bliss.

"Dom, I promise, next time—"

He sighs, exasperated. "I think you should take some time to get to know your body on your own."

His words reverberate around me, melting away the pleas on my tongue. "Wait . . ." I sink into the booth cushion, hearing that *on your own* loud and clear. "Are you breaking up with me?" It's our two-year anniversary. He gave me a necklace. He can't be . . .

He rubs his hand over his mouth, not answering right away. And to me that's answer enough. I lean back, my eyes watering. So, there really won't be a next time? Twenty-nine was our last attempt—not because I succeeded, but because Dom's finally giving up on me.

6

The porch light is on—my parents are waiting up. We're ten minutes past ten, but I don't have the mental capacity to worry about that.

Dom and I are over.

It's not like we've seriously talked about marriage and kids and being together forever, but everyone thought we were headed that way—including me. Love is understanding, and Dom understands me better than anyone. He understands how hard it is being the pastor's daughter—he practically grew up as the pastor's son. Being with him was time away from all that responsibility and respectability and all those impossible expectations to be pure and perfect. I didn't have to pretend with him.

But I guess I took that for granted.

It's like when someone is always around, all one hundred and forty pounds of them, you never consider what it'd be like to have that weight drop from your side. And then, when they do, you question everything, like what was keeping them there for so long in the first place. At what point did they start slipping like old Velcro? I guess, despite our issues, I never thought we would break up. At least, not over this.

When he walks me to my front door, he hesitates at the bottom of the steps. Any other night, he'd knock on the door and deliver me directly to my father. *Be the perfect gentleman.* Daddy would invite him in, and they'd talk about something boring like sports or the deck they're building together in our backyard. I'd go to my room and start to decompress from the night, when Dom would sneak in and kiss me one last time before leaving.

He knows that can't happen tonight, so he doesn't climb the steps. "Guess I'll see you around?" he asks, like I'm just a friend who he sometimes hangs out with—not his girlfriend of two years, who he's seen at least every other day this summer.

"Will you?" I ask.

"Yeah, I mean . . ." he says, and stops. He looks at me like I should know what he means, but how can I? Dom was my first boyfriend, so I've never been dumped before. I have no idea what any of this means.

When I raise my eyebrows, he sighs. "I just think we need space."

And that gives me a little hope to land on. "How much space?" I ask.

"I don't know." He holds his head back and sighs through his nostrils. "I mean, that's kind of up to you."

If it weren't for your messed-up body, we'd be happy and perfect and still together, is what he wants to say.

"How long are you willing to wait for me?" I ask, stomach clenched, waiting for him to say *forever.*

"I don't know, Mo. I might be done waiting."

And there it goes, the hope-filled landing strip pulled right out from under me. Now I'm free-falling, flailing, crashing.

He turns and walks away from me, like it's easy, like he's been thinking about this for a while, building up to it with every failed attempt—twenty-seven, twenty-eight, twenty-nine . . .

I stare into the darkness overlaying my front yard, watch as his taillights dim and listen as the chug of his engine fades into the distance. I stare and stare and stare, because if I stop staring then it becomes real.

But then the front door opens behind me. "Mo?" Aunt Dee asks.

"Mo-Mo? What are you doing out here?" Uncle Raven says.

I'm still standing with my back to them, trying to hide the tears sparkling in my eyes, because I'm afraid if I see their concerned faces, the pain will rush out of me all at once.

But they don't give me a choice. They come around and block my view of the night. "Kiddo," Aunt Dee says, "you're late."

The night is silent and still and so dark. He's not coming back.

"I tried to stick up for you, but your mom is pissed," Aunt Dee says. "You should head inside before it gets worse."

When I don't say anything, her face scrunches and so does Uncle Raven's. She asks, "Are you okay? What happened on your date?"

That snaps me out of it. Because I realize I'm not ready to talk about it—I mean, I don't know what to say. I can't exactly tell anyone the real reason Dom broke up with me. But her question makes me realize that I'm not ready to try and come up with a lie, not for her and especially not for my parents. "Sorry. I'm fine," I turn away. "Thanks for sticking up for me."

"Yeah, good night," Aunt Dee says, skeptical.

"Night." I go inside without another word.

Okay, I have to play this right. I'm late because there was an accident on I-45. I didn't call because my phone died. As I'm turning it off so that it looks dead, Mom comes sliding around the corner. "Monique Breann Tinsley."

I slip my phone back into my purse. "Sorry, I'm late—"

"Sorry?" She breathes a hot breath. I can feel it from here. "I let you go out in that dress. And so, what? You thought that meant you could do whatever you wanted?"

"Of course not."

"I knew I shouldn't have let Dinah talk me into letting you wear that. Give a kid an inch, and they'll take a mile."

I sigh, slipping off my sandals, then I lumber past her into the living room, already tired of this conversation. But I stop in my tracks because he's everywhere. Eight-by-ten photos hang on the wall, showing him and my parents in their Sunday clothes in front of the church. Him and me on the football field after he won homecoming king. Him and his dad in Austin after winning the basketball state championship last year.

How are we supposed to get any space when we occupy so much of each other's lives? We can't break up without breaking our families apart too. My daddy's gonna be devastated. Dom was truly like a son to him.

Mom hustles after me and grabs my arm. "What took you so long to get home?"

"Baby," Daddy sighs from the couch. "Ease up. I'm sure Dom had a good reason for getting her back late."

Mom turns on Daddy. "But I specifically told Dom there was no excuse."

"She's only ten minutes late, B."

"Ten minutes turns into thirty, turns into an hour, turns into two. Then, before we know it, we have another Myracle on our hands—out partying, out *drinking*, coming home in a squad car."

I freeze at the mention of Myracle.

Daddy scoots to the edge of the couch. "That would never happen, because Mo is nothing like Myracle."

Yeah. I don't have Myracle's guts.

But I'm stunned, because I didn't know they could say my sister's name without catching on fire—just judging by the way they've skirted around the subject. Like if they even think about

Myracle in my presence, I'll morph into her right before their eyes.

While they argue about whether I'm a "good girl," and whether I'll end up rebelling like Myracle did, I take one last glance at Dom plaguing our walls, then turn on my heel and head to my room.

"Oh, no, ma'am. We are not done here."

She's right on my heels, so I stop, tilting my chin up to the ceiling. "Mom, please," I say, my self-control waning. "I really don't want to do this right now."

"I specifically told you two that there was no excuse for you to be late. I want your phone. I want your laptop. I want your TV. And don't think you're going out with Dom again next weekend—"

"Wait." Daddy crinkles his brows thoughtfully. Then he stands up, glancing around the living room like he's missing something. He asks with a tilted head, "Where is Dom?"

The house falls silent, except for the sportscaster on the television.

"I know he didn't just drop you off and leave."

My tears are welling up.

"Mo-Mo?" Daddy asks.

I shrug, not ready to tell him the truth, because I don't know if I can handle coupling his pain with mine.

When Dom's mom died, Mr. Hudson was so overcome with grief that he could barely take care of himself, much less a seven-year-old boy. Dom started acting out and so my daddy stepped in. There were some nights that Dom would stay over. I would sleep with Myracle and he would sleep in my room.

At the time, he was my very best friend, so I'd get up in the middle of the night to check on him. Sometimes I would find him fast asleep, but other times I'd find him crying. He got homesick a lot, and he didn't want to sleep alone like a "big boy," and he really missed his mom. So, I'd stay with him and hold his hand.

He stopped sleeping over when he got to be ten, and we stopped calling each other "best friend." His best friends were all boys and mine were all girls. But I was still the person he came to when he missed his mom. And my daddy was still there when Dom's dad couldn't be. Daddy would pick Dom up from practices for football, basketball, track, baseball, would drive across Texas just to watch Dom play, and would give him cash for As on his report card.

I'm not ready to tell Daddy that Dom and I are over. I'm not ready to crush his dreams of Dom becoming an official part of our family.

When I don't answer him, his face hardens. "Dom and I are gonna have to have a talk." Daddy reaches for his phone on the coffee table.

"Daddy, no!"

"Dom knows better than that." Daddy points his phone at me. "I *taught* him better than that. If he steps foot on my property, he's due to come speak to me. Especially if he's dating my daughter—"

"Well, that's the thing," I say, without enough air to support my wavering voice. "He's not dating me anymore. We broke up."

Daddy's face falls. "What?" He sounds devastated. Almost as devastated as I feel.

Mom's eyebrows go up. "You broke up on your two-year anniversary?" She's looking at me closely, scrutinizing me.

"What happened? Did you get in an argument? What did he say?" Daddy asks, trying to get to the bottom of this.

I force away Dom's hurtful words—*I might be done waiting.* Instead, I think back to when we were laughing hysterically in his truck. When the sun had gone down but there was still light in the sky. When his smile lit up the sky. When he talked about Deacon Hanson and we sang "Wade in the Water" together. I flash back through all the times he's made my abs hurt from laughing so hard, and through all the times he turned my lips extra pink from all the kissing. When we weren't struggling over sex, we were perfect.

"Did he upset you?" Daddy asks.

"*He* broke up with *me.*"

His brow furrows. "Why?"

I suck my bottom lip into my mouth. I don't know what to say. I wish I could tell him the truth. Daddy has always been my rock—the chest I fall into when I'm too overwhelmed for my own good. He's always made everything better, but he can't help with this. He can't know about this.

"I'll talk to him," he says, nodding reassuringly.

"No, Daddy."

"I'm sure he's just acting on impulse. He'll come to his senses in the morning. Whatever the issue is, I'm sure it's nothing that can't be fixed."

My eyelids flutter. I want to latch onto his certainty. I want to nod my head and let him call Dom and let him try to fix this, but only I can fix this, and I don't even know if it's possible. Nothing that Dom tried has worked. What can I possibly accomplish on my own?

Mom is silent. And her expression is unreadable. She looks almost . . . sympathetic. But then she reaches out her hand. "Give me your phone."

"Baby, just—" Daddy squeezes his eyes closed, frustrated.

"No. She came in late. There's no excuse. Give me your phone," she says, wagging her hand at me. "Now."

But what if Dom changes his mind and calls me? What if the future of our relationship hinges upon me answering him?

She's not sympathetic. I don't know what that look was, but it wasn't sympathy. Here I am, broken in pieces, and all she cares about is the ten minutes I was late.

I hand over my phone, and she immediately turns away, brushing past my father. My lips quiver, watching her glide through the living room, the bottom of her robe flapping in the wind. Then I meet Daddy's sorrowful eyes. "Do you want me to call him tonight?" he asks.

It won't do any good. There's nothing my daddy can say that'll convince Dom that he's made a mistake. And I don't need Daddy prying into our business. Dom might accidentally tell him the truth. I shake my head. "No. Please don't." Then I turn away and hurry down the hall.

"Do you want to talk about what happened?" He follows after me.

"No." *Not at all.* Then I slam my bedroom door in his face. I have no business slamming any door in his house, but Daddy lets it slide. He lets it stop him from entering, because he's always respected my space and my feelings and my boundaries. And I've always taken advantage of that.

I wait until he's gone, wait until he's cut off the TV and all the lights, then I run across the hall and turn on the shower. My skin is covered in Dom's sweat and his saliva and his cologne. The smell of his cologne makes me miss him already. When the hot water hits me, I close my eyes and run through the good parts of today—the way he checked me out in church, the way his arms looked when he was beating his drums, the way he combed his fingers through mine when he grabbed my hand.

I run my fingers up the inside of my thighs, then cup my hand around my pelvic bone. My fingers tap, tap, tap at my vaginal door, remembering how Dom lay on top of me not too long ago, remembering how he walked me through breathing. *Inhale, baby . . . now exhale.* He told me I'd feel an urge to push him out, but to breathe in *hehe* and breathe out *hoohoo*, to stop myself. I tried. I swear, I tried to breathe through it.

I'm trying *now*, trying to get my finger up there, but all I feel is a wall of flesh, and I can't get myself to push any harder into it. So, I cry. I finally admit to myself—we weren't failing to have sex because I wasn't turned on enough, or because Dom was coming at it from the wrong angle, or because of anything we were doing. The problem was and *is* me.

It's like a wake-up call, an alarm ringing in my ears. I was waiting for Dom to come up with a solution, but Dom is all out of ideas. And if I want him back, I have to get this figured out myself. It's about time I come up with some solutions of my own.

7

Mom is standing over me while I hand-wash every dish that
we own, despite the fact that we have a perfectly capable dishwasher right-freaking-there. Apparently, her job this summer is
to make my life a living nightmare. But let's be real, that's every
summer, her being an elementary school teacher and all.

After both my hands have morphed into prunes, she finally
dismisses me. "Get back to your room."

My bedroom is white—pure. My pillows all say some vari-
ant of "I love God," yadda yadda yadda. And on my walls,
surrounding all the pictures of me and Dom, are Bible quotes
that Mom probably hopes will inspire me to not be a heathen.
I don't think they've worked. I mean, at this very moment, I'm
cooking up a plan to sneak out. But does that make me a heathen? Or does that just make me determined?

I'm doing research on my laptop when she walks in. Quickly,
I close out of the tab. "Come on, let's go," she says.

I freeze. "Where are we going?"

"To get our hair and nails done, like we always do."

I look back down to my computer screen, surprised by her mercy. She was ready to take everything away last night, and she's been on my back about cleaning all day, but now she wants to reward me? So, I say, "What do I need to look pretty for? I don't have a boyfriend anymore," hoping she'll feel so bad that she'll return my phone.

Instead, she looks shaken. "Monique Tinsley, we don't do this for *men*."

"But Daddy literally pays for it." I raise a brow.

"I don't keep my hair and nails nice for him. I do it for me." She lays a hand over her heart. "It's a way that I show love to myself. Your dad just . . . appreciates it."

I nod, keeping my eyes on the picture of me and Dom that I set as my background. "That's great, but I think I'd rather be alone right now."

"Really?" She places a hand on her hip. "You're just gonna sit here and wallow?"

I shrug.

"He's not worth it, Monique."

I look up, stunned. "Isn't he, though? You and Daddy loved that I was dating Dom."

"Your *dad* loved that you were dating him. I've always thought you were too young to date."

"We're the same age as when you and Daddy started dating."

"Yeah, but your dad was different."

"How?" I ask, getting defensive.

"He had values."

Values? Like, wait until marriage to have sex, and wait until marriage to kiss with tongue, and wait until marriage to see each other naked? I refrain from rolling my eyes. "Dom has values," I say, because she's supposed to believe that he does.

She makes a qualifying face. "Your dad was different."

"How?" I ask again.

She sighs. "Come with me and I'll tell you."

Hmmm. It's tempting, but I already have plans. I drop my eyes back down to my laptop. "Pass."

She grunts and says something under her breath. "Fine. Make sure those dishes are put away before I get back."

I nod, not making eye contact.

"And do not leave this house."

I look up then. "No problem. I've got nowhere to be and no one to see." And I'm being facetious, but realizing how alone I am hurts me more than I expected. Realizing that without Dom I have absolutely no one stings and makes me wonder how I got to be so isolated. It's been a while since I've talked to my girlfriends, Donyae and Brittaniya. One might even say *years.* I mean, we're friendly at school, but I haven't talked to them outside of school since freshman year, before Dom and I started dating.

Back then, me, Donny, and Brit-Brit were all about getting our first boyfriends and our first kisses. We had this notebook that we'd trade off every other day, full of journal entries about our crushes. Donny could never settle on one boy. She had a crush in every class period, while Brit and I had our "one and onlys." Mine was obviously Dom, and Brit was madly in love with this skinny Black boy named Curtis.

Back then, Dom was all I could think about, and when he finally asked me out, he was all I had time for. When Donny and Brit would call, I stopped answering, "Hey! What's up?" and started answering, "Hey, I'm with Dom. Can we talk later?" Then, when I never called back, they stopped trying.

I never had to notice how empty my life was, because Dom filled every corner, every second, every hole. But now that he's gone, I can feel the gashes in me—the ones left by my old friends, the one left by my sister, and this extra-big hole left in my heart by Dom.

Mom rolls her eyes at my self-pity and shuts my bedroom door behind her. I wait until I hear her car door slam before running to grab my keys off my desk.

Now I'm sitting in my Kia, one town over, staring up at the building. The Women's Clinic stares back at me. I read online that seventeen-year-olds can get a standard exam without their parents' permission. I also read that it'll cost me about a hundred bucks without insurance. I only have a hundred and seven dollars, so hopefully that's enough.

Surely, a standard exam will reveal whether I was born with the proper parts—you know . . . the vagina. Like, what if I'm shaped weird down there, and that's why I can't get anything inside? Or what if the hole is too tiny?

But I'm terrified because I've never been to the doctor by myself. Mom has always set up my appointments, filled out the papers, and talked to the doctors for me. But this is something she can't know about. This issue with my body is probably something she prayed for.

I make myself get out of the car and shuffle up the concrete path.

I don't want it to be the case that I don't have a normal, penetrable vagina, but it would explain a lot. Like, look, Dom, I wasn't pushing you away on purpose. There's literally no entry down there.

As I approach the building, a woman and her teenage daughter push through the front doors. "Wasn't so bad, huh?" the mom asks.

"God, Mom, stop," the daughter growls, speed walking across the parking lot.

The mom holds the door for me with a smile. "Here ya go, sweetie."

I thank her and walk inside, consumed by jealousy. That girl doesn't know how lucky she is to have a mom who would take her to the gynecologist. And I bet it wasn't even serious—the reason she came here. She's probably getting birth control. I bet if she *was* having the problems I'm having, she could talk about it without fear of losing her parents' love.

While here I am, completely alone in a waiting room full of pregnant women, with a few expectant fathers by their sides. But look on the bright side, at least I don't recognize anyone here. . . .

Then, to my misfortune, I turn to my right. There, tapping away at the front desk, is Sasha Howser.

Every ounce of determination I had is squeezed out of my already suffering heart. God, why? Of anyone who could be sitting in that chair, you thought Sasha Holier-Than-Thou Howser would be hilarious?

She looks away from the screen, smiling until she sees me. "Monique?"

I almost turn and run, but I'm sure that would look worse. "Do you work here?" I ask.

She shakes her head. "I'm watching the desk while my mom uses the restroom. Do you have an appointment? I can get you checked in."

"Wait, your *mom* works here?" Her mom is the secretary of our church, not to mention, she's friends with *my* mom. Nope. Never mind. "Look, can you not tell anyone you saw me here?" I start backing away.

"Are you—do you need help? Are you okay?"

"I'm fine."

"Are you *pregnant*?" she whispers. I bet she can't wait to spread that rumor about me.

"No! Absolutely not. I'm, like, the opposite of pregnant."

She raises her brows. "What's the opposite of pregnant?"

"A virgin?" *A chronic virgin.* I look around the waiting room to see if anyone is listening—everyone is listening.

"So, you're here for birth control? You know, since you're seventeen, you can't get that without your parents' consent, right?"

Oh, would you just look at the smugness in her eyes. I snap, "Yes, I know that." I did a lot of research before coming here. I know my rights. "I'm only here for a checkup, but I think I'll just go somewhere else." I turn away, certain with all my heart that she's going to tell everyone she saw Pastor T's daughter at the Women's Clinic. I feel like she thinks she's better than me, but I don't know if these feelings are because of anything she's done, or if it's the way my mom is always comparing me to her.

"Wait! I can help you!"

I turn back, ready to snap at her again about how I don't *need* her help, but the way her eyes are drawn in, she looks genuinely concerned.

"What are you experiencing? Weird discharge? Fishy smell? Bad period cramps?"

I hurry back to the counter. "No," I hiss, trying to get her to stop. I swear, she's being so loud. "It's none of that. I just . . ."

I know I shouldn't trust her. If anyone would report back to my mom, it'd be her. If anyone would shun me for my impurities, it'd be her. She'd say, "I'll pray for you," then give me those disgusted eyes, while wearing that grandma-esque blouse that hides *everything.*

"I won't tell anyone," she whispers. "I had a yeast infection once, and so many girls we know come through here with

UTIs, it's totally not a big deal." When I meet her gaze, I expect to find pity, maybe repulsion, a hint of a fake church smile, but her eyes hold honest care.

"You've had a yeast infection?" I ask. I barely know what that is, but it sounds bad.

She nods with a smile. "Yep. There's absolutely nothing to be ashamed of."

I search her eyes, letting that sink in. There's nothing to be ashamed of. *She* doesn't think there's anything to be ashamed of, so I take a deep breath, take a *huge risk*, and say, "I can't get anything up there."

She doesn't even flinch. "Like tampons?"

"Like anything."

Her eyes soften with recognition. "Painful penetration?"

I nod, hopeful and scared and confused to hear those words come out of her mouth.

Then she looks over her shoulder. "My mom's coming back. Go, go, go! I'll come by your house later."

I take off to the double doors, exiting the building before Mrs. Howser can see me.

8

I get home, caught up in a whirlwind of confusion. *Perfect Miss Sasha Howser* is coming over to help me figure out why I can't have sex. What kind of sense does that make?

She called my problem "painful penetration." I've never heard it put like that. Painful penetration sounds *fixable*. My stomach fills with flutters. What if I'm able to call Dom tonight and tell him *my body works now, wanna give it another try?* He'd be so excited. Then we'd have so much room to grow together without sex getting in the way all the time.

I wish I could call him right now and tell him everything about Sasha, about "painful penetration," about how hard I'm trying now. I need to get my phone back.

As I approach the kitchen sink to run myself a glass of water, I look up and out the window to spot my daddy bent over the deck with a hammer and nail. He looks like he's explaining something, while Reggie stands two feet back, looking at his phone, not paying attention in the least. I smirk, amused. He just can't be bothered to do anything that he doesn't want to do.

Then Mom comes clicking in with her kitten heels. Her hair looks amazing, stopping at the nape of her neck. She got it dyed chestnut brown to cover her grays, with honey-blond highlights. She runs her French-tipped manicured nails through her bangs, stops behind me and peers out the window. When she sees Reggie scrolling through his phone while Daddy hammers away, she shakes her head with a disgusted frown. "Complete waste of time. That boy ain't gonna amount to anything," she spits, walking away to her and Daddy's bedroom.

My smirk returns along with a breathy laugh. She hates him *so* much. She's never been defeated by any child, but Reggie is like a brick wall—nothing gets through to him, and it gets under her skin. Sorry, but I love seeing her so bothered.

When I turn back to the window, smile on my lips, Reggie's face is lifted from his phone and his eyes are on me. He's smiling, I think. I don't know, because I drop my eyes down to the sink so quickly, busying myself with the glass in my hand, pushing down that weird fluttering in my stomach. Right. Water. That's why I'm here.

As I'm filling the glass with tap water, the patio door slides open. My eyes cut over, expecting Reggie, but my daddy steps in. "Mo-Mo," he says, breathing heavy. He smells like sweat and grass, and his hands are black with dirt. I peek out the window. Reggie's holding the hammer in one hand, but he's back to scrolling through his phone with the other.

"You got Reggie to help with the deck?" I ask, scooching over so Daddy can wash his hands.

He looks out the window. "He's not really helping, is he?" Daddy asks, looking at me with a disappointed smile.

I shake my head.

"I just gotta earn his trust, is all." He drops his eyes back down to his soapy hands. "Reggie's not a bad kid. He's just . . . defensive, always on guard. Just takes some time and patience."

I watch the water run and remember when Daddy first asked Dom to help him with the deck, when it was just a big square with nothing inside. All those weekends I'd watch as Dom would sweat out of his T-shirts. All those salty kisses he'd steal when we thought nobody was looking. I'm sure Daddy's hurting for Dom's help, especially since Reggie isn't really doing much to take his place.

God, I gotta get this figured out. I would hate for this to become our new normal. I don't know *what* Daddy will do without Dom around. I mean, they lift weights together, they get haircuts together, they mow the grass together. Who will help Daddy build the gazebo after the deck is done? Reggie?

Not if I can help it.

I press my hip against the counter, watching as he rips a paper towel from the holder. "Sorry about last night," I say.

He looks at me carefully. "Do you want to talk about it?"

"Umm." I nibble the inside of my cheek, thinking about *painful penetration* and ways to talk around the truth. "We just had a . . . misunderstanding."

"When I talked to Dom, he said that you two were only taking a break."

I look up then. "You talked to him?"

He throws his paper towel in the trash, trying to hide his guilt. "I only wanted to help."

"I asked you not to call him."

"I know, but you wouldn't talk to me, baby. I just wanted to understand what happened."

My brows furrow; I'm unsure of how to feel about that. I feel betrayed and hurt and disappointed in him. But I also get it. For him, this breakup is sudden. In the blink of an eye, he lost his son.

Besides, my pain is overshadowed by my burning curiosity about Dom and what he's been doing since he dropped me off last night. Is he hurting as badly as me? Does he want me back? "What else did he say?"

"He said that you two were taking time to figure something out—that you were at odds about something, but he wouldn't tell me what." Then Daddy lowers his chin, waiting for me to spill the beans.

"Oh," I say.

"What is it that you have to figure out?"

"I can't tell you."

"Monique," he says, deepening his voice.

"You were never supposed to call him, Daddy. This is between me and him, and I *don't* want to talk about it." I hold his gaze, standing my ground. As much as he wanted to help, he had no right to call Dom and pry, especially when I specifically asked him not to.

"Fine. That's fair." He nods, but I can see the dissatisfaction in his eyes. "Anyway, I thought your mom was being a little rough on you last night. Being ten minutes late is forgivable, especially considering what happened between you and Dom. So . . ." He digs in his pocket and pulls out my phone. My eyes zero in on it, like it's all I have left in this world. I'll do anything to see what kind of messages I have. "Why don't you give Dom a call? You've both had time to cool down. Maybe you can work this out."

I look up at the hope and desperation and worry in his eyes. And I'm transported back to just a few months ago—back to him sitting on the edge of the bleachers between me and Dom's dad. He had his hands clasped tight, leaning over his knees. "That boy's gonna give me a heart attack," he said.

"His head ain't in the game," Dom's dad said.

"His head ain't nowhere *near* the game."

They were right. Dom's head had been clouded by attempt number twenty-five. The attempt where I tried being on top . . . but I guess *try* isn't the best word. I didn't really try. Dom said, "You just sat there and closed your eyes. Baby, I can't do this by myself. I need you to try."

And I said, "What if this is hopeless?"

"You can't be so pessimistic, or it'll never happen!"

I'm not a pessimistic person. But the reality was stark. We'd tried twenty-five times. *Twenty-five.* It's hard to be optimistic after failing that many times. And I didn't realize then that my "pessimism" was driving him away. I thought we were safe.

So, I let him drop me off without a good-night kiss. And I let him get away with not telling me good morning the next day. And I let him ride on that bus all the way to Austin for the basketball state championship without texting me once—I didn't text him either. Not even to say good luck.

I sat beside my father in the bleachers, feeling guilty that I didn't "try" that night, guilty that we might lose the championship all because of attempt number twenty-five, guilty because my father kept saying, "I just hope he's okay. I don't care if we win. I just hope he's okay." Because he looks at Dom like he looks at me, and like how he used to look at my sister, like Dom is a part of him.

I take my phone out of his hand. "Okay, Daddy, don't worry. I'll get it figured out." And he actually looks relieved. His hope for Dom and me to "figure it out" is like a shove to my back.

If only he knew what he was asking me to do. If only he knew that the thing he's pushing me to figure out is how to have premarital sex.

9

Sasha Howser embodies everything people assume about me. Church girls only talk about God. Church girls don't ever take risks. Church girls are celibate. Church girls aren't any fun. "Church girls" means Sasha. Period. And I resent that.

Mom lets her in with the warmest welcome I've heard her give any visitor *ever.* When I told her that I invited Sasha over to work on that Christian club she's starting at school, Mom was so excited she wasn't even suspicious of my sudden change of heart.

I come out of my room, tense. "Hi," I say with shifty eyes. I half expected Sasha to rat me out as soon as she walked in the door. *Hey, guess who came to the Women's Clinic complaining of "painful penetration."* I wouldn't put it past her to sell me out like that.

"I'm so glad you girls decided to work together," my mom gushes.

"Me too! Monique's so wise. I know she'll have a lot of

great ideas for the church club."

Wise? I almost vomit on the spot.

My mom holds her hands over her heart, then turns to me with hearts in her eyes. "So sweet."

I lead Sasha to my bedroom, and as soon as I shut the door, she sheds her backpack *and* the act. "I think you might have something called vaginismus."

The transition between the sweet girl she was at the door and *this* is nonexistent, so I'm standing beside my desk, reeling from her sudden change in tone and personality. "What?"

She sits on my bed, opening her backpack. "Sometimes at the office, Dr. Marion lets me shadow her—like, she'll explain some of the conditions and the treatments and stuff. There's this one patient who has something called vaginismus. It's like when the vaginal muscles contract"—she balls up her fist to demonstrate—"when you try to penetrate. I'm guessing that's what's happening to you." She raises her eyebrows.

I take a slow step forward. "I don't know. Maybe."

"Grab your laptop real fast."

I do as I'm told, spinning out from how bizarre this all is, and lounge beside her on my stomach. She hands me a pamphlet titled *Curing Vaginismus—You Have Options.* I unfold it, and on one side it defines vaginismus. My back stiffens. "This sounds like it." *This sounds like it!*

I read a section that brings moisture to my eyes: *It is not normal for sex to be too painful to endure. If you are experiencing perpetual pain during sex, you should see a doctor.*

It's not normal? Well, I guess I knew my experience wasn't *normal*. I knew that sex shouldn't be this hard; I just thought that every other woman goes through this amount of pain during their first time, like a rite of passage, and that I've just been too *weak* to follow through.

"If I have this, how did it . . . why is this happening to me?" I ask, looking at Sasha for guidance.

Her eyes soften. "I'm not a professional or anything, but I could take a guess. Did you take Coach Dale's health class?"

I nod, pressing my lips together.

"So, I'm guessing you didn't learn anything about sex in that class. And I'm betting your parents didn't help."

"Absolutely not." My parents help with my sexual education? Sex is something they assume will come naturally when the time is right—that time being after marriage.

"Sometimes it comes from trauma . . . like if you've ever been sexually assaulted."

"I haven't been," I say.

She nods. "And sometimes it's because the girl grew up in a home where sex is said to be dirty and bad." She lowers her chin, like she's waiting for me to say *that's me!*

I don't say it, but we both know that it *is* me.

"So maybe you feel guilty about wanting to have sex because you think it's bad? Maybe you even feel shame? Or maybe you're just scared."

I still don't say anything.

Shame of engaging in premarital sex. Shame because my father is a pastor—I'm supposed to be the holiest of them all. Fear that it'll hurt. Fear because I *know* it'll hurt. Guilt that I've made Dom wait all this time to have sex with me. Guilt because doesn't he deserve it by now?

I meet Sasha's gaze, incapable of saying all that, then I avert my eyes, because I don't understand why she knows so much about this.

"Maybe you were just born this way," she says with a shrug. "Vaginismus is still a huge mystery in the medical field, because—"

I interrupt her, "Why are you helping me with this?"

She looks surprised by the question.

We're both lounging on our stomachs, side by side on my bed, like best friends at a sleepover, even though we're far from that. Before now, I've wanted nothing more than to see her fall off her high horse, fall into drugs or get pregnant or *something* that would keep my mom from thinking she's better than me. But now, I have no idea what to think of her. Are we sure this is the same girl who got up and prayed in church yesterday?

She says, "Why wouldn't I help you?"

I look at her, and the genuine compassion in her eyes, and I instantly feel awful, because maybe the animosity between us was entirely one-sided—*my* side.

She rolls her eyes up to the ceiling, twisting her mouth in

thought. "Okay, so it's like this: Dr. Marion is my hero. She's so passionate about what she does, and she's just so cool." Sasha glances at me with a sheepish smile, then looks down at her hands on my mattress. "Vaginismus is like her specialty—well, not specialty—just, like, she's really passionate about raising awareness of it, because it's not as well-known as it maybe should be. A lot of girls don't know what's happening to them and why they can't use tampons—"

"Tell me about it," I mumble.

"I really wish you could make an appointment with her, but she can't even diagnose you without your parents' permission."

I nod with a sigh.

"But," she says with apprehensive eyes, "I know a lot about it too. If you're cool with it, I'd love to take a shot at treating you."

"Treating me?" I ask, my eyebrows rising into my hairline. "Treating me how?"

"Like, through therapy—physical and mental. I'll come up with a treatment plan just for you." She looks excited. She looks *really* excited.

But I'm not as enthused. I mean, I get that she knows a lot about it, but this is still *Sasha* we're talking about. I'm supposed to just divulge all my feelings and all my pain (physical and mental) to her? What if this is just some elaborate plan to expose my wrongdoings to my parents?

"Only if you consent to it, though," she says. "Like Dr.

Marion says, I can't help anyone who doesn't want to be helped."

"And you won't tell anyone?" I ask, nervously scraping my teeth against my top lip.

She scrunches her brows. "Of course not. That's the very first thing they teach you in medical school—patient confidentiality."

I smile despite myself. "How do you know?"

"I just figure." She shrugs. "It seems like the most important thing—trust between a patient and her therapist." She lowers her chin. "I would never tell a soul. Even if you don't want my help, I won't tell anyone about this." Then she holds up her pinkie.

And for the first time in a while, I think I might be lucky. Or, at least, on the right path. Because what are the chances that I show up to the Women's Clinic, and instead of being immediately busted by Sasha's mom, I run into Sasha? And what are the chances that the girl who I thought was perfect and pure knows more about what's going on with my body than I do?

I think I'll take my chances. I'm so tired of feeling helpless. If this is an elaborate plan to expose me, then at least I can say that I tried. I didn't just sit here and close my eyes. I *tried*.

So, I link my pinkie with hers. "Okay, Dr. Howser, where do we start?"

Her eyes light up. "Wow. I got so excited I think I just peed a little."

I laugh, leaning away from her. "Gross."

She laughs too. "Okay, so the first step is to get educated. The most important thing for you to know right now is that your vagina will stretch. It's not made of concrete."

I tense up, and my cheeks get hot. I don't think I can get used to hearing her talk so freely about reproductive organs. And she goes on and on about how stretchy it is. I try to keep my discomfort out of my expression.

"Actually," she says, "open your laptop, go to images and search *vagina diagram*."

My eyes snap back to hers. "I can't search that. My parents monitor my search history."

"So delete it afterward."

"But they can still see it."

"How?" she asks.

"Like, through our internet provider."

She tilts her head. "Do they actually check that?"

"I mean, I don't know. Maybe they get alerted when I look up bad stuff."

"Diagrams of vaginas aren't bad. They're educational."

"Not in their eyes."

"So just tell them I had your laptop. Besides," she says, "you should already know this stuff." She shrugs. "Coach Dale should have taught you this in health, but alas, he's just a coach . . . who also goes to our church." She pushes her lips to the side, and it makes me uneasy.

Not just uneasy—furious. When I took health class last year, we colored diagrams of the human body with *crayons*, like two-year-olds. We copied vocabulary from the textbook, but I still don't know the technical terms for the parts of my V because Coach Dale skipped that chapter. When anyone asked him about the sexual health chapter—to be fair, anyone who asked was laughing hysterically—he refused to explain.

So now I'm learning from a girl who's a year younger than me (do you know how embarrassing that is?) that vaginas don't get permanently stretched out after copious sex, and that they're capable of stretching enough to fit the girth of most penises. I seriously had no idea. I've witnessed girls, widely known as tramps, get shamed for their supposed loose vaginas. Boys would say, "I bet it's like throwing a hot dog down a hallway." And I thought those stupid boys knew what they were talking about.

Fear comes out of ignorance, and I've been ignorant about my body far too long.

I type in *vagina diagram*.

"Okay." She scoots closer to me, her hair tickling my arm. "Click this one." I open a very detailed diagram of a vagina, pubes and all. Sasha points to the "vaginal opening" and says, "This is what's contracting. The opening is literally closing."

"Yooooo, what are y'all looking at?"

We whirl around to find Reggie standing in my doorway. I slam my laptop shut and jump off my bed. "What are you doing in here?"

"Your mom told me to come get you. Why were you looking

up . . ." He checks over his shoulder, then dramatically whispers, "Vaginas?"

God, this is like when he caught me and Dom at the back of the church all over again. I rush to pull him inside, then shut my bedroom door. "Why are you always sneaking around?"

He snorts. "I don't sneak around. You're just sloppy when you do inappropriate things." He walks toward my bed. "If you're gonna look up pictures of vaginas, then maybe, I don't know, *face the screen the other way?* Anyone could have walked in." He shakes his head at us lowly amateurs, then picks up the pamphlet sitting on my mattress.

My eyes widen. "Wait, no—"

"What's vagineesmus?" he asks, reading the cover.

"Give me that." I snatch it from him before he can open the flaps.

"What is it?" He looks at me with a curious smile. "An STD?"

"NO!"

"Look, it's fine." He puts his hands up and shuffles around me. "That's none of my business."

"It's not an STD," I say.

"You don't have to be ashamed. People get STDs all the time." He opens my door. "I just came to tell you that your mom is looking for you." Then he walks out of my room.

"Reggie!" I hiss. Sasha and I follow him down the hallway, and I'm trying to whisper/explain. I don't want him to think I'm diseased.

"La la-la la-la," he sings with his fingers in his ears.

In the kitchen, my parents are surveying the refrigerator and all our cabinets. "Girls," my mom says, "I need you to run to H–E–B for milk and onions." She looks at Daddy over her shoulder. "What else did I say?"

"Flour for the pork chops."

She nods. "Right."

"And Reggie, you can go with them," Daddy says.

Mom's face freezes. "Aren't you taking Reggie home now?"

"No, baby, I told you he's staying for dinner."

She slams the refrigerator door. "You did *not* tell me that." Hand on her hip, she says, "I already asked Sasha to stay for dinner."

Daddy kinda laughs. "They can both stay. There's plenty for everyone."

"Well, I was hoping it would just be the girls." Then she smiles her church smile. "They're working on ideas for the church club."

"Yeah, and Reggie can help with that too."

Mom stares at Daddy for five silent seconds, then she looks at Sasha and me. "Girls, go on to the store." She tries waving us away, but neither of us is sure about leaving Reggie.

Especially not when Daddy says, "Reggie, go with them."

Mom's face tightens. "Jesse," she says with a fake laugh. They don't usually do this in front of company, and I can tell she's having a hard time keeping it polite. Mom whispers to

Daddy *loudly* because she's never been a talented whisperer, "I just got her to start hanging out with Sasha. I don't need some *troubled teen* with a rap sheet long enough to stretch from here to China getting in the way of Monique getting back on track."

My stomach drops. When I glance at Reggie, he's looking down at his shoes.

First of all, *ouch*. He's right here, for God's sake. Second of all, when exactly did I get off track? And what is "on track"?

"Kids," Daddy says, looking between the three of us, "y'all head to the store. Come right back. *All three of you*," he emphasizes. Then when he digs in his pocket for his wallet, Mom turns and storms to their bedroom. Daddy hands me a wad of bills. "Get what your mother needs. Keep the change." He waves us away and heads after Mom to their bedroom.

"Okay," I say, uncrinkling his money. I look at Sasha and Reggie with an awkward, confused shrug.

Sasha takes the front seat of my car. Reggie sits in back. We're quiet on the way out of town, not discussing what just happened. And it's really uncomfortable because my mom just blatantly insulted Reggie, and part of me wants to apologize, but a larger part would rather ignore it like it never happened.

Also, he thinks I have an STD. That bothers me more. That eats at me to no end.

I try to keep the words in, but I can't. "It's not an STD, you know." I glance at Reggie in my rearview.

He meets my gaze and shrugs. "Again, not my business."

"Yeah, but I just want you to know . . . I've never even had sex, so." When he doesn't say anything, I keep going, really hammering in my mortification. "I don't want you to think I'm dirty."

He says through a heavy exhale, "I didn't think you were dirty. Plenty of *clean* people get STDs. It's fine."

I nod, my cheeks burning up. "But I'm not one of those people."

When I look in the rearview again, he's smiling at me, amused. "Got it. So, then, what is it, if not an STD?"

I drop my eyes back down to the road, trying to get the heat out of my cheeks. It's one thing to talk to Sasha about my dysfunctional vagina, but Reggie? A boy. A cute boy. A cute boy with a terrible reputation who's probably had countless girls in and out of his bed. I glance at Sasha. She looks as hesitant as me. "You don't have to tell him," she whispers.

"You really don't," Reggie agrees. "I was just fine thinking it was an STD."

"It's a condition," I say, *not* fine with him thinking it's an STD.

Then when he doesn't say anything, I check his reflection in my rearview. He's got his eyebrows raised. "What kind of condition?"

"It, um, makes it impossible for me to have sex."

"Well, not impossible," Sasha says gently. "It *is* curable."

I stare straight ahead at the license plate in front of me.

"Yeah, according to the pamphlet, you have options," Reggie adds.

Sasha glances at him over her shoulder and rolls her eyes. "But seriously, you do," she says to me.

"Like what?"

"I'm still working on your treatment plan, but there are exercises you can do at home, and . . . you'll probably need to get vaginal dilators."

"What are those?" I ask, glancing at her.

"They're like plastic tubes that vary in size, so you can work your way up. Here, just look." She shoves her phone in my face. I glance at the picture of vaginal dilators on her screen. They're little pink tubes with rounded tips that are supposed to magically fit in my vagina.

"I bet they sell them in, like, adult toy stores," she says with uncertainty. "There's a patient who's going to therapy to help work through her fear, but she's also using dilators. Last I heard, she's making progress."

"Good for her. I'm glad she has access to therapy and to doctors," I say bitterly. "But it's not like I can go into an adult toy store. I'm only seventeen."

"Maybe I can help with that," Reggie says.

We both look back at him, surprised. I'm still a little horrified that he's listening to us talk about this, that he knows every intimate detail about what's wrong with my body. And, I mean, like, why should I care about what he thinks of me? Right? It's not like I want him to think of me as a viable sexual partner or anything. But I do care. For whatever reason.

"How?" Sasha asks.

"I know a guy who works in a sex shop. Sometimes he lets me chill there."

"You think he'd let us do *more* than chill, like purchase an item?" Sasha asks.

"Definitely. Pretty sure he's working today."

"Okay, whoa. Wait," I say. "We can't go there."

"Why not?" Sasha asks. "His friend can get us in."

I look at her, appalled. "That's not the problem here. It's illegal . . . I think. Your friend could go to jail. And then we'll be on the news in front of an adult toy shop, and our parents and our whole town will find out."

"Why would the news care about some kids going into a sex shop?" Reggie asks.

"Because it's scandalous!"

"Hardly." He scoffs. "We'll get in, get the things, and get out."

I look at Sasha. She's nodding like it's a foolproof plan, but I'm still not even sure how these "dilators" will cure me. I thought when she said there was a cure, there'd be like a pill or something. *Here, just take this with food twice a day for a week and then you'll be able to have sex.* I don't want to have to do *grunt work.* I say under my breath, "If I can't get a finger up there, how am I supposed to use these?"

"Dilators were *designed* for this. They'll work, trust me. There's one girl who used dilators, and after a month she was able to get the biggest size in." She widens her eyes like that's an astonishing accomplishment.

I widen my eyes too, but I'm not as impressed. "A *month*?"

"That's a short amount of time."

"Doesn't sound like it."

"You've probably been struggling with vaginismus for years. It's gonna take some time to cure."

"But a *month*?" By then Dom will have completely given up on me. In a month, he'll have found a girl whose body isn't broken, a girl who would never let a condom go to waste. In a month, I'll have lost him completely. I say, "I don't have a month."

She's about to argue, but then Reggie says, "So, I guess we should head there right now, then. No time to waste."

Sasha looks at him, then closes her mouth. I do too. Neither of us can argue with that.

Because it's already been way too long. I was supposed to be done with this the night of my junior prom. That night was supposed to be the night. That night is supposed to be everyone's night, right? I thought to myself that I wouldn't give up. That we would try every position. That I would hold in my gasps and hold back my tears, and once he got inside, it would feel good, and everything would be perfect.

But it didn't work out that way. It has never worked out that way.

This, *vaginismus* or whatever, has been ruining our nights—nights that were supposed to be perfect—for far too long. The sooner I get the dilators, the sooner I can finally have sex with Dom, so maybe he can finally look at me and not see a dead end.

I move my eyes back to Reggie's and his raised eyebrows. Then I nod. "Okay. Where is this place?"

10

Reggie points out the shopping center. My heart races at the sight of the sex shop. Then I'm parked outside it. Signs cover the door barring teens under the age of eighteen from entering. That's us! We're those teens who aren't supposed to enter.

Reggie confidently gets out. So does Sasha. But I'm frozen, worry lines creasing my forehead. I watch as they go to the door, grateful that we're all in agreement that I'm staying in the car. But then, I guess, Sasha realizes that I'm not behind them. She turns, frowning, and comes knocking on my window.

I let it down, continuing to look straight ahead.

She lowers herself, crossing her arms over my door. "Hey."

"Hi." I don't look at her.

"How's everything going?" she asks.

I nod. "Fine. Everything's great."

"Yeah? That's good. Well, I noticed that you haven't gotten out."

I sigh, then finally turn to look at her. She wears her hair in long black faux locs, religiously. Today she has them pulled back in a ponytail, her edges slicked down, and her eyebrows are high, waiting for me to say something. "Can't you just go in for me?"

"I could, but once I get them, I can't use them for you, Monique."

"What?" I furrow my brow. "I know."

"Do you *want* to have sex?"

I roll my eyes, frustrated. "Of course I do. But this is breaking the law," I hiss.

"So is having sex," she hisses back. "At least, according to your parents."

I pause, mouth open. She has a point. It's not like I'm *allowed* to have sex.

"Buying dilators is the first step in your treatment."

"I thought education was."

She shifts her eyes. "No, yeah. Buying dilators is the second step."

"But I hardly feel educated." I sigh.

"Okay, maybe steps isn't the best way to think of this. Going inside will be like exposure therapy. I think if you're brave enough to go in here and buy them, then maybe you'll be brave enough to use them."

"Let's goooo," Reggie whines from the front of my car.

I push my lips to the side, considering Sasha's point. For years, I've been too afraid to touch myself. As determined as I am to get dilators, will I be brave enough to actually use them? Hmmm, maybe my therapist has a point. I need to get out of my head and cultivate some courage.

"Fine," I say, letting my window up. I turn off my car and hurry to take off my seat belt, letting the momentum of my decision propel me forward before my fear can slow me down.

Reggie leads Sasha and me to the entrance, but then he stops in the doorway and whispers, "That's not my friend." The bell on the door chimes, and a white man, thin and wrinkled, looks up. My skin crawls.

"It's fine," Reggie says. He and Sasha keep walking forward. My footsteps falter, but I continue through as well. What choice do I have, at this point?

Suddenly, I'm surrounded by sex. I don't allow myself to stare at anything for too long. Honestly, I'd rather close my eyes. Even if I were old enough to be here, I would feel perverted. Like, what does the attendant think of me?

DVDs, Blu-rays, and magazines line the wall. So many boobs. At the very back of the store, lingerie and costumes hang on racks. Reggie starts down an aisle of dildos. "Where would they be?" he asks, inexplicably comfortable, like we're just looking for a new mop.

Sasha, on the other hand, is busy trying to therapize me. "How does being here make you feel?"

I look down at my shoes on the tile. "Uncomfortable?"

"Uh-huh," she says, nodding, like this is *new* information. "And *why* do you feel uncomfortable?"

I give her a look. I mean, I get that she's trying to be my therapist or whatever, and I'm appreciative, but this is laughable. "Um, because I'm too young to be here. And I'm surrounded by naked women and *dildos*."

She nods again, studying me. Then she motions around the store. "None of these products are going to hurt you."

"I don't think—" My voice is raised. I have to reel myself back in, because I don't want to lash out at her, but I really don't want to be here anymore. This isn't helping me at all. "I don't think any of this will hurt me. I think my *image* will be hurt if anyone catches me here."

She does that thoughtful nod again. "Well, here's the thing: no one's going to catch you here, because no one you know would ever come here."

I shift my eyes. "That doesn't really help."

"Yeah, I realized after I said it . . . What I meant to say is, it's very normal for people our age to be curious about sex."

Then Reggie comes over to us, giggling uncontrollably. "Hey, look." He hands me something, and it isn't until he's waving his butt in my face, saying, "Spank me," that I realize it's a whip.

I'm trying not to stare at his (cute) butt or the exposed band of his black underwear. I glance up toward the front and make eye contact with the attendant. "Reggie, stop," I hiss.

"Spank me!"

Sasha looks at him, furious. "Reggie, stop! This is serious."

"What about this is serious?" He looks back at her, annoyed. "We're in an adult toy shop, for God's sake. Emphasis on the toy part."

"Emphasis on the adult part," she counters. "We're supposed to be mature enough to be here, and here you are, acting like a child."

"Oh, my God, live a little." Then he looks at me. "Spank me." He smiles. "You know you want to."

"What I want to do is *leave*."

And just as I say that, the store attendant stops at the end of the aisle to answer my prayers. "Can I see some ID?"

We freeze. Reggie is still bent over, and I'm still holding the leather whip, mouth wide open. This is a nightmare—*my* nightmare. I swear, I can already hear the sirens. See, this is what I get for going anywhere with Reggie.

He straightens up and laughs. "Hey, man, it's cool. I know Demarcus."

"Who?" the man asks, confused, then his face turns annoyed. "I don't care who you know. If you're not eighteen, you need to leave now."

"We're seventeen, so what does it matter?"

We might be seventeen, but Sasha is sixteen.

"You need to leave now, or I'm calling the cops."

My stomach drops. *Here we go.*

"Okay, geez," Reggie says, herding us down the aisle. I leave the whip on a random shelf and hurry outside, embarrassed to my core, glancing around the parking lot to see if anyone just witnessed that—a news van, maybe. I sprint to my car and jump in.

When Reggie and Sasha join me, I have my face stuffed in my palms. Reggie's laughing in my front seat and Sasha's chastising him in the back. "That was mortifying," I say, my voice muffled by my hands.

"That was hilarious," Reggie says.

I pull my hands away from my face, scowling at him. "I thought you said your friend was working today."

He shifts his eyes with a sketchy little smile. "Okay, so get this—" He laughs, then says, "I don't actually have a friend who works here."

All of that whooshing traffic on the interstate behind us fades to nothing. I could *not* have heard him right. He's over there laughing with the brightest of smiles. No, yeah, I must have misheard him.

"I'm sorry, what?"

"I don't know anyone who works here. I didn't think you guys would actually go for it!"

"Are you serious?" Sasha says.

There's a whirring in my head, like my ears are ringing. I just did the most mortifying, terrifying, illegal thing of my life for absolutely nothing but his enjoyment?

I don't say anything to him for a whole minute. In my silence, he looks at me with an unapologetic, infuriating smirk and asks, "You mad?"

My eyes widen. When I look at him, my skin catches fire. "I'll kill you!" I screech, and lunge for his throat.

He yelps, throwing his door open and launching himself out of it. My fingers graze his T-shirt, but he slips out of my grasp. I throw my door open too, sprinting around the front of my car to his side. But it takes him a while to realize that I'm actually trying to murder him. When he finally does, he tries taking off, but his shoes betray him—karma.

I've got a grip on the bottom of his T-shirt and start pulling him back. He whips around to face me, ripping his shirt out of my hand. Now he's backing away, hands up. "Hey, calm down," he cries, his voice cracking. "Let's talk about this."

"I don't want to talk." I'm approaching like a lioness on her prey.

"Okay, listen," he begs, "when I decided to prank you, I was . . ." He shakes his head and sighs. "I was young and dumb."

"That was ten minutes ago!"

"Yeah, but my growth is exponential. You know, most people's growth is linear, but I grow more and more each day, each second." He nods, trying to talk me down with freaking algebra. "Have you ever seen it graphed?"

"Shut up about math!" I shout. "Why would you do this to me? I thought . . ."

His brows pinch as he waits for me to finish.

"I thought we were on the same side," I say quietly. "After yesterday, in the car. . . ."

He drops his head, and he says, "It was just a joke," like that's a good enough reason to betray me.

"Nothing about this is funny."

Sasha joins us then. "This is your idea of a joke? Monique has a serious medical condition and you thought bringing us here would be funny?" Sasha points at me while yelling at him. "Your little stunt might have just traumatized her even more!"

He looks shaken by that.

But I'm not *that* fragile. "I'm not traumatized," I say, raising my hands. "I'm just upset."

"You hear that? You upset my patient, you idiot," she spits at him. "You apologize to her right now."

He cocks up an eyebrow. "Look, I'm sorry, I really am, but if you have a serious medical condition, shouldn't you tell your parents? Sounds like you need to see an actual doctor, not this wannabe."

Sasha scoffs at him.

"How am I supposed to tell my parents about this? What am I supposed to say? Hey, Mom and Dad, Dom and I have tried doing it twenty-nine times, but every time my body has failed me. Yeah, I'm sure they'd love to hear that."

"Wait, twenty-nine times?" Sasha asks.

Reggie looks stunned too. "So, why isn't Dom helping you, then?"

"Because he broke up with me yesterday." The words are still so raw. I can feel tears heating up behind my eyes.

Reggie's face falls, as does Sasha's. She says, "Did he break up with you because of . . . sex?"

"You mean the lack of? Yes."

"That's really messed up," Reggie says.

"It's been two years." I look away, not exactly feeling up to justifying why Dom broke up with me, but I mean, twenty-nine times in two years. Of course he broke up with me.

"So, you think if you can fix your condition, you can get him back?" Reggie asks.

I blink down at the ground. "I know you probably think that's stupid. You don't have to help me, but please don't . . . don't make a joke out of it again."

His brows twitch, almost like a wince.

Sasha says, "Maybe we should get what your mom wanted, then go back home. We'll find another way to get the dilators, Monique. I promise."

I look at her and her compassion and think to myself how much I don't deserve it. I've said such awful things about her in the past. I thought I knew who she was. I thought she was a stuck-up church girl. But here she is, determined to help me.

I nod at her. "Yeah, let's go."

We walk close, heading back to my car, still parked outside the toy shop. She says, "Even though it was a joke, I'm still proud of you for going in there."

I smile to myself.

"I know that was probably really hard."

"It was really uncomfortable," I say.

"I know, but you did it anyway. That was a good first step—"

"Hey!" Reggie calls after us. "Wait!"

I roll my eyes and she sighs, but we both stop and look at him over our shoulders. "What?" she spits at him.

He approaches us slowly, like we might run if he makes a sudden move. "We should go see if Target has them."

"Target?" I furrow my brow.

"Sometimes Target sells sex toys. They're the most basic pieces of shit, but still."

"How do we know this isn't another joke?" Sasha says.

"Because this whole thing stopped being funny ten seconds ago." He tilts his head. "Come on. Your dad gave you a wad of cash. Target is *right there*, and we're actually allowed to be there. There's literally no risk. So, I say we go to every department store, every drugstore, every gas station in the area until we find them. We don't go home until we get you those dildos."

"Dilators," Sasha corrects him.

"Right." He raises his wild brows as if to ask if we're in.

I've been on an emotional roller coaster for the past twenty-four hours, and I'm not sure that I'm ready for another loop the loop. But maybe, by some miracle, Target has exactly what I need. I look to the shopping center over my shoulder, then back up at Reggie. "We can go on one condition: no more pranks."

He makes a face like I'm asking too much of him. "No more pranks *on you*." Then he whips past me and runs to the car.

"That's not what I said!"

"Let's go!" he hollers, jumping in my passenger seat.

I walk slowly to the driver's side, knowing that I probably

shouldn't trust him—*the* Reginald Turner, the boy who just got me kicked out of a sex shop for the fun of it, the boy with a record longer and even taller than him.

But I also don't have much of a choice. I need those dilators if I want Dom back, and if that means spending a little extra time with Sasha Howser and Reginald Turner, of all people, then that's exactly what I'm going to do.

11

Reggie said there was no risk going to Target, but he didn't mention the fact that going *anywhere* with him is a risk.

As soon as we walk through the sliding doors, Reggie, strutting like he's ready to start a riot, grabs a red shopping cart and takes off running. Why would he need a cart? And why would he run with it? So I run after the madman, because I don't know why—I'm stupid?

"Reggie, stop running! We don't need a cart."

People scowl as he whips around them and their families. Then he says, "Of course we need a cart! How else will we carry all of our sex toys?" loud enough for people three aisles over to hear. Families upon families turn to stare at us.

I stop. Sasha keeps after him, trying to wrangle him in. But I don't like the attention. And suddenly I hate that the two of them know about my condition. I hate how much Sasha is trying to help. I hate how she keeps watching me, like any second

I might shatter. And I hate that Reggie thinks this whole thing is a joke.

I just want to go home.

I wander through the racks of clothing on my left, running my hand over a row of hats and stopping at a display of men's belts.

And I miss Dom. I run my fingers over the necklace he gave me yesterday.

There's nothing in particular that I miss. I mean, I saw him yesterday. It just hurts knowing that he's not mine anymore. That he's not mine because my body is broken. I feel so broken.

"Hey." Reggie appears beside me, breathing kinda heavy. "Where'd you go?"

I think I have tears in my eyes, because when I look at him, his face falls. I say, "I don't want to do this anymore. I want to go home."

"Why?" he says, disappointed, then he points his thumb over his shoulder. "Because of that prank back there?"

"No, I mean . . . yeah. But also no."

He inspects my face, and he's standing pretty close to me. I have to look up to meet his gaze, but I don't feel brave enough to. He rests his arm on the top of the belt holder, crowding my space even more. "I'm sorry. I thought it would make you laugh."

I shift my eyes, confused. "What about that was funny? Everyone was staring at us."

"Did you see their expressions, though?" Reggie asks,

smiling. "All those white women—they were like, 'Sex toys? My *word*.'" Then he clutches his invisible pearls.

I can't help it. I laugh.

"See?" he says, grinning. "You know it was funny. Sasha keeps saying that I need to be more *sensitive* about your condition." He rolls his eyes.

"You think we're full of baloney, don't you?"

He raises a brow. "You mean full of shit? Yes. I think *she* is." Then his hazel eyes drop down to my mouth. "But I don't think you are."

My pulse beats out an irregular cadence. I feel something lift in me, or maybe lift *off* me. That sudden desire to go home is gone. And I realize I like standing this close to him.

A family passes us by with their shopping cart. Reggie watches them go, still resting his arm atop the belt display. Then his eyes fall back to mine. "I think she's babying you too much. You're not some helpless baby bird. So, you can't have sex!"

I look around to see if anyone heard him.

"It's not the end of the world," he says with a shrug. "It doesn't mean you can't have a little fun."

I grin sheepishly. "I think our definitions of fun are very different."

He laughs at that. "Stick around. You may be surprised to find how similar we are."

Before I can ask what he's getting at, Sasha cuts the corner in a half jog, half walk. "There you are," she says, out of breath.

Then she points at Reggie. "You're an idiot." To me, she says, "Monique, if you're uncomfortable, we can go. Reggie clearly can't take anything seriously."

Reggie rolls his eyes.

I smile up at him because he's right—she is babying me. I appreciate her sensitivity and her compassion and her willingness to help me, but her carefulness is making me feel even more helpless, and I don't like it. I say, "No, it's fine. We can stay." And Reggie smiles back down at me.

"Really?" Sasha asks.

Then I meet her apprehensive gaze and nod. "Exposure therapy, right?"

At that, she tilts her head thoughtfully.

"Well, all right," Reggie cheers, clapping his hands. "Let's go find you those dildos!"

My cheeks warm as I look around the men's clothing section. Yep. Several families turn to stare at us, aghast. When I look back up at him, he's smiling deviously. *Oh God, what am I getting myself into?*

The way he smiles, he's challenging me. I'm not some overly sensitive, helpless baby bird. I'm gonna prove to him that I can hang. "Dilators," I correct him.

"Yeah. Those." He smiles harder. "So, where should we look?" he asks, turning to Sasha like she's the expert. I look at her the same way.

"As if I know. Probably with the condoms. Right?"

So, we head to the health and beauty section and stop at the "feminine products." At the cap end we find the condoms and such, but nothing that says "dilators."

There's a worker restocking nearby, while we're looking at the lubricants. When she's finished, she lingers, watching us. Three teenagers ogling condoms and lubricants—of course she's watching us. After I make eye contact with her, she walks over with a painted-on smile. "Can I help you find something?"

Poor girl.

Reggie nods with his hands on his hips, like somebody's dad, and with all the confidence of one, he asks, "Yes, we're looking for"—he turns to Sasha—"what are they called?"

"Vaginal dilators," Sasha answers.

Reggie tilts his head, waiting for the employee to help us find them.

"I'm sorry. What are they?" she asks.

"They're like dildos. Right, Sasha?"

"They're tubes that condition the vaginal muscles."

I wipe my hand across my sweaty forehead. *Whew,* this is . . .

The employee's smile fades.

"Yes, we need tools to condition a vagina," Reggie repeats slowly. "Do you have those?"

My hand falls to my mouth. I almost turn and run, but the employee does it first, quickly replying, "No. We don't."

When she's gone, Reggie busts out laughing, and Sasha actually joins in. I'm on the brink of hyperventilating, full of panic and embarrassment. Then a laugh bursts out of me too.

It's a bit hysterical, shaky, like it's coming from a place in me that's not often awake. "You're insane," I say, looking up at the smile on Reggie's face.

He bites down on his bottom lip, summoning my eyes there. I swear, he has the deepest Cupid's bow I've ever seen in my life. Then he shoulders past me, his entire arm colliding with mine. "And you, Monique, are having fun."

I blink a couple of times, pushing away the heat in my cheeks. He looks over his shoulder with that up-to-no-good smirk and nudges his head. "Come on. Let's try another store."

Fun with Dom was trash-talking church people. It was getting out of the house, hiding away at the creek, getting out of our clothes.

Fun with my old girlfriends, Donyae and Brittaniya, was fantasizing about our lives with boyfriends. It was gushing and dreaming and writing. It was sleepovers with brownies and nail polish and romantic comedies.

This? This running in and out of stores, disrupting the peace, bringing attention to ourselves, adrenaline coursing through our veins, this smile trespassing on my lips—I don't know if I'd call this fun. Can fun be scary? Because fun with Reggie is scary.

I'm out of my league trying to run with him. This boy breaks into places, late at night, and steals things. Shouting the word *dildos* in an otherwise quiet CVS drugstore is kid's play to him. Fun with Reggie doesn't wait for you to get yourself ready, so every other second, I find myself far, far out of my comfort zone.

Then, amidst all the running around in Conroe, Daddy texts: **You kids go see a movie or something. If you're gonna be out later than ten, just text.**

My eyebrows shoot up. Wow, I've never been afforded that privilege. It's always *be back by ten or die.* So, after ripping up every department store in Conroe, we decide to take our festivities to Huntsville—in the complete opposite direction. As I'm pulling out of my parking space, Reggie in my passenger seat, Sasha reaches from the back. "Can I have the aux?"

I make a face without thinking about it. It's just that church girls only listen to gospel music, and I am not up for that right now.

"Please," she whines, leaning her cheek against my seat.

"Okay." I sigh, pulling the long, twisted aux cord out of my cup holder.

After a few seconds of anticipatory silence, Megan Thee Stallion bumps over my speakers, and suddenly the airwaves are full of cuss words and sex. So much sex.

My eyes widen. "Wow," I say, turning the volume down. "You listen to Meg?"

"From time to time. Do you?"

My mouth opens to answer, *yes,* but I actually don't. I don't ever get the chance, because obviously, I'm not allowed to, and even though Dom is a Houston rap fanatic, he hates Meg.

Anytime I ever tried to play her music, he'd make this grossed-out face and insist I turn it off.

I turn the volume up, *way up*, enjoying my freedom to. Then the impossible happens: Sasha sings along. Loudly. Energetically. *Accurately.*

My eyes bulge. I glance over at Reggie, and his face holds the same surprise, his mouth shaped like an O. With every cuss word that comes out of her mouth, I jump. I click the volume off and look in my rearview, appalled.

"What happened?" she asks, the rest of the lyrics caught up on her tongue.

"What was that?" Reggie asks at the same time I say, "Who are you?"

Reggie follows up with, "Did you just say the word *fuck*?"

I follow up with, "How do you possibly know the words to that song?"

"Guys, *chill*. Everybody knows that song." She turns back to her window like nothing happened—sitting innocent in her wholesome turtleneck and long pants in the dead of summer—then she reaches forward and clicks the volume back on. We let all the windows down, letting the wind drive us faster and forcing us to turn up the music louder. I sing along too, skipping out on the cuss words, because somehow, I'm not as brave as Sasha. Which makes me feel all kinds of conflicted. How has Sasha perfected the art of cussing before me? Sasha, of all people.

It's in this moment that I realize that "church girls" is *me*, not Sasha.

No, but she's the one who praises God like a grown woman! She's the one who suggested we bring church into our school. She's like my mom's lapdog. . . . But clearly, it's all a lie.

The things we resent about other people, aren't those always the things we hate most about ourselves?

I drive a little faster, feeling self-conscious about how much further along Sasha is than me, how much braver she is. I embrace the fact that I've tried to have sex against my parents' wishes, that I'm searching for dilators, against their knowledge. I embrace that I'm not all good either. As far as I can help it, "church girls" won't be me. Not anymore.

12

In Walmart, Reggie takes off without us.

"Where did he—"

Sasha shakes her head. "He's weird."

So, we decide to go to the women's clothing section. I fully expect her to pick out a couple more turtlenecks, but she holds up a pair of blue jean shorts that are much, *much* shorter than any I own, and a crochet crop top. "I wanna try this on." Then she disappears inside a dressing room.

While I wait for her, my eyes wander over to the shelves of underwear. All of my underwear came from those shelves. They fit high on my waist and cut lines into my butt cheeks. Forget wearing a tight skirt because I always have a panty line. They are, by definition, granny panties. Made it pretty embarrassing when Dom and I would fumble around in his truck.

But then he bought me that lingerie. . . .

I never thought he cared about my granny panties. He'd take them off so fast I thought all that mattered was my skin underneath. But maybe he took them off so fast because he couldn't stand the sight of them. Now I can't imagine driving out to the creek with him in my regular underwear. If I'm going to fix my body, I have to fix *everything*—the inside and the gift-wrapped outside—so he knows for sure that I'm ready.

I search through the red lace bras for my size, but all I see are Bs and Cs. I almost give up, until I find one lonesome 34A at the very back. I hurriedly pull it off the rack, grin on my face, when Sasha runs up behind me. "What do you think?" she asks, excited.

I turn, caught.

She's wearing the crop top and the short shorts. I've never seen so much of her body. My God, she's gorgeous. But her eyes are zeroed in on the red bra in my hand. She raises her eyebrows. "Are you getting that for Dom?"

I lower my eyes and shrug. "Yeah, I guess."

When I look back up, she's got her eyes lowered too, hands shoved in the front pockets of her shorts. She looks up then and catches my eye. "For the record, I think Dom's an asshole for breaking up with you over this. You are more than what your body can do for him."

I think it's supposed to make me feel better, but it just feels too soon. Like I'm not able to take that perspective, because all

I want is to win him back. "I don't think a therapist would say that to a patient."

I'm a little bitter about it, and I think she hears it in my voice. She says, lifting her head, "I didn't say it as your therapist. I said it as . . . your friend."

My eyes widen. It's the kind of declaration that begs for a response, but I'm not sure what to say. I never thought I'd call Sasha my friend. I'm still not sure that I will. I've spent so much time hating her, I can't do a one-eighty flip in less than twenty-four hours.

Thankfully, Reggie shows up just in time, running, full speed. And in a flash, he rips the bra out of my hands.

"Reggie!" I call after him. "Stop!"

He does not stop.

So I jog after him. "That's the only one in my size. Give it back!"

He's laughing maniacally, running much faster than me. People stop and gape at us, but I can't even be bothered by it, because I can't stop laughing either. I've learned how to laugh, instead of freaking out about people staring.

Then suddenly he stops, and his head disappears. When I get to the spot where he vanished, I see his shoes hanging out from beneath the rack of clothes. I roll my eyes and push back the hangers.

He's sitting on the floor, smiling up at me. "Hey."

"Come on. Give it back."

He shakes his head like a child. "You come in here, then I'll give it back."

I sigh, popping out my hip.

"It's like a whole other world in here. Come on. Just try it."

His eyes are so youthful. Everything about him is youthful. The crazy stuff he does just reminds me how it feels to have fun, how it feels to *play*. "Okay, fine," I grumble. Then I open a spot next to him and crawl inside.

His back is pressed against the metal bars, crisscrossed at the bottom of the rack, making tiny triangles of space that used to be big enough when we were kids, but now our shoes hang out, no matter how tightly we hug our knees to our chest. My back is pressed against his, and so is my right arm.

"Isn't this cool?" Reggie says giddily.

The curtain of clothing shields us from the harsh fluorescents. All sound outside blurs into white noise, while everything inside is amplified—like Reggie's breathing, and the pounding of my heart, and my racing thoughts. This whole time, I haven't had one second to think, and it's been great. But for some reason, being in this little closet of clothes allows my thoughts to swarm me.

Dom broke up with me. He was my entire life, my entire future. And my parents think we just got in an argument. If they find out the truth, they'll banish me for sure. Kick me out on my butt. Disown me like they disowned my sister, because I don't fit into their plans, into their perfect cookie-cutter world. *And* I have a disorder! I can't even go to the doctor for it. All

I can do is find dilators and hope that they work. And even finding the dilators is proving to be impossible. I will have this disorder forever, and Dom will never get back together with me.

I take a deep breath, leaning farther back against the bars. Dread washes over me in a cold sweat.

"It's kind of relaxing, huh?" Reggie asks.

I laugh a little. "I would say the exact opposite."

He looks at me over his shoulder. His face is close, but he's so tall, my head only comes up to his shoulder.

I whisper, "You know how sometimes when you go to bed, you turn off all the lights, and it's quiet, then everything you've been avoiding, all of your nasty thoughts and worst fears, swarm you at once, and everything just feels . . . hopeless?"

His eyebrows pinch. My hand is braced against the cold tile floor, so he lays his hand over mine, getting my full attention. "Hey, are you having an anxiety attack?"

My eyes get caught in his dark eyelashes and the concern in his hazel eyes. His hand is really warm and really long and slender.

"No, I don't think so." I turn away from his probing gaze, propping my hands atop my knees. "It just sucks, you know? This whole situation."

He hums thoughtfully, then he props his hands up on his knees too. "I don't know. From my perspective, it doesn't suck all that much."

I look at him with my face screwed up. *His perspective?*

"The way I see it, you, me, and Sasha—we're like Scooby-Doo and the Mystery Inc. We're solving mysteries and fighting crime."

I laugh and look up at him, leaning into his smile. "Except where the mystery is my vagina." I whisper the V-word.

He throws his head back, laughing. "Yeah, I guess that's true." Then he settles down and leans into my smile too. "But what I mean is that—" He bites the corner of his lip, unsure. "You're not alone. Not anymore."

My smile dims, as does his. That settles me, those three words: *you're not alone*. Realizing that scares away all my darkness and replenishes my hope. I don't have to figure this out on my own. I have him and I have Sasha—a very unlikely trio, but so far, our union has felt natural. As natural as it feels leaning against him, leaning *into* him, with his eyes scouring my face, and my eyes scouring his, hoping he can fill me with more hope and more warmth and more comfort.

Then the clothes that are hiding us from the world are ripped open. Reggie and I jump apart, falling into Sasha's wild gaze. "Hey," she barks, "we gotta go." She looks over the top of the clothing rack.

"Why?" I ask. "What's going on?"

She meets my gaze. She looks harried and scared.

"What did you do?" Reggie asks.

"I didn't do anything, we just need to go. *Right now*." She waves us out of the clothing rack.

I follow Reggie up off the floor. "Can you at least tell us why?"

"I'll tell you in the car."

I glance behind me and catch her looking over her shoulder again. "If you didn't do anything wrong, you sure are making us look suspicious." Three teenagers hurrying out of the store without buying anything, repeatedly looking over our shoulders. Except then I notice the Walmart bag clutched in her hand. "You bought something?"

"Yes," she hisses. "Now hurry. Y'all are walking so slow."

We speed walk through the sliding doors, bypassing the door greeter, not making eye contact. When we're crossing the dark parking lot, Reggie looks at me with a hesitant smile. "Listen, I need to tell you guys something."

"What?" I ask.

"Don't get mad."

I sigh deep. "What is it?"

He checks my expression, then he starts walking backward ahead of us. "Okay, get this"—he laughs a little—"I completely forgot that I hid this in my waistband." He lifts his T-shirt and shows me the red lace bra that neither of us paid for.

"Reggie!" I run to catch up to him and jerk his shirt back down over the stolen merchandise. Thankfully no one is watching us. "You need to take that back," I say.

"What? I can't take it back. Are you crazy?"

"Why not?"

Sasha answers for him. "If they catch him, you'll have to explain to your parents why you were stealing lingerie from Walmart."

I glance back at her, then glower at Reggie. "I can't believe you stole it."

"It was an accident!" He laughs and pulls his shirt up again. "I forgot—"

I can't help but notice how pale his torso is, compared to his face, and how thin he is and how defined his washboard abs are. I pull his shirt back down. "Stop that! Someone will see."

He looks down at me, smirking. And for a few steps, I'm walking backward in front of him, holding the bottom of his T-shirt, and he's matching my steps, holding my eyes. "My bad."

"Let's go, let's go, let's go," Sasha hisses, pointing out my car a few spots down.

After we all jump in and slam the doors closed, Reggie throws the devil bra at me. I frown. "I don't like this."

"Not quite your style?" he asks.

"No. I don't like that it's stolen!"

"Well, it's not like your parents would have let you *buy* it."

I roll my eyes, then I look over my shoulder at Sasha in the back seat. "And you. What did *you* do?"

"I didn't steal anything," she says reassuringly.

"But?" I prompt her.

"There is no *but*. I just . . ." She scoots to the edge of her seat. "Okay, so after you two ran off like children, I went to the books section." In her pause, she rustles her Walmart bag, pulling out a book. "I ran into Deacon Hanson, and he was holding one of these." She shows us the cover—*Nervous* by Zane.

I shift my eyes. "Okay?"

"Do you know what kind of books Zane writes?" she asks.

"Oh my God, my mom has those books," Reggie says. "You saw Deacon Hanson buying one?" He covers his mouth with his fist and busts out laughing.

"So? What's wrong with them?"

Sasha's smiling at Reggie, trying to contain her laughter, then she looks at me. "Zane writes Black erotica."

Erotica? I've heard this word before, but . . . I can't place the definition. Reggie looks amused at my confusion. "Oh my God, Monique, it's porn!"

My eyes grow as wide as his. "Ew. What!"

"Deacon Hanson was buying porn!" Reggie howls.

"Wait, are you serious?" I ask her.

"Yes." She laughs. "So I grabbed this one and ran out of there."

Reggie shakes his head. "That nasty old man."

I smirk, thinking back to when Dom and I laughed at Deacon Hanson after church. Ohmygod, I can't wait to tell Dom. He's gonna flip when he finds out.

"Wait." I narrow my eyes at Sasha. "Why did *you* buy one?"

"Oh." Then she slides the book across my center console. "I got this for you."

Reggie laughs. "You bought her porn? I think that's way

worse than me stealing you a bra."

My face tightens.

"Erotica is not porn. It's *art*."

"It's totally porn," he laughs.

"Look, I don't need this," I say, motioning to the dirty book, like merely touching it might set me on fire.

"It's exposure therapy," she says. "And I thought this one would be perfect for you—it's about a closeted freak."

—insert Reggie dying—

I scowl at him.

She says, "You need to get comfortable with the topic of sex." She tilts her head, like I'm not seeing her reasoning. And she's right, I'm not.

"I am comfortable with . . . the subject matter. I just—"

"Wait," she says, studying me with narrowed eyes.

"What?"

She nods her head. "Say it. Say *sex*."

"I don't . . . what?" I smile nervously. "Why?"

"Just say it."

My mouth dries and my body gets all hot, like I'm onstage and everyone's waiting for me to put on a show. I stare out the windshield at the car parked in front of me. "I don't need this."

"Yoooo," Reggie howls in disbelief, "say it."

"I don't need to be able to say it. I need to be able to do it."

"How can you expect to be able to have sex if you can't even say it?"

"Right?" Sasha agrees with him. "It's fine. Don't say it. But you need to read this book."

"I don't need the book," I argue. I can't read that. What if my parents catch me? They'll think I'm some pervert. I don't need that book. And I don't need to *perform* for these two. What I need is dilators. "So, to the next Target we go?" I ask, starting the car and pulling out of my parking space.

"Just say the word," Reggie urges me.

I blink at the windshield, then roll my eyes. "Will you leave me alone if I do?"

"Sure," Reggie says quickly. "Just say it."

"Sex," I say under my breath.

He looks at me, his eyebrows scrunched. "I couldn't hear you. Did you hear her?" he asks Sasha.

She says, "Don't push her. With time she can build up to it," putting on her therapist pants.

Reggie turns back to me, ignoring her *baby talk*. "You gotta speak up," he says.

I say it again, but it comes out weird.

"Did you say *sucks*?" he asks, laughing. "No, Monique. That's a completely different activity. Some consider it foreplay."

I laugh and push his shoulder. "Gross!"

"S-E-X. It's just a word."

"It's not, though." It's practically a cuss word in my house. Even my parents stick to *having relations* or *being intimate*.

Reggie's smile fades. Then he taps his finger on the console. "Well, maybe that's the problem. You've never even had sex, so why put it on this undeserved pedestal? That gives it way too much power. Just say it."

Because if I can just say it, then maybe I can just do it.

"Sex," I say loud enough for them both to hear. I don't say *six* or *sucks* or *sax*.

Reggie smiles, nodding. "Yeah! Say it louder!"

I laugh and say it assertively, above my normal talking volume. "Sex." I embrace the way it feels slipping between my lips, like seeing a fence and climbing it despite the "No Trespassing" sign, like crossing a border, exploring new territory.

"Woo!" Sasha howls.

Reggie turns to his open window. "Shout it to the world!"

Wind flies inside the car as we race past storefronts and parking lots. I turn my face toward my window. The night air feels dry and almost cold as it slaps against my skin.

I open my mouth and shout, "I want to have sex!" My voice is captured by the wind. Then I laugh, grasp the steering wheel tight, and glance over at Reggie.

He lets up his window with his eyebrows rising into his hairline. "Do you? Right now?" He motions to the edge of the street. "We can kick Sasha out and pull over right here."

I push on his shoulder again. "Shut up!"

Sasha grumbles, "Trust me, you wouldn't have to kick me out. I would run."

116

But I'm feeling a lot right now. Like, *a lot*, a lot. Because Reggie just alluded to having sex with me, and I think my body might be responding in a way it shouldn't be. My stomach feels like it's full of helium, trying to lift its way out of my throat. My heart is racing. And my mind, my dirty little mind, is feeding me images of him without his shirt on. Ohmygod, *stop*.

"But, anyway," Sasha says, "I'm leaving this book in your back seat. If you don't want your parents to find it, you better take it."

Some therapist *she* is.

13

The Target parking lot is empty when we pull in.

"Damn, what time do they close?" Reggie asks, looking at my dash. "It's only after nine."

I park in a spot close to the front, despite the fact that they're obviously not open. This was our last stop. I don't think any of us were expecting to find dilators here, but I'm still a little disappointed. This means we can't just walk into a department store and find what I need. We'll have to find another way to get dilators, or I'm stuck out of luck.

Reggie gets out. He runs up to the red doors. Sasha and I watch from the car as he looks at the posted hours, then turns around and shrugs.

"Where else can we go? Is this it?" I don't want this night to end so soon.

Then Reggie runs over to a loose shopping cart and shouts at us, "Get in!"

I look around the empty parking lot, the weight of how much we shouldn't be here heavy on my chest. "Is he crazy?" I ask.

"Yep," she says, "but that idiot *does* know how to have fun."

"Come on!" he shouts.

"He sure does."

"But if you're scared—" she starts, but I don't let her finish. I'm tired of hearing it. I'm tired of being treated like I'm fragile.

I open my door, get out of my car, and leave it running.

I just wonder where he got his compass. How he just knows where to go next. How he doesn't care about getting kicked out of sex shops, or earning disapproving looks from white women in Target, or possibly getting scolded by a disgruntled Walmart employee. But I don't question it. I follow him and his aimlessness, and Sasha follows me.

And now I'm laughing uncontrollably in the basket of a Target cart, back-to-back with her. Reggie's pushing us, running across the white-striped parking lot in zigzags and in circles. It's like a roller coaster that feels like freedom, like I've finally escaped the bars of my prison room. Like my mother would never approve, and I never expected it to feel so good to defy her, so I toss my head back and breathe in as much air as I can. This is what I hope losing my virginity feels like.

I look up at the black sky, trying to find the moon, then I tilt my head back down. Reggie's watching me, smiling. "What'd I tell you?" he shouts into the wind. "Our definitions aren't so different!"

I smile. No, I guess they aren't. Actually, I think all this time my definition of fun might have been wrong. It feels like I've never had fun before, not until tonight. "They were different!" I shout back. "Yours was just better."

He smiles too, his eyes taking me in with astonishment. After a while, he slows to a stop to catch his breath. Sasha leans back all the way against me. She's warm and soft and solid. It feels intimate, like the way I might lean against my sister. It feels like no matter how much I thought I hated her before this night, none of that can compare to how comfortable we are right now, leaning against each other.

I smile and relax too.

Maybe I can call her my friend, eventually.

Then all of a sudden, Sasha launches herself over the side of the cart. She runs to my car, hops in the driver's seat, and after a few seconds of questionable silence, turns a Vontae song *all the way up*, and lets my windows all the way down. I didn't even know my car had that much bass. She's dancing in the front seat, shouting the lyrics. "I got hunnids in the house, I got thousands in the car, I got millions in the bank, I got billions on the bar!"

Reggie joins in, pushing the cart toward my car. "Bitches wanna get a taste, they just wanna be a star!"

"Dropped a bill on the way in, never felt it leave the jar," I say.

Reggie smiles at me, surprised that I know the lyrics. "Pick it up, pick it up, pick it up!" He points at me.

"Pick it up, pick it up," I say.

Then we all shout, "Ayeeee!"

"You need it more than me," Reggie raps, holding his hand over his heart. "So don't let me get in your way."

Then I lift myself up, holding on to the sides of the cart. I'm standing as Reggie pushes me toward the cart hub. "Quick like a girl in stilettos to jumble the words that I say. You wanna mess on my name, then turn around and say hey."

"Monique, those aren't the lyrics!" Reggie says, cutting me off.

"Yes, they are."

He stops at the hub. "No, it's 'Quick like a bitch in stilettos to fuck up the shit that I say. You wanna piss on my name, then turn around and say hey.'"

I shift my eyes, keeping a straight face. "That's what I just said."

He throws his head back and laughs at the moon.

We're the only car in the parking lot, and the music is loud enough that people can probably hear us from the highway, but I'm at ease. I'm more than at ease—I love everything about this moment.

14

"How did this happen to you?"

Reggie's holding on to the console, staring at me, waiting for my answer. I know what he's asking, but I don't know how to answer.

"Did your parents pass it on to you?"

"Noooo," Sasha says from the back seat.

He turns to her. "Well, *I* don't know. I've never heard of vaginalismus."

"Vaginismus," Sasha corrects him, laughing.

"Whatever." He turns back to me, staring at the side of my face.

I finally say with a shrug, "I just learned about it today."

"If it's not hereditary, then how do you get it?" Reggie asks Sasha.

"There's not a lot we know about it. It could be sexual trauma or just, like, fear."

"Fear of sex?" he asks.

"Yeah, well, fear of painful sex. Or it could just be an unexplained muscle spasm. No one really knows for sure," she says.

They're talking about me like I'm not right here.

"Do a lot of girls deal with this?" he asks.

I inhale through my nose. "Why are you asking so many questions?"

He furrows his brow at me. "I'm curious."

"Why? It's not like you have to deal with it. It's not like you were cursed with a broken body. Just stop. Okay?"

He stares at the side of my face, silent. Then he asks, "Why are you mad?"

"Because! I don't know how I got this way. It's such a stupid thing to happen to someone's body. Like I'm so emotionally unstable that my fear is manifesting itself into a physical disorder? I'm so scared that it will hurt, so scared to disappoint my parents, so scared that if I give away my virginity I'll have nothing left of value. And now my body won't even *let* me give up my virginity. That's so . . . dumb." I take a breath. "And I don't understand why I have this and why Sasha doesn't."

"What?" she asks, bewildered.

"You went to the same church I did. You were part of the promise ring ceremony too. How did that not—"

"Fuck me up?" she asks.

"*Yes.*"

She's quiet for a few seconds. Then she says, "I think because of the way I view church. I love church."

My head jerks back. Wait, she loves church? How does she love church and still say the F-word on the fly? I'm so confused.

Apparently so is Reggie, because he asks, "Wait, so it's not just an act?"

"No!" she says with a frustrated laugh. "I love church, because . . . it makes me feel close to my grandma."

My stomach clenches.

Her grandma died just a little over a year ago. My dad officiated the funeral and let her family hold the services in the church free of charge—Ms. Rosie had been a member of our church for so long, there was no question about it. Sasha was pretty broken up, though. And I guess, yeah, shortly after the funeral, she was more active in church.

But that night with Dom, all those things I said about her, comes flying back to me, turning my stomach.

"Church was, like, Granny's foundation. It was her thing. So, when I go to church, I feel like she's with me. Like her soul lives in those songs. I don't know if that makes sense."

"No, yeah, I get it," Reggie says. "It's like an imprint. She left her mark in church."

"Yeah," she says quietly. "That's what church is for me. I've never really given in to the fear tactics. Like, I love the songs and the rituals, but I have my own beliefs about what God expects from me."

"So, you're saying I *did* give in to the fear tactics?" I ask.

"Didn't you?"

I bite the corner of my bottom lip.

"I mean, I get it," she says. "Your dad is a pastor. And your mom is really intense."

"Your mom is really, *really* intense," Reggie mumbles.

"You said yourself that you feel like if you give away your virginity that you'll lose value. That's kind of what the church teaches you."

"Yeah," I say, because that's exactly it. That's exactly what my mother means when she says to me, *your virginity is a gift for your husband*. "But I thought I stopped believing all that when I got with Dom."

I thought I had . . . but at the same time, I believed we would eventually get married, so it was okay if we had sex.

I can't believe it took me two years to figure this all out. And I can't believe I figured it all out through Sasha Howser.

When I pull into her driveway, she scoots forward, holding on to the backs of our seats. "So, that was fun," she says.

"Yeah, it was," I say, like I couldn't wait for someone to say it first, glad that I'm not the only one who had an unabashed blast.

She sucks the back of her teeth. "Didn't get what we went out for, but . . ."

"I almost forgot we were supposed to be getting dilators," Reggie says, smiling. "Damn, that trip was a total bust."

It didn't feel like it, I wanna say. But they're right. There's no way I can fix my body without those dilators.

"We'll figure it out," Sasha says confidently, opening my car door and trotting up her driveway with a lazy wave. I sure hope she's right.

Then I remember what Reggie said about me not being alone. Thank God, I'm not alone. I'm considering the bright side of things as I drive through the dark backwoods, about five miles outside of town, when Reggie sits back, pulling at the legs of his pants. I feel him glance at me. "Hey, so about yesterday."

I keep my eyes forward but scrunch my brow. "What about yesterday?"

"The way your mom came at you was . . ."

Oh. That. "Yeah," I say like a sigh.

"Shitty," he says, finishing his thought. "I had so much to say that I was speechless. I'm sorry I didn't say anything."

I look at him, appalled. "Don't be sorry. You were right not to." I turn back to the road as a pair of headlights bounce on the horizon. I wait until they flash past to say, "Besides, I purposely put the pressure on myself in order to . . . take the pressure off you."

I let that sit in between us for a minute, feeling extra exposed. Then, when I turn to look at him, he's studying me. *Closely.* He says, "I know you did. And thank you for that."

I blush at the sober look in his eyes. All day he's been planning his next prank. I didn't know he could be so solemn. "Of course," I say, just as earnest. "But while we're apologizing, I'm sorry about what my mom said today. She was out of line."

He waves it off. "It's whatever. I'm used to that kind of shit."

"Yeah, well, maybe you shouldn't be." I glance at him. He's trying to look unaffected, but the fact that it bothered him is written all over his face. "She's just so . . ." I shake my head.

"You have to know that nothing she says ever counts."

"So I shouldn't listen to her?"

I smile. "I mean . . ."

"No, I hear you. When she says to put my phone away in church, I should just ignore her."

"No." I laugh. "Don't ignore her. I just mean that her opinion doesn't count."

When I look at him, he's smiling, biting the corner of his pink plump lip. "Okay, I gotcha." He glances out his window, then back at me. "So, while we're apologizing—"

I laugh again. "Why are we doing this?"

"I don't know, but I like it," he says, laughing too. "I'm sorry I got us kicked out of that sex shop."

I roll my eyes. "Yeah, you should be sorry for that."

"I really, really am." After a few seconds of laughter that makes me think he really, really isn't, he says, "Your turn."

"Oh, um . . ."

"Don't tell me you're out of things to apologize for."

"I'm sorry that I ran out of things to apologize to you for." I laugh, glancing at him.

He shakes his head. "Weak."

"Wait, I got it." I twist my mouth, giving him my sincerest expression. "I'm sorry that my daddy is all up in your business all the time."

His face falls, but only for a half second. "Oh, well, that's okay." He looks down at his hands in his lap. "Your dad's actually cool. I thought he was just gonna lecture me. You know?

Try to convert me."

I nod, staring through the night.

"So, I just came out with it. I told him right off the bat that I'm an atheist."

"Wait. Seriously?" I didn't even know he was an atheist. Daddy was pushing me to hang out with Reggie despite knowing that he's an atheist? "What did he do?" I ask.

Reggie looks at me with a puckered smile. "He said, 'Okay, that's cool.' Then he babbled on about how to properly hammer a nail." Reggie laughs.

I smile, feeling a spike of pride for my daddy.

"But, for real, all he did was ask me questions about the stuff I'm interested in." He smiles to himself. "I don't think I've ever had anyone just talk to me like that. Especially not, like, an adult. Without them trying to change me or make me better."

I nod. Then I meet his eyes.

"Your dad's pretty cool, Monique. I mean, maybe there's a shot he'll be understanding about your condition."

I shift my jaw. "Yeah, no. Absolutely not."

"Why not?"

"Because this is way different. The only reason he even let me date Dom is because he trusted that we wouldn't do anything . . . unsavory. We had a whole ceremony promising to not have relations before marriage."

"Sex," he corrects me.

"Sex before marriage," I say, trying to get used to the way

it sounds coming out of my mouth. "My daddy would not be understanding about this."

I finally make it to town—driving through the meager streetlights, down the vacant streets and past the barren storefronts. I start down Highway 150, on the way to Reggie's house, about five miles out of town. That's the thing about living around here—hardly anyone actually lives in the city limits.

"That brings me to my next apology," Reggie says in the silence.

"Oh?"

"I'm sorry you've been dealing with vaginismus *alone* for so long."

My lips part slightly. "I wasn't completely alone. I had Dom. But neither of us knew I had vaginismus. We didn't know what was happening."

He nods. "I bet not."

"But, yeah. Thank you."

My headlights slice tree trunks at their base as I make my way down the curvy road. I wonder if I told Dom about my vaginismus, if that would change things for him. Would he consider taking me back? Would he take the reins from Sasha and Reggie and help me figure out how to cure it?

Reggie cuts into my thoughts. "Hey, but you're okay, though, right?"

I glance at him with a lift of my brow. *Okay in what sense of the word?*

"Outside of sex, it doesn't cause you any pain, right? Your vagina isn't collapsing in on itself?"

"Reggie, no!" I laugh so hard, my vision blurs.

He laughs too, saying, "I'm just making sure we don't need to rush you to the hospital or anything."

"No!" I catch my breath, trying to soothe the ache in my abs from laughing so hard. "No, it's only a disorder. My vaginal canal closes up when anything tries to enter it."

"Oh, *cooooool*," he says, nodding. "So, it's like a Venus flytrap."

"First of all," I say with an amused grin, "it is not cool. Second of all, I don't like that you just compared my vagina to a murderous plant."

He busts out laughing, curling over himself. "But I seriously do think it's cool!"

"Cool, but not sexy," I say.

He shrugs, tilting his head. "Well . . ." As if he maybe does think that's sexy.

If he actually had to deal with my Venus flytrap vagina, he wouldn't think it was so cool, and definitely not sexy. But I appreciate how comfortable he is talking about this—how comfortable he makes *me* feel. He isn't treating me like I'm some unfortunate freak with a broken vagina—like I'm damaged goods.

I pull into Reggie's driveway, my headlights shining on the dark, empty blue house. "Here we are."

He turns to me with a goofy smile that's mostly bottom lip. "Okay, sooooo get this."

I immediately brace myself. "What?"

He grins harder. "I don't actually live here."

I look at the blue house, my headlights shining in the windows. "What do you mean you don't live here?" I think of the literal month my parents have been dropping him off here. "Who lives here?" I say, my hand on the gear shift.

"No one." He shrugs. "It's just an abandoned old shack."

I stare at him, horrified and amazed and so confused.

"My mom is always home on Sundays. And I didn't want your mom inviting herself in to snitch. When they do it over the phone, it's so much better, so my mom doesn't have to pretend to care about the little things your mom freaks out about." He rolls his eyes.

"So we've just been dropping you off in front of an abandoned shack, thinking you lived here?" I'm smiling, and now I'm laughing. "Wow, we must have looked dumb."

"I mean, yeah, kinda." He laughs too.

I think of all the times he's walked up that driveway so slowly, just waiting for us to leave.

"What would you have done if we actually waited for you to go inside?"

"I would've gone inside," he says, nonchalantly. "Like I said, it's abandoned. The door is broken in."

I look at the shack and realize just how worn down it is. The windows are all boarded up. It is quite obviously an abandoned shack, but somehow we believed he lived here. I just thought he was really, really poor. Plenty of kids around here live in dilapidated houses just like this. "So, where do you actually live?" I ask.

He points to the dirt driveway, and I finally notice how it continues carving a line through the trees, along the left side of the shack.

After only about a quarter mile, we pull up to a one-story house, with white slabs, black window shutters, and a matching black front door. The front steps are rounded, made of red brick, and lit by a lantern-shaped porch light. It's small, but perfectly big for Reggie and his mom.

"Wow," I say with a laugh. "You've been hiding this for a month. You are . . ." I shake my head at him. "You're somethin' else."

"You've gotta admit it's pretty hilarious."

I roll my eyes, smiling. "I guess." I just wonder what prompted him to finally tell me the truth. He could have gone inside that spooky little shack, and I would have reversed, gone home, and not known a thing. But him showing me this means he trusts me. It pulls a smile to my lips. Next Sunday, I'll know where he goes. Next Sunday, it'll be our little secret.

When he opens the passenger-side door, the overhead light comes on, but he doesn't get out. "I learned a lot today." He looks at me pointedly, leaning his arm on my console.

I look out the windshield, shying away from his closeness, then brave it and turn back to him. "Yeah?"

"Learned a lot about *you*." He gets out, and before he shuts the door says, "Changes everything."

Then he slowly swaggers up his driveway, his long body making shadows with my headlights. He pulls up his pants, mid-step, then looks at me over his shoulder with a secret little smirk.

I take a shaky breath. What does *that* mean?

15

My sister used to stay up with me on nights like this. Nights that would pour into me past the fill line, so much so that I would spill all over her bed. I'd lie back on her mattress, close my eyes, and she'd pull out her sketchbook. While I described the scene that had my mind in a frenzy, she'd try to draw it.

One night, when I was a freshman and she was nearing the end of her senior year, I described a scene to her: "Daddy and I were sitting at the bottom of the bleachers, right by the court. The newspaper was there tonight, taking pictures of Dom. He's the youngest boy in the area with his stats. Daddy kept going on and on about it. Anyway, it was like there was a magnet between me and Dom. Every time Coach Dale called time out, he'd huddle up, sure, but he kept staring at me. I don't even know if he was listening to the plays. He had his hands on his hips. He was sweaty, breathing out of his mouth—"

"When he looked at you, would he smile?" she asked, her pencil scratching across the paper.

"No. He just stared. Like, he wasn't flirting. He was only observing me. And after the game, Daddy and I were taking him home. You know how Daddy is. He was going over the game, like his coach or something. Dom was nodding like he was listening, and I was walking behind them. But then Dom looked over his shoulder and said, 'Mo-Mo, don't walk behind us. I need to make sure you're safe.' And Daddy was like, 'Yeah, Mo, get up here,' so I did. And every time I looked over my shoulder, Dom was staring at me. I don't think he cared about my safety. He just wanted to look at my butt."

Myracle laughed. "He wouldn't be that bold in front of Daddy."

"He could get away with it. Daddy *loves* him."

Then I described the car ride home, listening from the back seat as Daddy coached Dom up front. And how it felt sitting behind him. How I just wanted to touch him. How I wanted him to notice me again. And then when we pulled up to his house, how he peeked into the back seat at me and told me good night with a smile. How my heart had still been trying to catch up after that.

I kept going and going, and if I'd pause, caught up in my emotions, she'd always bring me back by saying, "And then what happened?"

But when my words cut off for good, when I just lay there

on her mattress imagining the scene again and again, Myracle's pencil kept scratching. The sound was usually comforting, like the murmur of a television or the hum of a refrigerator—a sign of constancy. Lulled me into believing she and I would always be together—*close* together.

But that night, the scratch of her pencil clogged my throat. The end of us was looming. She'd been accepted to the education program at Sam Houston State. She'd be leaving in a few months to start her future career as a science teacher. Sam Houston was only in Huntsville, one town over. She didn't *have* to move out, but she was adamant about getting her own apartment. She was adamant about ending our being together—*close* together.

"Why do you have to leave? You could save so much money if you just stayed home."

She sighed, sick of having this conversation with me, but I was sick of getting half answers. "Mo, I've told you, I can't grow in this house. It's stifling."

"What does that even mean?"

"You'll understand when you get older."

"I want to understand now," I whined, sitting up on my elbows.

She stopped sketching and met my gaze. I always thought Myracle had the most beautiful eyes, slanted inward, long and catlike. She blinked, scratching her cheek. "Mom and Dad have this idea of who I should be, what I should want, and where I should end up. That idea is like a cage. I can't even *think* for myself in this house. I can't make my own decisions."

"Yes, you can. Daddy let you choose which apartment you wanted. He let you choose what car you wanted. He lets you choose a lot."

"He lets me choose between options that he's already picked out for me. That's not freedom."

I stared at her, frowning. I didn't understand what she needed so much freedom for. He paid her deposit on the apartment. He paid for her car, her insurance, her gas. What more did she need? "Whatever, Myracle." I lay back down and closed my eyes and tried to get back to thinking of Dom, instead of what life would be like when she was gone.

She got back to sketching the high school gym, the back of my and Daddy's heads, and Dom across the court from us—hands on his hips, eyes on me. She said, "This house is too tiny. You'll see when you get older."

But all I've seen since she left is how big and empty this house is without her. How big and empty my life is. I miss coming home to her being here. I miss *her*. So when I get home, feeling like a piece of the night that accidentally floated indoors, I don't have a way to spill my guts about tonight, and how it's been the absolute best night of my life.

Everything is on in the living room, but my parents are nowhere to be found. Actually, it looks like they never came out of their room. I tiptoe to their closed door.

"I have a say in the way we raise our daughter," Mom says.

"I know you do, but I need you to turn to God. God asks us to forgive."

"Jesse," she cries in frustration, "I need to talk to my husband and the father of my child right now. Not the pastor of my church. The father of my daughter wouldn't be so cavalier about letting troubled teenage boys into her life. The father of my daughter would guard her innocence."

Guard her innocence? Jesus, that sounds gross.

"I can't pick and choose when I'm your husband, when I'm a father, and when I'm a preacher. I'm all three, all the time. And as the father of that child, I know that my daughter will be a good influence on Reggie. That boy doesn't need another adult telling him who to be. He just needs love and someone to tell him that it's okay to be exactly who he is."

My heart softens hearing my daddy's passion. It really is crazy, the dynamic here. Daddy thinks I could be a good influence on Reggie, while Mom thinks Sasha could be a good influence on *me*. It's crazy how they're both so wrong.

While my parents are occupied with their "discussion," I figure this is the perfect time to sneak in the book Sasha forced on me and my new devil bra. I stuff them into my biggest purse, smuggle them inside the house, and hide them in the same place that I hid the lingerie Dom got me: far, far beneath my bed.

Then I wander into Myracle's room (the effective guest room). Mom might have changed the bedding, put up a few paintings of horses, and put in a few rustic chairs, but there was nothing she could do to get rid of the carvings in the desk or the dried candle wax in the carpet. Myracle was an artist—she was messy. Mom *hated* that about her. But I loved her mess. I loved to become a part of her mess, to listen to her thoughts and share mine.

My feet take me to the corner of the room, past her old bed and her old dresser, and I stop before her desk. When I open the top drawer, there it is—the one and only project Myracle and I did together. She sketched a cover for a book I wrote when I used to do that kind of thing—when I had time and fantasies too big for my brain. The cover is of me, sitting in a classroom, biting my bottom lip, staring at the back of Dom's head. He's looking down at his desk, completely unaware of my desire for him—the story of my life as a freshman.

I pick up the packet of notebook paper, stapled together in a corner, then I flip past Myracle's drawing to the first page, written in purple ink. I used to spend so much time making all my letters look bubbly and cute. I used to write in colorful ink. Each chapter is basically a diary entry, a different fantasy I had of Dom and me—him admitting his love for me at my locker, him kissing me in the middle of the cafeteria, him waving to me right before making a jump shot during the basketball championship. It was a dream relationship—one that didn't end with me having vaginismus and him breaking up with me.

I drop the homemade book back in the top drawer and slam it shut. Myracle's gone, Dom's gone, and so are all those dreams. But I don't want to think about that right now, not after the amazing night I had. God, I wish Myracle was still here, so I could tell her all about it.

I lie on her mattress, just like I used to, and replay the last seconds of the night when Reggie said *changes everything*. What changed?

Somehow, tonight it felt like me and him and Sasha were on our own little planet. And it didn't feel like Daddy was forcing me on Reggie, while Mom forced Sasha on me. We all got so comfortable, so fast. And of our own accord.

What changed about us tonight?

Everything.

Myracle's bedroom door creaks open. I sit up on my elbows, watching Daddy walk into the room, looking around like he doesn't remember when it got to be so unrecognizable. "Hey, baby," he says distantly. Then he sits on the edge of the bed.

I lie back down, eyes trained on the ceiling fan.

"You miss her, huh?"

My eyebrows flick up. "Don't *you*?"

He doesn't say anything for a while. This is one of those off-limit conversations. But when he does finally speak, his voice is cold. "Of course I miss her, but Myracle made her choice, and now she has to live with it," he says, unconcerned about where those choices might have landed her—if she needs help, she can no longer come to him, and that scares me. I swallow hard, trying to not imagine him saying that exact thing about me and the choices I've made tonight.

Then he sighs and immediately changes the subject. "Baby,

I want you to tell me something."

My stomach drops. *Does he know something? Does he know what I did tonight?* I try not to show my immediate fear on my face.

He says, "How did Reggie behave when you all hung out together?"

Oh. This is about Reggie. Not me. I release my breath. "He was fine. Normal."

"Did you have fun?"

Flashes of the night pull my lips up into a smile. "So much fun."

"What about him did you find fun?"

My eyes widen slightly. "Um." The way he screamed *sex toys* in the middle of Target, and the way he asked for dildos in CVS. I say, "You know, he's just really funny." And immature and bold. I say, "He makes everyone laugh." Everyone except for the employees and the shoppers and anyone who isn't me and Sasha.

"He doesn't take himself too seriously," Daddy says.

"Exactly." He doesn't take *anything* too seriously.

"But what I'm asking is, he didn't do anything bad, right? You didn't catch him stealing or anything?"

"No," I say immediately. The bra doesn't count, I tell myself. It was an accident.

Daddy nods. "Good." Then he pats my knee. "Let me know if he ever acts up around you. Okay?"

I nod. And I don't make eye contact, because if I do, I might spill everything.

Daddy might be a pastor, but his advice is never "pray" or "God will make it better." He gives real, compassionate advice. If only I could tell him everything. But if I tell him, I already know that'll be the key to turning off his ears, like he did for Myracle.

He gets up to leave but stops in the doorway. "So . . . did you ever call Dom?"

I freeze. My whole body stiffens. The mention of Dom sends me spiraling, because of course as soon as I got my phone back, I texted him. He hasn't texted back, though. He hasn't even opened it. But I can't say that to Daddy, because then he'll try to help, and I don't have the energy to fend him off. "Not yet."

"What are you waiting on, baby?"

"I'll call him soon. I just gotta get my words together."

He studies me for a few seconds. He probably has so many questions. I'm so glad he decides to not ask, because I don't have answers.

When he leaves, he closes the door, and my body sinks into the mattress. If only Myracle was still here. I could tell her everything. If only I knew how to get in contact with her. But when she left, Mom cut the service from her phone, and then she fled social media, and I haven't heard from her since. I don't even know if she's okay.

16

Sasha's sitting at my desk, wearing fake glasses and the smile of a kindergarten teacher. I stare back at her, shifting my eyes uncomfortably.

She's here under the guise of planning the church club for school, but really this is our first "therapy session." She has a pen and a notepad in her hands, and for some reason, she brought a yoga mat. I have no idea what's going on, and I'm not sure why we're just staring at each other. "Sooooo . . ." I finally say.

"Let's start with an exercise," she jumps in. "Close your eyes." I hesitate, but then I do as she says, crossing my legs on my bed and closing my eyes. "Now, when I say the word *penis*, what's the first thing that comes to mind?"

My eyes pop open.

"Close your eyes," she gripes.

"Wait, but, like, are you asking what *word* pops in my head, or what . . . image?"

She twists her mouth, unsure. She clearly has no idea what she's doing. She's a sixteen-year-old girl. There's no way I can expect her to seriously therapize me.

"What emotion do you feel when I say the word *penis*?"

"Um." I frown. "Weird?"

"Weird isn't an emotion."

I shrug. "Sure it is. A person can feel weird. I feel weird."

She rolls her eyes. "Okay, close your eyes." I do, and she says, "What about when I say the word *vagina*?"

I smile. "Weird."

"Sex?"

I shift in my seat. "Weird."

"You can't keep saying *weird*."

My eyes are still closed. I swipe my tongue across my front teeth and shrug. "Uncomfortable."

"Okay. Why do you feel uncomfortable?"

"I don't know. I mean, my mom could walk in at any moment and hear us talking about it, and we'd get in trouble."

"Sex. Say *sex*."

"Talking about sex," I say, annoyed.

"So it feels risky?"

"Very," I say.

"When you would try to have sex with Dom, were you scared you'd get caught and get in trouble?"

"Most of the time, we were in his truck, and we'd be parked at the creek in the middle of the woods. For some reason, I never thought we'd get caught. That's not what I was worried about."

"What were you worried about?"

I open my eyes, peer over to the Bible verses on my wall. Her eyes follow mine. Then we meet gazes again, and her eyes are softer. "Were you worried about God or your parents?" she asks.

"My parents . . . I think. Maybe both. Maybe neither. I wasn't thinking about a particular person or entity. It was the idea of having sex before marriage. It was the idea that I could give him my virginity, and he could just walk away with it."

"And what if he did, where would that leave you?"

". . . Soiled. It's such a big deal who you give your virginity to. Like, whoever takes your virginity owns you."

"That's honestly bullshit. And that's not equally true for boys. It's not fair."

I press my lips tight, staring at her. Her tone surprises me, but she's right, it isn't fair. Having sex wasn't a thing for Dom. He wasn't even a virgin when he got with me—and I didn't think less of him for that. But he made such a big deal about wanting to be the one to take my virginity. It would seal the deal. Like a ring on my finger, it would make me his forever.

"If you date a boy and you're not a virgin, that doesn't make you less of a catch," she says. My eyes heat up, because it's something I need to hear, but for some reason, it's too solid to soak in.

"So, let's do this." She suddenly looks excited. "Let's talk about what makes you a catch."

I laugh a little. "Uh."

"I'm serious. Okay, I'll go first. I'm a catch because I don't change myself to please others. I'm a catch because I can sing and dance and I'm really good at math. I have goals. I'm going to be a financial adviser, or maybe an accountant. I'm a catch because I believe in myself, and I don't limit myself. I'm going to get a scholarship to go to a school outside of Texas. I want to move to California. Stanford."

"Stanford? Wow."

"That's my dream," she says, smiling.

"An accountant? I could have sworn you wanted to be a therapist or a gynecologist."

"A gynecologist is just too ironic." She rolls her eyes.

I laugh. "How?"

Her lips part slightly, like she realizes she's said too much. Then she drops her gaze to the blank sheet of paper on her notepad. "I guess I'd like to be a therapist or a gynecologist, but I hate science, and I really don't want to go to medical school."

I nod. "But you seem really good at it."

And her eyes light up. She ducks her head down, sheepish. "Thanks." Then she takes a deep breath with a big smile. "Well, anyway, what about you?"

My smile fades. I honestly don't know what makes me a catch.

"Who are you outside of your relationship with Dom? What are you other than a virgin?"

"I'm . . . not sure," I say delicately.

She nods. "Well, that's your homework." Then she stands up, placing her pen and paper on my desk. "In the meantime, let's do some physical exercises to help open you up."

I grimace. "Open me up?"

"Relax your pelvic muscles. To dilate your vagina—"

Then my bedroom door opens, and in comes my mom.

Sasha's quick with the switch. "God forgives. He loves us unconditionally. All we have to do is repent. And I think maybe we should focus on that every Thursday." Then she turns to my mother with the biggest church smile. "Oh, hi, Mrs. Tinsley."

Mom has an equally big smile as she watches the two of us get along, talking about God and whatnot.

"Hi, Mom," I say, then to Sasha, "I think that's a great idea. Maybe Tuesdays, we can do Bible study?"

"Yeah," Sasha says enthusiastically.

"Those sound like great ideas," Mom says, grinning. "Girls, listen, I'm running to Huntsville to run a few errands. I'll be back in a couple of hours. Call if you need anything."

"Okay, Mom," I say.

"Bye, Mrs. Tinsley."

"Bye, girls." She smiles, and Sasha and I wait until we hear the front door shut before looking at each other and bursting into laughter.

"Oh my God!" I squeal. "You were amazing."

"Why thank you." She bows, her faux locs falling over her shoulders.

Wow, how I misjudged her. I never in a million years thought Sasha would willingly deceive my mother. I never in a billion, zillion years thought she could say the word *penis* with such ease. Or, for God's sake, be the one to help me with this sex thing.

She rolls out her yoga mat and allows me to sit on it while she takes the floor. Then she instructs me to spread-eagle my legs. She does the same and mirrors me as I rest my body toward my right leg.

"Oh, God, I'm tight," I grumble, feeling the tension in my hamstrings.

She laughs. "Yeah, that's essentially the problem. Try to relax as much as possible."

I take a breath and close my eyes, letting my shoulders sink. After a minute of silence, I open my eyes again to find her nose touching her knee. *Geez*, she's flexible. "How do you know about this stuff? Dr. Marion?"

She lifts a bit and turns her face to meet my gaze. "No, well, Dr. Marion typically refers her patients to physical therapists. So, before I came here, I found a video on YouTube of stretches we could do."

I smile. "You did research for me?"

She smiles too, then drops her nose back to her knee. "Of course."

We stretch to the other side, then we pull our feet together into butterfly stretches. We're facing each other, but we're not comfortable enough to look at each other. I stare at the carpet blankly, then she calls my attention back to her when she says, "That's a really cool sketch." She nods her head to the drawing on my wall.

I look at it, even though I know exactly which sketch she's talking about. My face instantly gets cloudy. "Oh, that . . ."

It's a sketch of me and Dom in the back seat of my daddy's car. We're facing each other, smiling, moments before we kissed for the first time. It was after a revival program all the way in Corsicana, Texas, where my daddy had been invited to preach.

Dom and I had been flirting heavily for weeks, and that night, when my parents left us alone in the back seat of the Cadillac while they conversed with the congregation, Dom finally made a move.

It was tense at first. We were quiet and there was a whole middle seat between us. But then I turned to him. "Good job, by the way, on the drums."

He looked at me with a smirk. "How would you know? You don't know anything about music, remember?"

I smiled back at him, because that was something I'd told him weeks before. "I could tell by how many people were into it. And, I mean, I know what sounds good."

He laughed gently and stared at me. Just stared. Then he unbuckled his seat belt and moved to the middle seat. Got real close to me, stopping my heart. "I was wondering something kinda random."

I bit my bottom lip and squeaked, "Okay?"

"Would you be willing to wear my jersey number on your cheeks when the season starts in the fall?"

I raised my eyebrows and lost my breath. "Usually . . . only girlfriends do that."

"I know." He smiled and peered down at my lips. That was all he said. That was all he needed to say. *I know.*

He leaned in slowly, until the tip of his nose brushed mine. I sucked in a shaky breath. "Okay," I whispered. "I will."

Then he kissed me.

I told Myracle that story, in a fit of excitement. She hadn't gone with us to the revival, because at that point, my parents couldn't get her to do anything she didn't want to do.

I could barely stop smiling and squeeing enough to lay out the scene. She drew it, capturing that moment forever. Every time I look at it on my wall, I remember how it felt to have my heart burst into flames and how it felt to have a stomach full of butterflies, *perpetually,* and how it felt to think that life was perfect.

That moment with Dom was the most perfect moment of our relationship. And sharing it with my sister, being able to describe my desire to her without feeling ashamed (that we'd kissed on church grounds), that was the foundation of our sisterhood. I lost that when I lost her. That sketch was the last sketch she ever gave me. Not even a week later, she left and never came back.

When I look at Sasha, the pain shines in my eyes.

"Oh," she says. "Sorry. I shouldn't have asked. I know you and Dom just broke up."

"No, it's okay," I say, pushing my feet together in the butterfly pose. "My sister drew that."

"Myracle?" she asks. "Wow, she's really amazing."

I nod, not making eye contact.

"I always wondered . . . like, what happened to her. I mean, I know she was supposed to go to SHSU, but she ended up not going. So where did she go?"

I'm not sure I want to talk about this. I'm not sure I know how. When I look at Sasha, though, her soft, dark eyes make it hard to not want to spill my guts. After all, it's been so long since I've been able to talk to anyone so candidly, not since my sister left.

"Myracle wanted to go to art school." I take a deep breath and press forward, leaning over my butterfly legs, stretching and relaxing farther down. "My parents thought she wanted to be a teacher, like my mom. They got her an apartment and everything. Then, in the middle of the summer, she told them that she had declined her admission."

"Oh, shit. Seriously?"

I nod. "My parents lost their deposit on the apartment. They had no intention of spending money on art school. And they were really mad that she declined the offer at Sam without even talking to them. At the same time, Myracle had been really . . . rebellious. She was getting into arguments with Mom, she was staying out past curfew, hanging out with people my parents didn't approve of. One time, she was brought home in a squad car after being caught drunk at a party. So, my daddy thought the best thing for her was to spend the rest of the summer at my granny's house in Mexia—which, I don't know if you know, but there's *nothing* to do out there."

"No, I know," she says, nodding.

"They packed her bags, and said they'd try their best to get Sam to give her back her spot in the fall, but Myracle wanted nothing to do with it. She grabbed her stuff and just *left*."

"Where did she go?"

I shrug. "No idea."

"Wait . . . so you don't know where she is? Have you talked to her since?"

I hesitate, but then I shake my head, because I feel kind of ashamed. What kind of sister am I that I don't know where she is, or if she's okay? "My parents cut off her phone, and she hasn't been on any of her social media accounts. I don't really have any way of contacting her."

"That's . . ." she says, not finishing her thought. I can think of a few words that she probably wants to say. *Shameful. Awful. Disgusting.*

"I'm sorry," she says instead. "I'm sorry you lost your sister like that."

My lip starts to quiver a bit, because I guess I've never been able to admit to myself how hard it's been without my sister. Maybe things would be different with my body if Myracle was still around. I look up at Sasha, vulnerable and grateful. "Thanks, Sasha."

She nods, then we move on to the next stretch.

"Have you started reading that book I got you?" she asks me, after we've stretched and rolled and thrown our legs in the air. Thank God Mom is gone, because she would have a lot of questions about the poses we were doing.

"I can't exactly whip it out in front of my parents."

She frowns. "Well, your parents aren't home right *now*."

"You want me to read right now? What are you gonna do, watch me?"

"Oh, wait, I got an idea! Do you have HBO?"

"Absolutely not."

"No, yeah, of course you don't. It's fine. We can use my brother's login." She gets up and grabs my laptop.

"Wait, for what? What are we doing?"

She doesn't answer—only smiles sinisterly. I don't know what I'm getting myself into by sliding my laptop over to her, but I'm intrigued, if not a little scared.

She goes to HBO Max, enters her brother's login information, then immediately goes to the *Insecure* series. "You've heard of this show, right?" she asks.

I shrug. "In passing."

Then she just smiles at me, studies me like she knows something I don't.

"What?" I finally say.

"Okay, so we don't have time to watch the whole series, but I'll explain as we go." She clicks on season one, episode five, and sets it up on my desk. Then she joins me on my bed.

I have to ask. "What does this show have to do with me reading that book?"

"It doesn't. This is an alternative way to get exposure therapy."

"*How?*" I ask, almost horrified.

"Because it shows two Black women who talk about sex in a very . . . open way." I narrow my eyes, not trusting her. "Just watch," she says. "It's a really good show."

"But why are we starting on episode five?"

"It's an important episode. Just *shhh.*"

So I do. I watch, not knowing who anyone is or what's going on or why we couldn't have just started at the beginning. But then there's talk of someone's *broken p***y*, and I get it. "Is this what you think of me? You think my . . . vagina is broken?"

She laughs, "No! I would never!"

I lower my chin with tight lips.

"I'm serious. That's not why we're here. Just keep watching."

I watch the whole episode, and sure, it's interesting, but again, no context. We get near the end, and Issa is with Daniel in the music studio and suddenly I scream. There are naked man buns on my computer screen! I cover my eyes.

Sasha laughs. "No, come on! You have to watch."

"How is this allowed to be on TV?" I exclaim.

"Just watch! I promise, your eyes won't fall out of your head."

"I'm not sure about that." I uncover my eyes and wrinkle my face at the full-blown sex scene unfolding on my laptop.

Then everything gets worse.

My bedroom door opens. Aunt Dee walks inside. "Mo–Mo, where's your mom?" Then she notices Sasha beside me. Then she notices the show on my laptop. The sex. Our young eyes. On the sex. And she says, "Oh, shit, are we marathoning?" She turns to us, excited. "I haven't even seen the new season, yet, but I'm the biggest Daniel fan."

"Wait, are you serious?" Sasha sits up, appalled. "Daniel's the worst. He . . . *you know*, in her eyes. Like, on her face. And he's just, like, cold and opportunistic."

"How is he opportunistic? If anyone is opportunistic, it's Issa. I mean, if we're being honest, Lawrence would have never gotten his shit together if Issa hadn't left."

"But she didn't just leave! She cheated on him."

I sit, scratching my head. So, are we just gonna not talk about the fact that she practically caught us watching porn? We're just gonna . . . Okay. Cool.

Aunt Dee smirks, hand on her hip. "I've had this argument several times with my girlfriends." Then she narrows her eyes at Sasha. "I like you."

Sasha smiles. "Thanks."

Then Aunt Dee looks at me and back at my computer screen.

"But are y'all even allowed to watch this?" She scrunches her eyebrows at me.

Okay, here we go. The discussion. The talking-to. The *I'm gonna have to tell your mom about this*. My mouth opens but no words come out.

Instead, Sasha shrugs. "Sure we are."

Aunt Dee studies the two of us as the episode ends. She laughs and walks away. *Like everything is fine.*

I release my breath, hand over my heart. And the only thing Sasha has to say for herself is, "Wow, that was really close. You should really get a lock on your door."

I look at her, almost furious. "Can we be done for the day?"

"Oh, yeah. Right. Therapy." She rolls off my bed, and I feel kind of bad, because maybe this stopped being a therapy session for her and started being something else. Something like two friends hanging out.

"Maybe we can do something not so risky—give my heart a break," I say.

She stops, hands on her hips, hope in her eyes. "Yeah, sure. I'm up for anything." She turns off the episode, and while she does, she asks, "But who was that just now?"

"My aunt," I say with wide eyes, so hopefully she'll understand the weight of what just happened.

She says, "That was your *aunt*? She was really cool. Maybe you should tell her about your issue. She seems like . . . she could understand."

"Oh, I don't think so. She's still my mom's sister. She wouldn't be *that* cool."

"Monique, she just caught us watching a real-life sex scene and laughed. She likes *Insecure*. You haven't seen the whole show, but if she can watch that series, I think she would have a lot to say about your condition. She might even take you to the doctor."

I rub my hand over my neck. "You think so?"

"She's your aunt, so you know her better than me, but what just happened"—she circles her hand around the room—"was really cool."

And surprising. I never thought *any* adult in my life would react that way to catching me watch sex. It makes me wonder how else Aunt Dee could surprise me.

17

Aunt Dee and Uncle Raven live in a single-story brick house in The Woodlands. They live in the type of neighborhood where the houses all look the same, and it usually takes me ten minutes more than it should to find the house. I know it when I see it, though, what with the neatly trimmed shrubs lining the front of the house, the perfectly green grass, the brick-encased flower bed on the left side of the yard, and the rock garden on the right—all courtesy of landscape designer Uncle Raven.

They always have the most beautiful yard in the neighborhood, despite the fact that Uncle Raven designed over half of his neighbors' yards. There's no way he'd let anyone outshine his *own* yard, though. That's why I always tense up when he insists on seeing how far my daddy has gotten on building the deck. I'm just waiting for him to insult Daddy's work and for Daddy to be inconsolably discouraged. But it hasn't happened yet. Uncle Raven is prideful, but he's not mean.

I park behind Aunt Dee's white BMW, get out of my car, and hesitate in the driveway. Sasha thought this would be a good idea, but maybe I didn't think this all the way through. Aunt Dee is cool, but she's still loyal to my mom.

She doesn't give me time to reconsider, though. The front door bursts open and she comes speed walking down the driveway with Zula, their black-and-white border collie, right behind her. Zula gets to me first, jumping up, paws on my thighs. "Hi, Zu-Zu," I coo, running my hands all over her furry head. She licks my chin, and I duck away.

"Mo-Mo, what in the world is going on? Are you okay?" Aunt Dee asks, hands on her hips.

"I'm fine," I say, dodging Zula's kisses.

"What was so important that you couldn't tell me over the phone? Spill it."

I look at her with my face scrunched. "Can we, like, go inside first?"

She stops and stares at me, then rolls her eyes. "Whatever. Come on, Zula." She leads me and Zula inside, Zula circling my legs the whole way there.

I slide out of my sandals, leaving them at the door. Zula scampers alongside Aunt Dee into the kitchen. "Is Uncle Raven here?" I ask.

"Yeah, baby girl," he calls from the living room. I slide across the tile, peering through the doorway at the big-screen television, playing what looks like a fishing show. Uncle Raven is always watching boring stuff like that—golf or swimming or

159

tennis—I mean, the *least* interesting sports.

"Hey, Unc."

He doesn't turn his head away from the program. "Hey, Mo." He's sitting in his leather recliner, in a white muscle shirt, cracking pecans over a TV tray. He's honestly too young to be engaging in such "old people" activities. He may live in this posh neighborhood, but he's a country boy at heart.

In the kitchen, Zula is lying at Aunt Dee's feet while she probes the refrigerator. As I pull out a bar stool at the island, she asks, "Want some water, lemonade, Kool-Aid?"

I shake my head. "I'm okay." I'm *nervous*. All I can think about are the words I'm supposed to say. The words that escaped me the second I pulled into her driveway.

She opens the freezer. "Vodka?" she asks, and pulls out a frosty bottle full of clear liquid. I stare appalled as she fills a shot glass and slides it to me.

What is this, a test? "No," I say with furrowed brows.

Then her eyes flicker between mine. She looks scared. "I knew it. Oh *God*, you're pregnant! Oh God! Do your parents know yet?"

"What?" I screech. "No!"

"Of course they don't. Of course, I'm the first person you tell."

"No! I mean—"

"Who's pregnant?" Uncle Raven shouts from the living room.

"No one! I'm not pregnant!"

But Aunt Dee is still looking at me like I'm a tragedy. "That's why that eggheaded boy broke up with you," she says. "I'll fuck him up, I swear. He's gonna take care of this baby."

I slap my hands against the counter. "Aunt Dee, I swear I'm not pregnant. It's not even possible for me to be pregnant. I can't have sex. I have—"

"You're a virgin?" she asks, then assumes she's right and keeps going. "Oh, thank God! Now I can tell your mom to stop freaking out."

"Wait, tell my mom? About this conversation?"

She grabs the shot glass and dumps it in the sink. "That's all she worries about—Dom pressuring you into sex. I'll just tell her you confided in me that you're still a virgin, so maybe she'll get off your back. I'm always trying to tell Bianca that you're not even *thinking* about sex."

She's rinsing out the shot glass and putting the vodka back in the freezer, while my leg is bouncing on the bar stool. "But . . . what if I *am* thinking about it?"

She pauses, stone still. My eyelids flutter, vision blurring into her black Nike tank top. She's wearing a silk wrap on her head, black-rimmed glasses sliding down her nose. When she turns to look at me, she looks like she wishes I hadn't said that. "Thinking about it how? You have questions about how it works?" She tilts her head down, prompting me to *please God* tell her that's what I meant.

I say, with my eyes closed, "Thinking about doing it."

"Why, Monique?" she asks. I open my eyes and watch the

confusion take over her face. "For that boy? Is *that* why he broke up with you? And you think having sex with him will get him back, don't you?"

I bite the corner of my lip. This wasn't the reaction I was hoping for when I imagined having this conversation with her. I imagined I'd tell her about my condition, and I imagined her eyes softening, and I imagined her getting pissed at the fact that I don't feel safe enough to tell my parents, and I imagined her packing me up in her car and rushing me to a doctor. But I can't even get to the vaginismus part because here she is overreacting to the sex part.

"Don't you?" she asks again.

"Not exactly."

"But a little bit," she says, nodding, resting a hand on the counter. For the first time ever, she actually looks like the most responsible adult in the room. She's got that same look in her eyes that Mom gets when she's about to give me a talking-to. "Sex is not the way to win a boy back."

"But the thing is, Aunt Dee, I can't even have sex."

She misunderstands immediately. "I know you can't. Your mom would kill you. Your *dad* would kill you." She says it in list form, like she's reminding me of all the reasons I shouldn't be thinking about this.

Then I ask, "Would *you* kill me?" I peek up from under my brow, and she looks pained by that question. I can tell how much she hates having this conversation right now.

"Mo-Mo." She sighs and then takes a seat on a bar stool across from me. She crosses her hands on the island counter and wrinkles her nose. "I can't tell you when to have sex, and neither can your parents, for that matter." Then she leans forward, forcing me to make eye contact, attempting to penetrate my soul with how deeply she means the next part. "What I *can* tell you," she says, "is that you are a phenomenal young lady."

My brow furrows. What does that have to do with me having sex?

"I remember when you were a little girl. You were always so careful. Always on time for everything. A *big* planner." She smiles at me. "When I would take you and Myracle anywhere, I knew I didn't have to worry about you. It was always Myracle that I had to keep my eye on. You're responsible, smart, beautiful, and if I remember correctly, a very talented tree climber."

I smile at that. She's right. I was a fantastic tree climber, because I took my time with it. I planned out every step, searched for the next limb, made sure that it could support my weight before I went any farther. I would get up so high and I never fell. Myracle fell. Myracle rushed. But I never did.

"I know you," she says. "I know what you look like when you're thinking about your next move. You get this faded look in your eyes, and your whole face gets still." Then she slides her hands back across the counter. "Look, I can't make you keep your virginity. I just hope you'll give it as much consideration as you do everything else. If you have sex, make sure it's because you want to, not because some stupid boy asks you to."

She stands up, and Zula's already at her feet. "I have to get back to work, my girl. Was that all you came over to talk about?"

"Um." My face gets still. I guess this is the look she's referring to when I'm thinking about my next move. And maybe this would be a great time to tell her that I can't have sex—like physically can't—but I'm still thinking about what she said. Am I doing this for me? Is having sex something that I want to do? Or is it just something that Dom wants? "Yeah," I say. "Yeah, that was all."

She starts to leave the kitchen, but I call out, "You're not gonna tell my mom about this, are you?"

"*Fuck* no," she says. "Can't even imagine having that conversation with her."

I flick my eyebrows up and murmur, "Yeah, me either."

"Help yourself to anything in the fridge," she says, leading Zula down the hall, back to her home office.

"Thanks! I'm probably just gonna go, though."

She doesn't respond. I don't think she heard me. I stand, and as I'm about to leave, I glance at the refrigerator. Usually, she keeps word magnets stuck up there. Myracle and I would make little stories out of them, insulting each other, calling each other pumpkin head and big head. And there were a few magnets with cuss words that I refused to touch, but Myracle didn't care.

There's something else, though, stuck to the fridge. A small postcard with a sketch drawn on the front. A sketch of Aunt

Dee doing someone's makeup. My makeup, in my bathroom, on the night of my anniversary with Dom. That was only a few days ago. How? Wait, what?

I stare at it, recognizing the drawing style. Terrified and confused about what this means. Aunt Dee has been in contact with Myracle? Recently? *Very* recently. The inside of me drops and splats on the floor. Why Aunt Dee? Why not . . . me?

18

I couldn't sleep. My heart just wouldn't slow, and my mind kept going over what happened that night—the night Myracle left.

She'd been gone for two whole days, no calls, no texts. We had no idea where she was. When she finally came home, as soon as I heard the front door slam, I ran out of my room and hung on to the edges of the hallway, watching the scene unfold.

She stumbled past the boxes lined up by the door—boxes of all her stuff. She looked hurt, like her every step was painful. Our parents were on the couch in the living room. And they just watched, stunned, as she trudged closer.

Myracle stopped, looked over her shoulder at the boxes by the door, then back to our parents, her voice weak. "Is that my stuff?"

It was the push they needed to jump out of their stupor. Daddy popped up from the couch, Mom right behind him.

"Myracle, where have you been?"

She looked at them, blinking slowly. "Out."

"For two days?" Daddy asked in disbelief. "You couldn't have answered your phone? We were worried sick."

"Couldn't have been too worried if you were packing up all my shit."

I inhaled sharply. Myracle cussed around me all the time, but never in front of our parents.

Mom growled, "You watch your mouth."

"My-My," Daddy said, "*where were you?*"

When she looked at Daddy, her eyes softened. She always softened when she looked at Daddy (I always do too). She said, "I was . . . doing a lot of thinking."

"You couldn't have done your thinking inside the house? What were you thinking about?"

She shrugged. "Who I am, and what I want."

Mom scoffed.

"Okay." Daddy nodded. "Who are you, and what do you want?"

"Jesse, don't even entertain her ridiculousness," Mom said.

Myracle scowled at her, but when she looked at Daddy, her eyes watered and her lips trembled. She said, "Daddy, I . . . I declined my admission to Sam. I don't want to go."

"You declined? You . . . what?" He was speechless. "You did it already? Without talking to us first?"

"I don't want to be a science teacher."

"Okay, but you could always change your major. You didn't

have to *decline* your admission." He slapped his hands by his sides. "So what? You're not gonna go to school at all?"

Then a smile cracked across her face, a genuinely excited smile. "Actually . . ." She pulled out her phone and handed it to him. "I got in at the Art Institute."

"The Art Institute?" Mom asked. "We can't pay for the Art Institute."

And then they listed all the reasons she should have come to them first, and how irresponsible she'd been, and how much money they wasted putting a deposit down on her apartment. Daddy said, "I don't think being here has been good for you. Your new friends have been putting all kinds of ideas in your head. So we're sending you to your granny's for the rest of the summer."

"In Mexia?"

"Yes. Then your mom and I are gonna do everything we can to get your spot back at Sam. How dare you make this decision without talking to us first."

"I'm eighteen. It's *my* decision."

"It's *our* money," Mom said.

And they were right. It was their money. If Myracle wanted to do art, she could have done art at Sam. She could have stayed close and just gone to Sam, but she insisted on getting as far away from me as possible.

They sent her to her room, said they'd take her to Granny's in the morning. She stormed past me as I was still lurking in the hallway, and slammed her bedroom door. So I went back to my room, a little scared for her, but mostly hopeful that she'd learn to enjoy being at Sam, hopeful that maybe she would still live at home.

But she was not hopeful. She came to my room at one thirty in the morning, shook me awake. My eyes popped open, scared. "I'm leaving, Mo-Mo. I can't let them take my future away."

"What?" I spat. She turned and headed to my bedroom door. "Wait, where are you going?"

Over her shoulder, she hissed, "You have to be quiet." Then she wagged her hand for me to follow.

I hurried out of bed, the sound of my own breath clouding everything, making it hard to be as quiet as she needed me to be. I was terrified. I was confused and frustrated. Just, *God*, why couldn't she just stay put? Why couldn't she just stay in line?

She opened the front door for me and quietly closed it behind me. Then she led me to her car. I wasn't wearing shoes, so I could feel every rock in our driveway poking into the fleshy parts of my feet. And it was so dark. We weren't the type of people to leave our front porch light on all night, so I could barely see my hands in front of me.

Myracle had a duffel bag on her shoulder. She opened the passenger door and the overhead light came on. As she dropped the bag in the seat, I noticed her appearance. "Did you cut your hair?"

"Yeah," she said nonchalantly, quietly closing the door and consequently turning out the light. "I'll message you when I get where I'm going."

"Where are you going?"

"A friend's."

"Which friend?"

"I'll message you," she said, walking around the front of the car.

"Wait, but Myracle, why?"

"I have to get going."

She wasn't listening to me. She was moving too fast. I was about to lose her. "Stop!" I shouted too loudly.

She hurried over to me, whispering, "Mo-Mo—"

"Why'd you do that, Myracle?"

"Why'd I do what?"

"Decline your admission."

She sighed, resting her arms by her sides. "Mo, I don't want to be a teacher. I don't want anything to do with what our parents want for me. I don't want to marry a church boy. I don't want to go to church *ever again*. I don't want to stay in this shitty town, teach at that shitty school, be near these shitty people. It's all so limiting."

I dropped my head, because it didn't feel like I was an exception to any of that. She counted me as one of those crap people in this crap town. "If you want to do art, can't you do art at Sam?"

"No." She laughed. "What kind of art scene does Huntsville have? Absolutely none. There's nothing inspirational around here. I have to get out there, Mo. I have to find my people and my scene."

"What are you gonna do with your degree?" I asked, vibrating with anger.

"Whatever I want." I could hear her getting just as frustrated as me. "But I'm too good to not even try."

She started taking backward steps. She was pulling away. I could feel the threads that bound me to her snapping one by one. And I would say anything to keep them intact, to keep her here. "Yeah, you're good, Myracle, but so is everyone else."

As soon as I said it, I heard the implications—that I didn't believe she could make a career out of art, that I didn't believe in her. I heard her surprise in the silence. I heard how much it hurt her. The last thread between us broke, and that ended up being the last thing I ever said to her.

She got in her car and left me shaking in the driveway. I was mad and she was mad, but I thought she would still message me when she got where she was going. She didn't. In fact, every one of her profiles on every social media platform had been disabled.

I spent years telling her how amazing an artist she was. I spent years fantasizing with her about a future where she was a makeup artist/fashion designer/illustrator, while I was a model/novelist/actress. I would write the books, and she would illustrate the covers. I would play the part, and she would design the costumes. That's always been our joint dream. But how could it be a joint dream if she wasn't around to hear my stories?

I get it, though. I get why she wanted nothing to do with me. But it still hurts that she'd stay in contact with Aunt Dee and not me. It feels like being abandoned all over again.

When morning comes, I hear my phone vibrate on my nightstand. I honestly think it's the first time I've gotten a notification since I got my phone back. Having a dry phone has been the biggest reminder of how alone I am.

I grab my phone and squint at the light. It's a text from Sasha: **How did the talk with Aunt D go?**

I take a deep breath and sigh it out. **Terrible.**

Oh no! She's not gonna tell your mom, is she?

I text back, **I don't think so. But it wasn't very helpful.**

I'm sorry . . . but don't lose hope. We still have work to do. Have you read that book yet?

. . . No.

Come to my house later this evening, and we'll brainstorm ideas to get the dilators, but I want you to have read at least half of that book.

I roll my eyes. When did she get to be so bossy? I guess when I agreed to let her call herself my therapist.

I put my phone back on my nightstand and stare up at the ceiling. The sun dusts across the floor, making shadows on my wall. I might as well get up. It's not like I'll be able to get any sleep now.

So I go to the kitchen, still wearing my bonnet, unsuspecting. I grab a glass and look out the window, only to get an eyeful of the back of Reggie's head. Like, he's *right there*. If he turns around at this very moment, he'll see me in my most I-just-woke-up-I-look-awful state.

I duck down. The sink is still running and everything. I reach up and turn it off without pulling my head above the counter. Then I jet back to my room.

How dare my daddy put him to work so early! That is cruel and unusual punishment . . . for *me*. I would have been so mad if Reggie caught me looking like this.

By the time I get outside, my skin is shining with cocoa butter, my hair is pinned up, and I'm wearing the shortest pair of blue-jean shorts I own and a frilly little tank top. I've got a glass of iced tea in one hand and the book Sasha gave me in the other—the outer jacket replaced with a jacket from an "appropriate" young adult novel void of sex—then I slide the patio door open and step into the morning sun with my summer sandals, toenails freshly painted.

Reggie's across the way holding a handsaw. When he looks up, he does a double take. My daddy pulls his head up from the deck, drill in hand. His eyebrows draw in. I might have overdone it a little. "Good morning, sunshine," he says. "Little dressed up just to be lazing around the house, huh, Mo?"

"I'm not dressed up. This is how I always look."

"I know for a fact that it's not." He laughs.

My face catches fire. "Well, you're wrong," I say.

"Okay, whatever." He puts up his hands.

Jesus. Way to embarrass me, Daddy.

I catch Reggie's eye as I head toward the porch swing beside Mom's garden. He smiles and ducks his eyes away, back to his task at hand. And so I try to focus on my task too—reading this book that's supposedly not porn, but is *art*, as Sasha put it.

I kick my feet up on the swing, getting comfortable against the pillows, open to the first page, skipping past the introduction and the dedication and all that, and I kid you not, language is already dicey one page in. Then I get to page five, and I'm, no lie, right in the middle of a full-on sex scene. My skin tightens. It's so soon!

This is not art. It's too graphic to be art. Something carnal stirs in me. I sit up a little straighter, reading every single dirty word, tempted to just skip past it. But I have to wonder why. Why is this so uncomfortable for me?

"Whatcha reading?" Reggie asks.

I gasp, holding the pages close to my chest. And when I look up, I feel like I've been transported into my own Zane novel, because at some point he took off his shirt, and he looks like he should be on the cover, sweat dripping down his muscular chest, work gloves on his hands. It's too much.

He gives me a weird look, noting my nervous behavior. "What *are* you reading?" Then he tilts his head to the side. "Oh my God, are you reading porn right now?"

I glance at my daddy still drilling nails into the deck and hiss, "It's not porn. It's *art*."

He tosses his head back and laughs.

"Shut up," I say.

"And you've got it covered with this adorable-looking book cover. What is this? *I Wanna Be Where You Are*. You're bad."

I'm having a hard time keeping my eyes on his. I keep

peeking down at his abs and his arms. "Hush, okay? Sasha basically threatened my life about this book."

"Yeah, whatever, dirty bird." He takes his work gloves off
and lays them on the swing next to me. "Can I get a sip of
that?" he asks, pointing at my glass.

"You want a sip of my iced tea?" I raise my brows.

"Wait." He snorts a laugh. "Why did that sound dirty?"

"It didn't sound dirty." My cheeks get hot again.

"Five seconds with that book and you're already talking
dirty to me?"

The heat spreads all over. "I was *not* talking dirty."

He says, "Okay, whatever. *Yes*, I would like a sip of your iced
tea." Then I can't help it, I snort too. It does sound dirty.

He smiles. "See!"

"I don't let strangers sip my iced tea. Sorry."

He points at me, grinning ear to ear. "You are so bad."

I laugh wholeheartedly. I can't believe we're laughing about
this while my daddy is right there. We *are* bad.

"You can have the rest of it," I say. "I'll get myself another
glass."

Then Daddy comes sauntering over, taking off his work
gloves. "What's so funny over here?"

I freeze. "Nothing. Just talking about this book."

Reggie grabs my glass of iced tea and takes a long sip.

"What's your book about?" Daddy asks casually.

I shift my eyes, thinking fast. "Um, God."

Reggie spits out a mouthful of tea in the grass.

"You all right, son?" Daddy asks, concerned.

Reggie nods, hacking. I smile up at Daddy, trying not to laugh. "If you would excuse me, I have to get myself a new glass of tea. Would you like some?"

"No, I'm good, sweetie."

I stand up and take my book with me—can't risk Daddy getting curious, because I'm almost certain if he flips to any given page in this book, he's bound to find something unsavory.

As I'm heading toward the patio door, my daddy's voice booms authoritatively, "Reggie."

"Yessir?"

"Eyes on the deck, son."

I look over my shoulder and catch Reggie's hazel eyes on me, smirk on his lips. He says, "Yessir," then drops his gaze to the slabs of wood on the ground.

When I get inside, butterflies flock to the pit of my stomach. They're begging me to go back outside, to feel that again—the way it feels to be checked out by Reggie. And there—there's that familiar heat between my thighs. The heat that usually only shows up when Dom and I are fumbling around in his truck.

19

When Sasha opens her front door, I thrust the book into her hands. "I finished it."

She looks down at it, then up at me, amused. "Okay, but did *you* finish?"

Reggie snorts next to me.

I shift my eyes. "Yes, that's what I just said."

Sasha just stares at me.

"I don't think it was my cup of tea."

"But did you finish?" she asks again, emphasizing every word.

I look at her like she's crazy. How many times do I have to say it? "Yeah, I read the whole thing," I say.

Reggie laughs. He *howls*, following Sasha inside the house. Sasha's shaking her head, leading him toward the stairs. "Why are you laughing?" I ask, closing the front door behind me. "You know, Sasha, I thought you would be proud of me."

She turns at the bottom of the stairs. "I would be proud if you were able to *use* the book to *finish*."

I narrow my eyes, and then it sinks in. "Oh. I see."

Reggie howls louder, holding on to his knees. Sasha winks at me, and my cheeks get hot. Can we *not* talk about masturbation in front of the B-O-Y?

She leads us to her bedroom—which is surprisingly dark. The walls are literally painted black, which looks pretty cool with the sun streaming in from her floor-length window. She sits at her desk and opens her laptop. Reggie plops onto her white duvet cover on his back, like he's been here before. So I do too, lying on my back.

"So, you read the book—fantastic. How about your other homework?"

I can't see her from this angle, but I imagine she's staring at me, so I shake my head.

"Wait, what was your other homework?" Reggie asks, turning his head to look at me.

I mirror him, turning my head to meet his gaze. "To figure out who I am."

"To figure out why you're a catch," Sasha edits.

"Why you're a catch?" Reggie repeats, smiling into my eyes.

"What I have to offer besides sex."

"Well, you don't exactly have sex to offer, so . . ."

I smile, surprised at his tease. "Yeah, I guess not."

"Not penetrative sex," Sasha clarifies. "There's all kinds of other things you can do sexually, though."

Reggie hasn't looked away from me. "And you haven't figured it out yet?"

I shake my head.

"I think that's a pretty easy one," he says. A blade of golden light passes through the window at our feet, cutting across his multicolored irises. He says, "You're sweet and funny and fun." His eyes study mine, because the same blade of light is cutting across my cheek and into my dark eyes. Then his gaze dips down to my lips. "And full of surprises."

I smile and shiver at the butterflies breaking out of their cocoons, trying to hide how affected I feel.

"Great answer," Sasha says, "but she has to come up with her own."

He rolls his eyes away from me. "How exactly is this supposed to help with her condition, anyway? Aren't we still looking for dilators?"

"Yes, but getting dilators isn't the only solution."

"Yeah, but it's one." He rolls onto his stomach. "If we can't get them in a store, how about we try online?"

"How? We don't have credit cards," she says.

"I was actually thinking about this," I say. "Your mom works at the Women's Clinic. . . ."

"Yeah. So?"

"Well, if you're diagnosed with vaginismus, don't they give out dilators there?"

She looks uncomfortable. "It's not like we have a stockpile, but yeah, there are some in the supply closet."

"So, couldn't you easily grab one?"

"No. I'm allowed to sit behind the desk with my mom, and that's it. If I go in the back, it's because Dr. Marion's letting me sit with her, but she never lets me out of her sight."

"Never?"

Sasha's face contorts immediately. "I'm not stealing dilators from my mom's job."

"It's not stealing if we leave them cash," I argue.

Sasha looks at me, then at Reggie. "I don't want to lose my privileges with Dr. Marion. I'm learning so much from her. And if I get caught stealing from the clinic, it's over. She'll never mentor me again, and . . ."

"And what?"

"She'll never write me a recommendation letter. Do you know how weighty a letter from her would be?"

"But I thought you wanted to be an accountant."

Her eyes bulge for a second, then they flick down into her lap. "I did . . . but I've been thinking about what you said, and maybe I wouldn't be such a bad gynecologist."

I have to smile at that, especially because, during our talk, she was so sure of herself—sure of who she was and what she wanted. At least, she *seemed* sure. But maybe she's just guessing like me. Maybe it's okay that I don't have an answer to her question yet.

"Anyone gonna ask me about *my* idea?" Reggie says.

Sasha looks at him, already annoyed. "What's your idea?"

"Your brother," he says simply. Sasha raises her eyebrows,

waiting. "My sources tell me that Terrence buys shit on Amazon all the time."

"Who are your sources?" Sasha asks, perplexed.

"All we have to do is break into his account, order the dilators—"

"If we order something, he'll get an email about it," Sasha points out.

"So break into his email and delete it before he can see it."

"But he'll get it on his phone, instantly, and it'll show up in his order history."

Reggie grumbles, "I'm trying to help here! How about you come up with something, instead of shooting down all our ideas?"

"I'm shooting down your ideas because they're stupid."

"So, let's hear it, freshman!" Reggie swings his body around so that he's sitting on the edge of the mattress. When she doesn't say anything, he stands up with an impatient grunt. "That's what I thought." Then he walks out of the room.

When he's out of sight and out of range, Sasha looks at me completely unbothered and says, "Okay, now that the idiot is gone"—then she scoots closer in her desk chair and hunches down—"were you able to finish with that book?"

My face ices over. "Are we really talking about *masturbation* right now?"

"Yes." She tilts her head, disappointed. "Masturbation isn't some terrible thing. It's normal. It's *good* for you. I masturbate all the time, and I'm sure that idiot in there has his hands down his pants at least three times a day."

I shift my eyes, highly uncomfortable. I could never admit to masturbating. Not in front of her, and not even in front of Dom.

"You don't have to be ashamed. Everyone masturbates."

"Not me," I murmur.

She looks at me, not convinced for a second. "Yes, you do. Don't lie."

"Well, how can I?" I hiss, motioning to my crotch. "I'm broken, remember?"

"There are other ways to get yourself off." Then she shakes her head at me. "It's fine. I know you're playing dumb, but that's your homework."

"To masturbate?" I ask.

"To *admit* that you masturbate."

I zip my lips shut. Well, I guess I'm going to fail this assignment, because *never* will I say those words. I *don't* masturbate. I don't even . . . like, know how. So. I guess there's no hope for me. I don't know who I am, if not *the pastor's daughter*. If not *Dom's girlfriend*. I don't know what makes me a catch. I don't even know if I want to have sex . . . or if it was just something I wanted to do for Dom.

A large part of why I want to cure myself is to get him back. But I don't know, this whole thing feels really hopeless. How is talking about masturbation supposed to help me? Or doing stretches on the floor? And how are dilators supposed to help if I've never even touched myself?

Wow, today is not going at all like I thought it would. I thought Reggie and Sasha would give me hope, like they did last time, but my hopelessness is swallowing me again. Before I can really commit to wallowing, though, Reggie bursts through the doorway wielding a massive Nerf gun with a revolving drum full of darts. He unloads on us, yelling "Roar!" while blasting darts at us innocent civilians.

"Stop!" Sasha and I squeal, holding our hands out in front of us. He does not stop. Not until he shoots us with all of the darts, and there has to be at least two dozen in the drum.

"What is wrong with you?" Sasha yells, jumping up from her chair, looking at her floor and her bed littered with orange darts. "Where did you get that?"

Reggie looks sheepish, lowering the gun. "Terrence's room."

"What were you doing in Terrence's room?"

"Well," he sings, picking up a few darts off the floor, "I broke into his laptop. I have the dilators pulled up on his Amazon account. All you have to do is press 'place order' and we're good to go."

My eyes widen, and Sasha is flabbergasted. She says, "How did you break into my brother's laptop?"

Reggie places the gun and a handful of darts on her bed. "It wasn't hard. He barely has a password. It's just a four-digit PIN. I used his birthday and voilà."

"How'd you know his birthday?"

"Why are you asking me so many questions?" Reggie says. "Are we placing the order or what?" He looks at her, then me, with his eyebrows raised.

"No!" she screams. "You idiot! You need to go close out of that window before—"

The front door slams downstairs.

We freeze.

"Sasha!" Terrence calls as he runs up the stairs.

We are so dead.

20

Sasha doesn't tell us how to distract Terrence long enough
so she can remove the dilators from his Amazon shopping cart;
she just says, "Go!"

So, Reggie and I are standing in the middle of the hallway,
sweating bullets as Terrence rounds the corner. I have every
intention to let Reggie take the lead, until I see Dom walk up
after Terrence. I nearly spill all over the floor when he looks at
me.

"Dom?" I say. My voice croaks, like I haven't spoken in
years. It feels like *we* haven't spoken in years.

"Mo?" He's just as surprised.

Terrence says, "Reggie? Monique? Where's Sasha?"

"Uh," I say, turning to Reggie.

"Uh," he says, looking at me with the same question mark
on his face. He raises his eyebrows, urging me to come up with
something.

So, I say the first thing that comes to mind: "She's pooping."

Reggie snorts and turns to me. I shrug. "Yep, she's pooping," he says, nodding. "She actually has explosive diarrhea, the poor girl. She asked us to guide you back downstairs, so the smell doesn't overcome you." Reggie waves his arms forward, trying to usher them downstairs.

Terrence doesn't budge. "Nah, man. We're just going to my room."

"You're too close, good sir!" Reggie says. "I can already smell it from here. We must go downstairs at once. Right, Monique?" He looks at me.

"What? Oh, yeah. Poop."

That's all I say.

Reggie looks at my face, and he can't stop himself. He busts out laughing. My mouth drops open, because I don't know whether to laugh too or to try to keep up these poop charades. But Reggie howls, "Really?" and I can't help myself when he laughs like that.

"Reggie, stop!" When I push on his chest, he grabs my arms and holds on because he can barely stand. It's not that funny, but his laugh is so contagious.

Terrence says, "Are y'all high or something?" He scoots around us, and there's nothing we can do to stop him, because we've lost our breath from laughing so hard. We've completely failed Sasha.

Dom, on the other hand, doesn't like how Reggie is holding on to me. He grabs my waist with one hand and pries Reggie's fingers from my skin with his other, saying, "All right, that's enough."

And it feels like it's been so long since he's touched me. When he does, I'm instantly entranced. Gone, up and out of my mind. The only thing I can concentrate on is being touched by him.

As Terrence nears the doorway of his room, Sasha suddenly walks out. "Sasha, what the—"

"Hey, bro," she says nonchalantly.

"The hell are you doing in my room?"

She shrugs. "It's where I go to fart. I don't want to stink up my *own* room."

"You nasty little . . ." He shakes his head. "How many times do I have to tell you to stay out of my room?"

"Just five more times, then I think I'll understand." She walks past him, giving me and Reggie a quick bulge of her eyes. "Well, we should get going." She grabs my hand on her way past, pulling me out of Dom's arms.

"Wait, Mo," he says, watching me walk away from him— watching me walk away with Sasha and Reggie, of all people.

"We're kind of in a hurry," she says, continuing to pull me along.

"Are we?" I ask. I haven't been able to talk to Dom in a week. He hasn't answered any of my calls or texts. I've been trying so hard to tell him about everything I've learned, but he hasn't given me a chance to explain. Now, here he is, begging me to talk to him.

I look back. Catch a glimpse of his body. God, I miss his

body. Catch a glimpse of his face. He looks jealous and over-protective. He's still jealous and overprotective of me. That has to mean something, right?

"We are, if we're going to the Women's Clinic," she whispers to me. "They close pretty soon."

My eyes widen when I look at her. She's smirking. Reggie's grinning. We're really doing this? Oh my God, we're really doing this.

"Talk later?" I ask Dom over my shoulder.

He doesn't confirm. His face scrunches, confused as to how I would choose them over him. But I don't really get a chance to think about that, or to honestly celebrate that he cares enough to be jealous, because Sasha pulls me down the stairs in a hurry. Then we're running down the driveway to my car.

"Do you have a plan?" I ask, my voice shaking.

"Of course she doesn't have a plan," Reggie says, laughing, jumping in my back seat.

Sasha gets up front as I get behind the wheel. "Yes, I do, thank you very much. And unlike your stupid idea, mine will actually work."

21

The plan is simple.

Dr. Marion isn't working today, but Sasha's mom is. Sasha will go inside, tell her mom that she left "something or other" in Dr. Marion's office. Mrs. Howser will give Sasha her keys, and Sasha will "go check Dr. Marion's office," but really she'll be sneaking into the supply closet.

Reggie and I have been instructed to wait in the car. He's sitting up front with me. The air is tense, for some reason. I think maybe with the way Dom pulled me away from Reggie. That's what I've been thinking about this whole time, replaying the scene in my mind, when my phone vibrates. I jump, and my heart skips a beat. Excited, I grab it out of my cup holder. It's a text from Dom! **Mo, what are you doing hanging out with Reggie and Sasha?**

I text back: **It's a long story, and I can't really go into it over text.**

So call me.

I glance over at Reggie. He meets my gaze with a questioning look. **Can't right now.**

"So," Reggie says, "does Dom know about your . . ." He motions his hand to my body.

"No." I slide my phone back into the cup holder. "I haven't really gotten a chance to tell him."

"Oh." Reggie nods thoughtfully. Then he turns and looks at me. "Do you think it would make a difference for him?"

"A difference how?"

"Like, if you told him that the reason you weren't able to have sex with him was because you have a *medical condition*, do you think he'd take you back?"

I search his eyes, then blink down to the gray shirt hanging loose on his chest. "I mean, I still haven't cured it, so I still can't have sex with him."

"I know." He nods. "But he'll know it's not your fault. It was never something that you could help."

"But still," I say.

"So, no? It wouldn't make a difference for him?"

I'm getting a little frustrated. "Let's be realistic," I say. "If a girl told you that she has a condition that prevents her from having sex, would you even date her? Knowing that you may never have sex with her? Eventually you'll get tired of that."

"Nah," he says. "Not if I don't get tired of the girl."

"So, if you were Dom, you would take me back?"

He pauses, inspecting my dark eyes, then dropping his gaze

down to my lips, making me aware of how suddenly dry they feel. I rub them together, spreading what's left of my gloss, and he smiles gently. "If I were Dom, I would have never broken up with you." His eyes pull back up to mine, sending my heart into a frenzy, lighting those butterflies in my stomach on fire. My phone vibrates in my cup holder, but I barely register it over the pounding in my chest.

Reggie breaks away first, gasping at the song playing on the radio, then he turns it way up. It's an old Ariana Grande song, and he knows every word. He's dancing in his seat and screaming the lyrics. My eyes widen, because I have no idea what to make of this. When the song comes around to the hook, he turns it up even louder, lets down the window, and starts shouting the lyrics in the middle of the parking lot of the Women's Clinic.

"Reggie!" I turn the music down to a whisper and stare at him, aghast.

"What?" he asks, like I'm the one acting a fool.

"We're supposed to be stealthy right now. We're *stealing* from this place."

"I'm not," he says with a laugh. "Sasha's getting the goods. You're driving the getaway car. I'm just here to have fun, baby." Then he turns the music back up and starts screaming again.

There's no one around, but I can feel a thousand eyes on us. I turn the music off completely and whir his window back up. "Hey," he protests. Then I lock his window so he can't roll it back down. "Oh my God, you bully!"

I laugh. "You're bringing attention to us. That is the opposite of what you're supposed to be doing."

"The more attention on us, the less that's on Sasha." He rests a hand on my console, then stretches his other long arm across me in an attempt to unlock his window.

I grab his hand. "Stop!" I laugh. My back is against my door. He's laughing too, trying to break out of my hold. Then he uses his free hand to tickle my waist. I squeal, grabbing his fingers.

Now we're holding *both* hands, and I think he realizes at the same time that I do. Our laughter runs out slowly, drip-dropping to a silent halt. His fingers are slender and long, like everything else about his body. His hazel eyes look green in this light, and they're flickering all over my face, like a dragonfly that can't decide where to land, until he finally chooses my lips.

His fingers wiggle in my left hand until they've found their way between mine, waffle-style. "I forgot one thing when I was listing all the things that make you a catch," he says in the silence. I take a deep breath, because I don't know if I'm ready for what he's about to say. As much as my heart is racing, and as much as those butterflies are stirring—as much as there's undeniable heat between my thighs—I'm not ready to admit anything about my feelings for him—feelings that I hadn't realized existed until now. And I'm definitely not ready to respond to his feelings.

But he doesn't say *you're gorgeous* or *you're everything I want in a girl*. He says, "You're not as sweet and innocent as everyone says you are. The pastor's daughter can do no wrong—*bullshit*." He smiles. "You're not some delicate pushover. You've got guts."

"You thought I was a pushover?" I ask.

He shrugs. "At one point."

"When did you realize you were wrong?"

"That day in your parents' car, when you took the heat from your mom for me."

Oh. That day was transformative, wasn't it?

When he caught Dom and me making out behind the church, and he joked about how my daddy called Dom the *perfect gentleman.* He realized then how Dom has my father wrapped around his finger. And I realized then that if my father's judgment of Dom could be so wrong, then maybe his judgment of Reggie was wrong too.

I know now that it was.

I look down and realize that our hands are still joined. And I realize that I don't mind. I realize that it doesn't feel uncomfortable, having his fingers laced with mine, having his eyes probe me, having him lean closer to me. I may not be ready to verbally admit my feelings, but this physical stuff feels . . . easy.

Then the back door bursts open and Sasha slides in. "I got 'em."

Reggie and I release hands so fast, you'd think she caught us kissing or something.

"Wait, for real?" Reggie asks.

I look in the back seat as Sasha pulls a box of dilators out of her bulbous purse, with a mile-wide smile on her face. My smile matches hers in width and wattage as we stare at each other. Then, out of nowhere, like we can read each other's minds, we start squealing out of excitement. I can't believe she did this for me. I can't believe after all our running around, coming up empty-handed, I finally have the missing puzzle piece to curing my mysterious body.

Reggie joins in with us at the same octave, until all three of us are bouncing in our seats, squealing like ten-year-olds at a slumber party. I don't know that I've ever felt this excited about anything. Even though I don't know how the dilators will work for me, I have hope. For the first time in a while, I have genuine hope.

22

"There's a whole documentary about it. There's plastic in these fries," Reggie says, holding up a skinny McDonald's fry.

"That's an old documentary. They've changed their recipes since then," Sasha says, chewing in my back seat.

"*Yeah*, that's what they want you to think."

"Shut up and eat the damn food," Sasha murmurs.

We're sitting in the parking lot, eating like it's our last meal. The sun is starting to go down. I have to get back home soon.

"So, Monique," Sasha says.

I look up at her in my rearview mirror, chewing a McNugget.

"Now that you have dilators, do you think you'll use them?"

The question kind of puts me on the spot. I chew and take my time before swallowing. Then I say, "Yeah, I at least want to try. I'm not sure how they'll work, but . . ."

"Okay, let me ask you this." She scoots forward, holding on to the side of my seat. "If there was no Dom, no boy in the picture at all"—tell me why my eyes shift to Reggie—"would you even *want* to have sex?"

I turn away from her, laying my head against the seat. This is kind of the same question Aunt Dee was asking me. And I haven't really thought much more about it. I want Dom back. I want sex to not be an issue. But do I want to have sex?

"I think so," I say.

"Okay, sure, you want to have sex, but do you want to wait until marriage?"

"No," I say immediately.

She raises her eyebrows, like *are you sure?*

"It's like—" I sigh, rolling my eyes up to the ceiling. "When Dom and I would be, you know, getting hot and heavy, I wouldn't want to stop. If there wasn't a condition stopping me, I would have had sex a long time ago. I don't want to wait until marriage."

"So," she says, twisting her mouth, unsure, "why are you still wearing that?" She nudges her head toward my hand.

I look down at my ring finger and the silver band my father gave me during the purity pledge ceremony. "Oh." It dawns on me all at once. "I've just never taken it off."

"It's been an ever-present reminder of your promise to stay pure. It might be a little confusing to yourself that you're still wearing it if you don't intend to wait until marriage."

I raise my eyebrows and look back at her. She's kind of close to my face, because she's hovering on the side of my chair. "Good point, Dr. Howser."

She smiles, really tiny at first, but it grows to take over her face.

"Yeah, her first good point in a while."

"Shut up, Reggie!" Sasha growls, and he laughs.

I slip off the promise ring, glancing at Reggie beside me. He's watching with an encouraging smile, and so is Sasha.

"Yeah, take it off!" Reggie howls.

"Strip, strip, strip," Sasha chants.

I laugh, holding the removed band in the air, then tossing it in my glove compartment. *Out of sight, out of mind.* And just like that, with the emptiness on my finger, the literal weight lifted off my hand, I feel that much freer to make my own decisions. I feel less like I owe my daddy my word, less like I owe Dom my body, and more like I belong to me and only me.

I feel like I just made room for myself.

I think the ease with which I can breathe is visible on my face, because Reggie smiles back at me and says, "You know what? We need to go out and celebrate."

My eyes light up. "Celebrate how?" I ask.

Then his smile turns sinister. "Let's go to Shenanigans. Tonight is teen night."

"Ooooh, I've never been there before," Sasha says.

"But I'm not allowed to go to Shenanigans."

"Obviously, we wouldn't tell your parents that's where we're going," Sasha says. "Just ask for an extension on your curfew."

"What makes you think they'll give me an extension?"

"I'll call your mom. She *loves* me," Sasha says.

Reggie's waiting on my response. "Say yes, say yes, say yes," Sasha whispers, and Reggie joins in. "Say yes, say yes, say yes."

I smirk, facing the windshield. Everything is on the up. I know what's wrong with my body. I've got dilators, and Sasha is confident that they'll cure me. I have hope and I'm vibing off their energy, so I reach back and hand Sasha my phone. "Call my mom."

Shenanigans is a beach-themed club that got split in two. On one side there's a country bar; on the other is the club. They put away the alcohol for teen night and only admit adults if they're parents.

When we walk inside the bar, people in cowboy boots, blue-jean booty shorts with extravagant belt buckles, and a few cowboy hats line-dance on the center platform.

There are *a lot* of kids from our school here. And as soon as we walk in, everyone's attention is on us. It's like they're grateful to see us, or more accurately, grateful to see Reggie. They shout his name in unison. "You're doing 'Copperhead Road,' right?" they ask.

"Of course." He smiles, slapping hands with a number of white boys and side-hugging a few white girls.

He. Is. Popular.

He leads us between round tables and bar stools through a dark tunnel-like hallway to the club side. And *this* is where all the Black people are. This is where Reggie gives daps to guys and full-frontal hugs to girls, who all, in turn, give Sasha and me weird looks, surprised to see us "church girls" here. Then Reggie begins to take inventory. It's definitely like a school dance because no one's dancing. "Damn, this place is dead," Reggie says, like a surgeon examining his patient.

Then an extremely thin Black guy comes running up, his pants just about falling off. "Reggie, thank God."

"Laser, what the hell happened here?"

Oh, so *this* is Laser. *This* is who was so important that Reggie answered his phone during church.

"I don't know." Laser shakes his head, hands on his hips. "The DJ's been playing all this old shit."

"Tell me about it," Sasha says, her nose scrunched. He's playing a song I barely recognize. Something I must have heard as a kid, from the early 2000s.

Sasha takes off. "Where is she—" Reggie starts, then takes off after her. Laser and I shrug and follow.

Sasha stops at the DJ's booth and tries to wave him over. The music is blaring, as we're right by the speakers. The DJ, a pudgy white guy with dark sunglasses and a baseball cap, comes over. Sasha shouts, "Do you have anything that came out this decade?" The guy looks taken aback. She pulls out her phone, types something in, then shows him the screen. He rolls his eyes, and she begs, "Please!"

He puts up his hands as if to say *fine*, then heads back to his MacBook. He fades the current song out, then, *wouldn't you know it*, the Vontae song we blasted in the Target parking lot comes on. "Ayyyeee!" Laser shouts beside me. Sasha presses her palms together and thanks the DJ, then she runs to the center of the dance floor with Laser right behind her. Everyone who had been sitting bounces their way onto the floor too.

Reggie turns to me. "Wanna dance?"

I look to the massive crowd, then back at him, and shake my head.

"You sure?" he asks, slowly backing away.

I scrunch my nose and nod. "Go ahead."

Then everyone in the room starts shouting the lyrics. I watch Reggie snake his way through the crowd, dancing with literally everyone. "Pick it up, pick it up, pick it up!"

"Pick it up, pick it up, ayeeee," I say too, taking timid steps closer.

"You need it more than me, so don't let me get in your way!"

I remember junior high dances—no one was afraid to dance. But when we got to high school, even if you could dance, you were never socially allowed. *But this?* This is like a junior high dance.

Reggie makes his way around the group, dancing with even the bad dancers. I smile. This is why everyone was so happy to see him. He really is the life of the party.

I head to the center of the floor and accidentally catch his eye. His left cheek lifts, and he starts making his way to me. I weave around bodies, never letting him leave my sight, until we finally stop in front of each other. I sing along too, leaving out the cuss words. "Cash and cars never question my heart, so why would I hesitate? You got a problem with how I make art, so"—blank—"everything that you say! Who the"—blank—"are you?"

Reggie grabs my hands and lifts them above my head. I wave my hips, watching his eyes. It's crazy how much lighting can change a face, and how being this close allows me to notice new things about him. Like how the freckles on his cheeks get darker the closer you get to his nose. The flecks of green in his eyes glimmer like lights of their own—neon lights that only turn on at certain times of the day, for certain people in certain situations.

He spins me around so that my back is to his chest, his fingers landing soft on my waist. Butterflies burst through my stomach, up my throat. I can barely register anything in front of me, or anything around me. All I see, feel, hear is him.

His chest bumps the top of my back; my back pockets graze his front pockets. Without my permission, my feet take a step back, until our bodies lock together like two puzzle pieces that finally found each other.

Then the song is interrupted by a succession of air horns.

Suddenly, Reggie spins me around with the wildest look in his eyes. Everyone else has the same expression. People in their cowboy hats and boots come rushing from the bar and join the chaos in the middle of the floor.

"What's going on?"

He grabs the tops of my arms. "You'll see."

There's a bang, like a gunshot, and everybody looks up. The ceiling seemingly opens up and a mess of confetti floats down all around us, flooding the floor with an array of colors. I laugh, overwhelmed with wonder. Then the music comes back on—an upbeat pop song by Rihanna that I've never loved until right now. Everyone starts jumping up and down, fingers grasping at the floating confetti.

I'm jumping up and down too, laughing with Reggie. I don't know what it is about him, but he has a tendency to make me forget the reasons I hesitate. He makes me lose all regret.

At the end of it, I'm exhausted. But I barely have time to catch my breath before someone shouts, "Reggie! Reggie, it's time!"

"Coming," he says, waving at them. Then he leans in, but he doesn't veer to one of my ears. We're nearly nose to nose. "Let's go to the country section."

"Why?" I ask, perplexed. I *despise* country music.

"Because it'll be fun. You'll see."

As we cross the dance floor, I stare at the curls on the back of Reggie's head. They look tight and loose at the same time, dark brown in this light. In the hallway connecting the two halves of the establishment, where the hip-hop 808s bleed into country banjos and fiddles, he turns over his shoulder and catches me staring. And when he does, he smiles.

My eyes get stuck there, stuck to his lips—plump and pink.

His lips were made for lipstick commercials. They say something, but I can't hear.

As we enter the bar, he repeats himself. "Do you know this dance?"

I look around. All the couples are lining up on the platform. "What's happening?"

"You don't know 'Copperhead Road'?" Then he starts backing away to line up too.

"How do *you* know it?"

"I'm from Texas," he says, like that's enough explanation. "How did you avoid learning this?" he asks, kicking his heels.

"I'm Black."

He laughs. "I can see where you're coming from, I really can, but even that's not an excuse." Then he and everyone else stomp their boots, turning to the side in unison. It's kind of alarming, but seeing Reggie in the mix, the only Black person in a crowd of white country folk, makes it hilarious. Then the beat picks up and so does the energy of the dance. Reggie swings his arms, kicking his tennis shoes, his hair flopping over his forehead.

A white boy from my class runs up and slaps Reggie on the shoulder. "Reggie, man, thank God you're here!" Then the boy joins in beside him. I watch them dance, the corners of my lips forever lifted. *Thank God he's here, indeed.*

When the song goes off, Reggie's out of breath. He walks over to me as a slower song fades in, hands on his hips. I meet him at the edge of the platform, applauding his performance. "Wow, that was . . ."

"Amazing? I know," he says.

I laugh, and then nod. "Something like that."

He's smiling, searching my eyes, then he reaches a hand out, palm up. "May I have this dance?"

My smile turns watery. I don't think I've ever been asked that before.

I take his hand, following him onto the hardwood. My hand reaches up to his shoulder and his hand falls to my waist. We two-step around the floor, my eyes strictly on the couples swinging around us.

When I dare to look up and find him staring down at me, my breath hitches.

He says, "You know, sometimes I feel kinda bad for corrupting you."

I jerk my head back, stunned. "Um. What? You're not corrupting me."

He laughs. "You don't think so? I mean, I got you here. And you're not allowed to be here. I got you *kicked out* of a sex shop—"

"Okay," I say, laughing, "that's all true, but I wasn't *good* to begin with."

He looks at me, unconvinced. "Why? Because you tried to have sex a couple of times?"

"It was more than a couple of times. If it weren't for vaginismus, I wouldn't be a virgin."

"And that makes you bad?"

"Doesn't it?"

He shrugs. "*I* don't think so. But that's kind of up to you to decide."

"No, it's up to my parents."

"No," he says sternly. "It's up to you. No one else can define it for you. I mean . . ." He falters, lowering his eyes to our moving feet. "Do you think I'm bad?"

The question catches me off guard. When I don't answer immediately, he says, "You can be honest. It won't hurt my feelings one bit." He smiles, but the smile doesn't reach his eyes.

Do I think he's bad? Ask me a few weeks ago, I would have said yes. But seeing the way he treats me and my vaginismus—like I'm not some helpless freak of nature—and the way people here praise him for being so *fun-loving,* now I know better. He's selfless. And he doesn't care what other people think. I have no idea what went down when he was going to school in Huntsville, but having seen him here today, I can't believe he's anything but good.

I say, "No. I don't think you're bad." I watch the smile on his lips make it up to his eyes. Makes me think it would have hurt his feelings if I *had* said I thought he was bad.

The smile fades quickly, though. "Well, your mom thinks I'm bad." He nods, looking over my head. "But it's not up to her. It's up to you. So, do you think you're a bad person?"

I shake my head, not even thinking about it.

"Even though you've tried to have sex?" He gasps dramatically. "You still think you're a good person?"

I laugh. "Yes. Okay? You've made your point."

"I know. I'm over here spitting facts."

"And now you've ruined it."

He laughs, and I smile, looking down at his gray T-shirt. Then my hand slips off his shoulder onto his arm, as his hand cinches tighter around my waist. Our steps—one, two, then back—are getting smaller and less defined. His thumb is rubbing my back and melting my bones, and when I look up, he's licking his lips as he looks down at me. It shoots a surge through my body.

This can't be real. Reggie is friendly. He's danced with just about every girl here, because he's sweet like that. There's nothing more going on between us, I remind myself. My body is broken. He can't possibly want me in that way.

But then I remember what he said in the car . . . *If I were Dom, I would have never broken up with you.* He thinks Dom was wrong for prioritizing sex, and I think the fact that Reggie doesn't is too good to be true. But, *God*, how I wish it could be true.

When the song ends and fades into another, I pull out of his hold. "We should go check on Sasha, right?" I barely give him a chance to answer before I'm hightailing it to the club side, trying to get ahold of myself. I can't want that from Reggie, when the whole reason I'm here is Dom. . . .

"Where *is* she?" he asks when we get to the entrance.

We look around the floor, looking for her long black locs and frumpy sweater. I find her and point. She's dancing, with every inch of her backside covered by the front of another girl.

"Oh, wow," Reggie says. They're swaying together, then Sasha bends over and twerks against the girl. Reggie laughs. "Who is Sasha, really?"

"I don't know!" I shout.

After a couple more songs, we drag her off the floor because it's nearing my extended curfew, but we can't seem to detach her from the girl she was dancing with. The two of them walk behind us all the way to my car in the dark parking lot.

We get inside and shut our doors, while Sasha talks to the girl at the front of my car with her back to us. I'm avoiding looking at Reggie, as it's uncomfortably dark and quiet, so I watch Sasha and the mystery girl—who is absolutely gorgeous, with dark brown skin, wearing a crop top and booty shorts. I watch as she pops out her hip and twirls her long wavy hair.

"Oh my God, is Sasha flirting right now?" I ask with a smile.

Reggie laughs. "Can you even imagine Sasha flirting? She's such a type A, know-it-all bossy pants. Sasha flirting sounds . . . stiff."

I roll my eyes back to Sasha and the way the mystery girl is biting her bottom lip. "That doesn't look stiff to me."

Reggie watches too and laughs again. "I bet this is what they're saying—" Then he starts talking in a ridiculously high-pitched voice. "Oh my God, I like you sooo much. You're so pretty, and I just want to touch your butt."

I look over at him, stifling a laugh. "What are you doing?"

"My butt? Ohhhh, okay. That sounds fine. Maybe not in public, but maybe next time."

Then the girls whip out their phones. Reggie says, "Oh, what's your number? I want to text you tonight and you can send me a picture of your butt."

"What is up with you and butts?" I ask, laughing probably loud enough for them to hear.

"My number is five, five, five—five, fuh, five, five, five—three, eight, five, ten."

"That's too many numbers!"

He laughs and keeps going. "Oh, cool. I'm gonna text you tonight and we'll talk about butts."

I turn to him, my cheeks hurting from how much I'm laughing. "What is wrong with you? What is actually wrong with you?"

He laughs, motioning to them outside my windshield. "That's what they're saying, I promise you."

Then Sasha leans in and they kiss. "Whoa!" Reggie and I both howl at the same time.

"Damn! How did I not know Sasha had game like that?"

"I don't know," I squeal, and after they're still kissing for another five seconds, I turn to Reggie with a giggle. "This makes me uncomfortable."

He meets my gaze, his expression serious all of a sudden. "Why? Because they're two girls?"

"No. Because PDA makes me highly uncomfortable." I clench my teeth, glancing back at them, then away again.

Reggie's studying me, studying my eyes. "Is that why you

and Dom would make out behind the church?"

Now it's my turn to get serious. "We'd make out behind the church because if my parents ever found out we kissed with tongue, they would have stoned us to death."

He nods big and slow. "Figures that this would make you uncomfortable, then." He points to the kissing couple. "You've been taught to fear this. But it's just love and affection. What's so scary about showing affection?"

I blink at him. "Besides what people will think of me?"

"Yes." Then he sighs. "I feel like people are more comfortable watching someone get bullied and judged in public than they are watching other people kiss and hug. That's pretty twisted."

When I look at him, I can tell how much he's trying to play off the fact that he cares. He's trying and failing to be nonchalant, but this is clearly something he's thought about at length. And I love that.

My daddy wanted me to hang out with Reggie because he thought I could be a good influence on him, but I think it's working the other way around. I've never met someone so . . . open. So unapologetic. He challenges everything I thought I knew.

We turn back to Sasha and her hour-long make-out session. "But geez, this is going on forever," Reggie says. He looks at the clock on my dash. "You've gotta get home soon. Let's go!" he shouts, reaching over to honk my horn.

Sasha and the girl don't even pull away from each other. Sasha lifts her middle finger and Reggie dramatically gasps. After another minute, they finally pull away and take slow backward steps, holding hands within the space. "Bye," I hear Sasha sing.

The girl tinkles her fingers in a wave, then turns around and heads back to the club. Sasha stands and watches for a few seconds.

When she runs and jumps in my back seat, Reggie asks, appalled, "When did you learn to pick up girls like that?"

I watch her shrug in my rearview. "Not something I had to learn. I'm just good like that."

"I'm gonna need you to show me your ways."

She smiles. "Like I'll tell *you* my secrets. You don't even have Monique's number and you've been fiending for a week now."

"What!" he shouts.

"What?" I say, turning to him, and then to her.

My face heats up, and we both laugh nervously, mumble *no* and *What! That's crazy*. Reggie says something about, "Monique is my friend." I say something about, "Dom." Then we both look at each other, mildly hurt by each other's rejection, but I'm a little relieved that neither of us can admit our feelings, because then I don't have to take responsibility for it.

All the way home, Sasha bounces in my back seat, telling us about the girl she met. Her name is Brandy. She goes to a Christian school in Huntsville. Sasha thinks she's in love.

When I pull into her driveway, she smiles. "Thanks, guys.

This was fun. We should definitely do this again." Reggie and I agree with her, then she quiets down and leans forward. "Could you guys keep the whole gay thing on the low? My family knows and a few of my friends know, but it's not something I want the whole town knowing."

Reggie nods with pinched brows. "Of course, Sasha."

"Yeah," I say with a smile. "It stays with us."

"Cool, thanks." Then she opens her door and gets out. "See ya at church tomorrow."

"Wait, Sasha!" I say before she can close the door.

She sticks her head back in. "Yeah?"

I close my eyes for a second, then I open them with a big sigh. "The answer is yes. I did."

She cocks her eyebrows up. "What are you talking about?"

"Yes. I finished."

Her eyes bulge. She screeches, "I knew it!" and slaps the back of my seat. "I am so fucking proud of you, Monique!" Then she slams my door shut and dances up the driveway with her fist in the air.

I watch, laughing to myself, the words *I'm proud of you too* on my tongue.

23

Let's get one thing straight: I did not enjoy that book. Not exactly. Once I got past the initial embarrassment, I realized that I'd never been exposed to the idea of a woman being openly aroused, taking control, and doing something about it. I'd only ever thought of sex as something that men wanted and that women gave.

She was a sex goddess. An unapologetic lusty dominatrix. She wanted sex all the time. And she *got* it.

Sometimes, when I hung out with Dom, I'd be desperate to go to the creek, but I couldn't get myself to say anything. I'd just get super touchy and hope to God that he'd suggest it first. Sometimes I worry that I get aroused too easily and way too often, especially for a girl who can't have sex. Like maybe I'm not supposed to instantly get turned on when Reggie touches me. But that book made me think my arousal might be my superpower, a tool, something to be celebrated about my body, rather than something to be embarrassed about. Like that song "WAP" by Meg and Cardi. That is actively me.

So, yes, I took a really long bath after I finished reading, but maybe I shouldn't have admitted that seconds before having to sit through a whole car ride alone with Reginald Turner.

I stare straight ahead, silent and stiff. He's quiet too, Childish Gambino whispering in the background, all the way to his house. When I pull into his empty driveway, I slowly shift the gear into park, really dragging out every motion.

He turns to me and says, "So . . ."

My spine zips up tight. *Please don't ask about the book.* When I look at him, he says with a quick laugh, "Was it fun, at least?"

I turn back to the windshield, sweating and taking extremely short breaths. "Listen, I'm sorry, but I really don't want to talk about *that* with you."

When I dare to look at him again, his expression is half confused, half amused. "Um. I was talking about Shenanigans. Did you have fun at Shenanigans?"

"Oh!" The sweat prickles on my forehead as I try to laugh it off. "Oh, yes. Yeah. I—it was so fun." I glance out the windshield, and then I can't help it, I start gushing. "I can't believe Sasha stole dilators from the Women's Clinic. And I can't believe we went to Shenanigans and she picked up a random girl and—" I stop, because when I turn back to him, he's leaning in slowly. My breath cuts off, gets caught in my throat.

His face is breaths away. His lips.

As his hand reaches up to my face, I look down at his mouth, then back up to his eyes, waiting for him to close the space between us. But his hand reaches past my face into my hair and pulls out a red sliver of confetti. He says, "This was in your hair."

I instantly realize I had been leaning in too, with my lips slightly parted. My hand flies up to my hair, my cheeks ablaze. "Yeah, I bet they're everywhere."

"Wanna come in and use my bathroom mirror? You don't want your dad asking questions."

"Uh." I look at his little cabin-like house. "That's true." Then I turn back to him, embarrassed of how much I thought he was gonna kiss me—how much I wanted him to. "Yeah, sure. That'd be great."

I pull my keys out of the ignition and follow him up the brick steps. He unlocks the door. Then, when we're inside, he switches on a lamp. I glimpse the cozy living room. Cozy but elegant. Reggie leans against the back of the tan wraparound couch, pointed at a plasma mounted against the wall.

He nods his head toward a dark hallway. "Bathroom is the first door on the right." But the hall is so dark. I'm feeling my way along the left side of the wall when I accidentally push open a door. Moonlight pours into the room through a big open window. I'm so disoriented that it takes me a while to realize I'm standing in the doorway of Reggie's bedroom.

His bed is unmade, sheets white, comforter black, floor the same clean hardwood as in the living room. But he hasn't attempted to decorate. Actually, it doesn't look like he's unpacked at all. Unopened boxes clutter the floor. Makes me remember just how new he is to this town and how much he might not want to be here.

"Wrong room," Reggie says, coming up behind me.

My mouth opens, surprised.

He's smiling, narrowing his eyes at me.

"Sorry, I accidentally . . . ended up here." As I'm saying it, I realize how unlikely it sounds.

"Yeah, yeah, yeah." He steps past me and turns on the light. "I haven't started unpacking, as you can see."

"Do you plan to?" I ask, taking a step inside as well.

"Eventually." He looks at the four empty walls, then he falls back on his bed, resting his head in his hands, peering up at the ceiling. "It just doesn't feel like home."

"New Waverly's not too far from Huntsville, you know."

"I don't mean the town. I mean this house. I miss our old house."

I nod, looking at all the boxes and the black permanent marker scrawled on the sides. One box says *Here's your fit, nigga.* I smirk, walking over to find it full of balled-up clothes. "You don't wanna at least put your clothes in the dresser?"

"Too much work," he says, rolling his neck over to me. He meets my eye and smiles. "You're welcome to do it for me, if it bothers you."

"No, I'm good."

He laughs.

I look at the labels on the other boxes. *Photographs and shit*; *Books & Movies & Music*; *RAS*. "What's RAS?" I ask.

"Random-ass shit," he says.

I laugh. "D'you label your boxes yourself?"

"Of course."

I'm curious about what's inside. I don't know why. I just have a hankering to open them, to see his photographs and the types of books, movies, and music he likes—enough to own physical copies—and what kind of random stuff is in *RAS*. Just to . . . know him, I guess.

He must see the curiosity in my eyes, because he says, "You can, like—" and then nudges his head.

"No, I don't wanna go through your stuff."

"It's cool." Then he rolls off the mattress and kneels down beside the *RAS* box. When he folds back the flaps, I close the distance and kneel next to him.

The first thing he pulls out is a miniature globe, ivory with its continents outlined in black. He places it on the floor without commentary, and next to that, a board game—it still has the shrink-wrap around it and everything. He says, "Oh, shit. I've been looking all over for this." He pulls out a bottle of leave-in hair conditioner, then reaches back and sets it on his bed. "Gonna need that later."

He tosses aside an old spiral. "Come on, get in here, Monique."

I smile faintly, then pull back the flaps. My eyes career over the contents in the box. My hand pulls out the first thing it lands on—a stack of old books, some of them with the front covers ripped off, all of them R. L. Stine.

"Yeah, I used to be a sort of horror buff."

"No kidding," I say, flipping through the series of Fear Street novels. "I was more a Goosebumps kid, until my parents told me, 'If you keep reading all that scary stuff, something's gonna catch on and turn you evil,'" I say, mocking my mother's voice.

He looks at me with a sad smile. "That sucks. My mom was even more into horror than me. She let me watch *Chucky* when I was, like, five."

"Wow. My parents would never."

He reaches back in the box and pulls out a sketch pad. Before he can toss it aside, I grab the edge. "Did you used to draw?"

He releases the sketch pad, letting me take it. "I do . . . draw."

"Can I look?" I ask.

"Um, sure," he says, but he looks hesitant.

So I open it slowly and carefully, because I can tell how much it means to him. The first drawing is of a lady sitting on a couch, smiling with her eyes closed. There's a speech balloon above her head that says, "Tomorrow's forecast is better for dieting. There's less pizza raining from the sky."

"That's, uh—that's my mom," he says, like he's embarrassed. "It's from a long time ago. I've gotten better since then."

"No, this is really good." His art style is much more cartoony than my sister's. Actually, it looks like a real-life comic.

"Wait, okay, but look at this." He shuffles over next to me, then flips through the pages to the very last sketch.

"Wow," I say, breathless. It's a landscape drawing, colored in with colored pencils. "Is this the town?" I ask, like it's not obvious. "There's the supermarket, and the doughnut shop, and the post office. You're so good."

When I look at him, he's smiling sheepishly. I've never seen him so coy. "Thanks," he says quietly, then he scoots back to his side of the box.

I lay the sketchbook down, reach back inside, and pull out a picture of a dark-skinned woman with lips just like Reggie's— she's sitting on a couch, smiling with her eyes closed. This must be the picture he used to sketch her. "I don't think I've ever seen your mom before. She's so beautiful."

"Thanks, I guess." He floats backward, leaning his back against the side of his bed.

I place the picture on the floor between us, then reach back in and pull out a picture of him as a baby. His hair used to be blond, and his eyes looked gray. I look up at him—his lanky body slouched against his bed frame, the tan of his skin, the curls on his head, the hazel of his eyes, his pink plump lips, and the freckles on his nose. *He's* beautiful too. He's always been beautiful, ever since he was born.

He stares back at me. "What?" he half asks, half laughs.

"Nothing." I smile, placing his baby picture next to the

picture of his mom. "So, what does she do?"

"She's a correctional officer at the Gulf Coast Trades Center."

"Oh." I try not to make a face. Everyone's heard about the trades center, how it's basically juvie, but no one really knows for sure what goes on in there. "Why doesn't your mom come to church with you?"

"She's not really into church like that. She just thinks it'll help steer me straight. She's so scared that I'll end up like the boys in her unit."

"Well"—I shrug—"you are kind of always in trouble."

"True . . ." He grins.

"Why *are* you always in trouble?"

He rolls his eyes. "I don't like to give respect to people who don't give it back to me."

I push my lips to the side, thinking of the horror stories I've heard about the reason he even moved to New Waverly. "So is that why . . . you stole all that stuff from your old school?"

He looks at me, surprised, like he didn't expect me to ever ask him that. I can't believe I actually did. After it leaves my mouth, I backtrack, "I'm sorry. You don't have to answer that."

"No, it's a fair question." He drops his eyes to the pictures on the floor, gathering his words. So I scoot closer and join him against his bed frame. He says, not making eye contact, "I didn't actually steal anything that night. That was just a rumor."

I furrow my brows, because I instantly feel bad. "Oh. Oh, I'm sorry. I thought—"

"No, it's okay."

"Everyone was saying that's why you got expelled. Even my parents were saying that."

"I know." He glances at me. "I just let people believe it because there was no point in trying to change their minds."

"What actually happened, then? Why'd you get expelled?"

He sighs big, like this conversation is exhausting him, but then he says, "I had this asshole teacher, right? Mr. Davis. Algebra II. That man hated my guts. And I get it—I could be pretty . . . disruptive. But that class was so damn boring."

"Tell me about it," I say. "I hate math."

"Well," he says with a smirk, "the thing is, I would show up to his class and ace every test, and he hated that. He hated that I was doing so well in his class. So one day, I was watching YouTube while he was teaching matrices and he got pissed. He said, 'You won't be able to just skip class in college and expect an A, like you do here. You're gonna get a rude awakening in college.' And I said that I doubted it." Reggie shrugs, then he stares into the empty space across the room, his face getting dark and cold.

"That just pissed him off even more. He said, 'I guess you're right. You're probably not even going to college. If you even graduate high school, you're probably going straight to prison.'"

I gasp, then my eyes start to water. Not out of sadness, but out of anger. "Are you serious? A teacher said that to you?"

He nods, pressing his lips together.

"That is so messed up. That man needs to be fired. How

dare he—" I pause, feeling myself getting overworked. *How dare he hurt you.*

"My mom thought the same thing, so she went to talk to the principal—that asshole. He basically told her that he has kids too and that you can't believe everything kids say. That if you look at my record, it's a little hard to believe anything I say."

"What?" My face falls. "So the teacher got away with it?"

"Yep." Reggie looks at me with a stone-cold expression.

"And you got *expelled* for that?" I ask, appalled.

A smile cracks across his lips. "Well, no, I did break into the school, but I didn't steal anything. It was just a prank!" He laughs. "I drew a bunch of dicks on his chalkboard and in his lesson plans and on all the desks."

"Oh my God." I smile at him.

"He deserved it!"

"He totally did," I say.

And he smiles back. "My mom was pissed, though. But I don't know, I hate when adults think they know soooo much more about what's best for me. I'm not here to change to make people happy."

He doesn't *need* to change to make people happy. Especially seeing the way people reacted to his presence at Shenanigans. Just being around him brings my mood up a thousand points. He's a light in a dark tunnel. He's so hopeful and fun and surprisingly sweet. I say, "I don't think you need to change. You're already pretty great." My cheeks heat up as soon as I say it. Geez, that was a vulnerable thing to say.

He meets my eye and releases a surprised, gleeful kind of breath. "I think you're pretty great too. You're, like, the only person in this town who didn't look down on me because of what you'd heard about me. You don't need to change *anything* for *anyone*. Not one thing."

My teeth clamp down on my bottom lip. Is he referring to my vaginismus? Is he referring to Dom? To himself? He couldn't possibly think I don't need to fix my body. He couldn't possibly want to be with me knowing that I'm broken.

In the silence, Reggie's eyes roam over my face and settle on my mouth. "Um," I say, watching the shadows of his dark lashes at the tops of his cheeks. I turn away quickly, desperate to not be feeling this *want* for him. I dip my hand back in the *RAS* box, searching for a distraction, and it lands on some kind of ball.

When I pull it out, confused, Reggie gasps. He reaches over and grabs it from me. "Holy shit! My Magic 8 Ball! Have you ever had one of these?" I shake my head, and he holds it up, eyes sober. "This thing has helped me make some serious life decisions."

"How does it work?"

"Well." He props up a knee. "You ask it a question, anything you want to know, shake it, and wait for the divine gods above to spit back an answer."

"The divine gods above?"

"Yes, Monique, the Magic 8 Ball gods." He inspects the black ball, then looks at me. "Once I was unsure about asking

May Parker to the homecoming dance, so I asked the gods. They told me 'don't count on it,' so I didn't ask her. Turns out she had a boyfriend, and she was already three-timing him, so I definitely dodged a bullet there. The gods always have my back."

"You don't even believe in God," I say.

"I don't believe in the Christian God," he clarifies. "But I'm not naive, Monique. I believe in the Magic 8 Ball gods."

I laugh, laying my temple against his mattress. "You know, you can just call me Mo. . . ." The words just kind of fall out of my mouth. I feel so incredibly comfortable here with him, it feels weird that he keeps calling me by my full name.

"Okay," he says, his voice soft. "Mo."

Watching his lips form around that one syllable twists me up inside. My stomach feels like the Mexican mountains in October—millions of butterflies clamber against my lining and rest along my forest floor.

He smiles, his eyes leaving trails all over my face but ultimately landing on my lips. After silently tracing their shape, he slowly blinks back down to the 8 Ball. "Let's see what the gods have to say. Magic 8 Ball, should I kiss Monique Tinsley?" When he says my name, he meets my eye and starts to shake the ball.

The butterflies all take flight, up and up and up.

He looks back down at the ball, waiting for a response, and I watch his eyes like my life depends on it. When he meets my gaze again, he's wearing a frown. "The gods have spoken." He shows me the window. *Outlook not so good.*

The butterflies all go poof, like suddenly it's April and they've migrated back north. Wow, I really hoped it would say yes. I come to ask myself: Who are these divine gods anyway, and why do I care what they have to say?

I've had enough of my parents telling me what to do. God and the Bible telling me what to do. Dom . . . I don't need some make-believe Magic 8 Ball gods getting in my way. I reach over and grab the ball out of his hands. "This is stupid. You shouldn't let chance decide for you."

He smirks at me. "I shouldn't?"

"No." I look down at the space between us. "The Magic 8 Ball gods don't know anything, and I don't intend to listen to them."

He reaches over, anchoring his fingers beneath my chin, and lifts my gaze back up to his. It sends my heart racing. "So then, what do *you* say, Mo? Should I kiss you?"

My breath comes out quick and sporadic as he leans closer, sliding his fingers along my jawline. The question turns my stomach back in time, back to October. I stare at his lips and lean in too, and then I close the distance.

His lips land soft upon mine, but I press harder, kissing his bottom lip, and then his top, paying extra attention to the dip of his Cupid's bow. The way he kisses me back and the way he braces his fingers against my jaw, it feels like he's waiting for me to instruct him. And I really like taking the lead. I like how hesitant his lips feel when I coax them apart. It makes me feel like the sexy dominatrix from that Zane book, like my body has power.

My head gets all fogged up. I let the 8 Ball drop. It rolls under his bed as I scoot closer. He exhales through his nostrils, his hand landing on my thigh, sending a shock up my spine. I'm floating out of myself, savoring every second with him.

Until a car door slams outside.

It jerks me awake. *Wait, what am I doing?*

Our lips rip apart, and we both look out of the wide-open floor-length window directly behind us. His mom's walking up the driveway, her body a dark shadow in front of her lingering headlights. Then she raises her hand and waves at us.

Reggie turns back to me with wide eyes, his lips extra, extra pink. "Holy fuck."

24

Turns out, his mom got off early.

We meet her at the front door, smoothing out our clothes and wiping at the edges of our mouths. The knob turns. Then she's right in front of us, caught off guard by the ambush. "Hi," she sings, cocking up an eyebrow as she closes the door. She's just as beautiful as in the picture.

"Hey, Mom," Reggie sings back, way too chipper, way too obvious. "This is Monique Tinsley, Pastor T's daughter," he says, waving his arm in my direction. We purposely placed about five feet between us.

"I know who she is," she says, smiling, like she's amused by our ridiculous charades. "It's nice to formally meet you."

"You too," I say, smiling back, but my smile wavers. I can't pretend like she didn't just catch me making out with her son in his bedroom. "I'm so sorry," I blurt out.

Her eyebrows shoot up. "For what?"

"I know I probably shouldn't be here when you're not here to supervise."

She lowers her gaze. "Yeah, I bet your parents would freak out if they knew." Then she takes a step around us, letting her hand fall on my shoulder. "So how about we keep it between us?" She winks at me.

A smile blossoms in my chest, then rises to my lips. "Yes, ma'am," I whisper, watching her walk past the bar stools toward the dark kitchen.

"I'm sorry, but I've gotten enough nasty calls from your mother to last me a lifetime."

That smile on my face turns into a laugh.

"Sorry. That was tacky."

"No, no, no! It was perfect." I stare after her, amazed.

"So, are you staying late?" she calls, turning on the light in the kitchen.

"No, ma'am. I should get home." I pull my phone out of my pocket and my stomach drops. "Oh no, I'm so late." I look at Reggie, panicked.

"Mom, I'm gonna walk Mo to her car."

"'Kay, good night, Monique. Tell your parents I said hi."

"Yes, ma'am! Good night, Ms. Turner. Sorry, again."

"Call me Jackie," she shouts as I'm walking outside.

I smile and whisper to myself, "Jackie."

Outside is cooler than I remember. And as soon as the front door is shut, I crumple in on myself. "Ohmygod, I'm so embarrassed."

"Why?" Reggie says, laughing. "My mom was cool about it."

"I know, but still."

"It was just a kiss," he says.

"Yeah." I avoid his eyes as I open my car door. "But it shouldn't have happened."

Reggie holds on to the frame as I bend inside and twist the keys in the ignition. When I come back up, his smile has subsided. "She shouldn't have caught us? Or we shouldn't have kissed?"

I slide my hands in my back pockets. "Both?"

He nods big, taking a slight step back. "I see."

"It's just that I don't know what's going on with me and Dom. . . . And I still have *feelings* for him. So I don't want you to get tangled up in that. And I don't want you to be my rebound, because you deserve so much better than that. Besides, I still haven't figured out my condition—"

"Listen," he says, holding his hands up with a smile. "You don't owe me an explanation, Mo. Like, *at all*. We can pretend like this never happened. Okay?" He lowers his chin, his smile actually reaching his eyes. "We cool?"

"Yeah, but—I need you to know, it's not you. It's me. I mean, I thoroughly enjoyed kissing you—" I stop and squeeze my eyes closed. "I probably shouldn't have said that."

When I open my eyes, he's grinning. "No, yeah. You shouldn't have." He shakes his head, taking a step away from me. "Guess I should have listened to the 8 Ball after all."

228

I let out a breath of surprising relief. How is he so cool about all of this? Then I laugh, my eyes filling up with water. "Yeah, I guess the gods were right."

"They always are. But really, Mo, it's cool. Okay?"

"Okay." I nod.

"Sometimes friends accidentally bump mouths. Happens."

I laugh, climbing in my car, watching him go inside. And I hesitate in his driveway for a second, pulsating. Because, *wow*, I was not expecting that reaction.

He didn't need an explanation after I said no. He didn't put me in a situation where I had to repeatedly reject him—I didn't expect to be so wildly turned on by that.

25

I get in twenty minutes late, so I guess Mom was right about the slippery slope. Next it'll be two hours, then maybe I'll disappear for two whole days like my sister did. But when I walk in, I'm surprised to find that Mom isn't at the door, waiting to rip into me.

When I get past the front hall, she's nowhere to be found, but I find my daddy's distraction—Dom's dad—sitting in the living room. They're both huddled over the coffee table with glossy smiles on their lips. Daddy turns over his shoulder, says, "Mo, come say hi."

And that's when I see him—Dom—sitting on the floor at the coffee table. He's looking directly at me, curious.

"Hey, Pops," I say shakily, because that's what Dom's always called his dad, and so that's what I've always called him, since I was a kid.

He stands and pulls me into a hug, burying my face in his chest. I relax against him and sink into the familiar smell of gasoline and tobacco. "Mo-Mo," he sings, rocking me. "I've missed you."

"I've missed you too," I realize. I've missed him coming over for dinner and the way he'd always bring me a plate of grilled hot dogs, since I'm apparently the only person in the world who doesn't like barbecue.

He leads me over to the coffee table. "Your daddy brought out these old pictures. Come tell me if you recognize any of these folks."

"She ain't gonna know 'em, Joe," Daddy says. His accent always gets twenty percent thicker when he's hanging out with Pops.

I scooch past to sit on the floor across the table from Dom. He's looking down at a photo, avoiding my eyes, but it's hard to not look at him. Hard to not concentrate on this bursting in my chest, this splitting of my atoms, this bomb ticking away in my mind. Being in his presence feels so heavy—everything we haven't been able to say to each other this week is flattening me, holding me down to the floor.

Then Pops taps my shoulder, snapping me out of it, as he slides over a photo of a young man—brown-skinned, high-top fade, and eyes like Dom's, wearing an outdated New Waverly Bulldogs basketball uniform. "You know who that is?" Pops asks.

I roll my eyes. "You."

He laughs, shaking my shoulders. "See, she knows, Jesse!"

"That was too easy. What about this?" Daddy pushes over a picture of a preteen Black girl with bone-straight hair and braces. She looks like Myracle, but not.

"Is that . . . Mom?" I ask, studying the dimples in her cheeks.

"That's your Aunt Dee," he corrects me.

"No fair, Daddy. They look just alike."

"How about this?" Pops asks, sliding me a photo of Daddy wearing the same outdated uniform and a buzz cut.

"She knows her old man when she sees him," Daddy says.

I nod, glancing over the other pictures of Daddy and Pops together—best friends since grade school.

"You know, yo' daddy could play some ball, baby girl," Pops says, bumping my shoulder. "He came in as a freshman and took over the varsity team. That don't happen very often."

I look at the smile on Daddy's face, but I already knew that. It's not like they don't stroll down memory lane every other month.

Pops continues, "Jesse and I set so many records for that school."

"Until Dom came in and beat every single one of 'em," Daddy says, gleaming.

Dom looks up then, smiles weakly at my daddy, then looks at me. Why does he look so sad? Or am I imagining that? No, because I've never seen him this quiet around my daddy. Usually he's quick to challenge the two retired basketball players, saying how his stats rank up against theirs. But right now, he looks . . . distracted.

"Yeah, but he's got himself a good team. You and me, we had to do it all on our own."

I look at Dom. And nothing. He's silent.

"That's true," Daddy agrees. "But I ain't ever seen anybody shoot with the kind of accuracy Dom shoots at."

Pops nods, smiling. It's like he's not even in the room. I wonder if it's been like this all night, them trying their hardest to pull Dom out of whatever this sadness is.

But then he looks up at me again. It's never felt so difficult looking him in the eye. Because it hurts so much—how much I miss him, and how much I want him, and how much I still can't believe him. But also, I feel guilty, because I've still got Reggie on my lips, and I'm not exactly ready to wipe him off.

Our dads continue talking stats when Dom nudges his head at me. "Come look at this." *There's* his voice. God, I've missed his voice.

I crawl around the table, leaving my purse on the couch, and sit next to him, but not as close as I used to sit next to him. He slides me a photo of his mom. I know it instantly. It's one of those rare photos of her that for some reason only exist in my family's photo album, so he rarely gets to see it. She's young and in her cheerleading uniform after what I assume was a football game. She's sitting on the hood of someone's car, posing, smiling, living.

When I look at Dom, his eyes are shiny. Daddy and Pops are still carrying on about basketball, so I silently mouth to Dom, *Are you okay?*

"Can we . . . ?" he whispers, nudging his head toward the wall separating the living room from my room.

"Yeah, sure." I stand up, step around, and grab my purse off the couch. "Daddy, we're gonna be in my room."

He only glances up, nods, and then immediately gets back to Pops—which isn't weird. Daddy would let us hang out in my room all the time *with the door shut* because he trusted Dom that much. And we weren't stupid. We never did anything in our parents' houses. We would never be that reckless.

When we get to my room, I put my purse on the bed, then we stand in the middle of the room, just staring at each other. "Mo," he whispers, a tear dripping down his cheek. I don't think about it. I wrap my arms around his neck and lay his head on my shoulder. He holds me tightly, breathing in and out. "It's just been one of those days," he murmurs.

"I know. It's okay," I hum.

This takes me back to sixth grade and seventh grade and eighth grade, when he'd come to me, just for a hug, because I was the only person he felt comfortable crying in front of. He's been crying in front of me since we were seven. I will always be that person for him—the person who was there when he found out his mom died of a random aneurysm, the person who asked what an aneurysm was because he was too afraid to, and the person who held his hand at the funeral. No matter what, I will always be that person.

I hold him, sinking into how it used to feel to be this close to him. Then he mumbles against my shoulder, "I miss you so much."

I stiffen, and my eyes widen slightly. His hands travel slowly up my back, and like instinct, my body presses tighter against him. "I've missed you too."

"You still have all our pictures on your wall, and that sketch your sister did of us."

"Of course I do. I haven't felt ready to take them down yet."

His hands pause on my back, then he pulls away suddenly, holding me so that he can look me in the eye. "Don't take them down."

I scan his eyes desperately. Does he mean . . . because we're not over? Despite everything, he's not completely done with me? A grateful smile starts to lift my lips. "Okay. I won't."

He wipes his face and sniffles, taking a step away from me. "So, you wanna tell me the story now?"

I shift my eyes, confused. "What story?"

"The long story of why you were hanging out with Reggie and Sasha." He raises his eyebrows.

Oh, yeah.

Then I'm back to feeling guilty because that story ends with me kissing Reggie. Actually, with me *insisting* that Reggie kiss me. And me quite honestly liking it.

"Um," I say, turning and taking a seat on my bed. "Well . . ." I stare at my hands in my lap and tell him about how I ran into Sasha at the Women's Clinic, and how she thinks I have vaginismus.

His face slackens. "A *disorder?*" He says it like I told him I have an STD—but unlike Reggie's blasé reaction, he sincerely looks disgusted. "So you won't ever be able to have sex?"

"No, no, it's curable," I say, reassuring him. "That's why I've been hanging out with Sasha and Reggie. They've been helping me find dilators, which—" I grab my purse.

"Why is Reggie helping you with this?"

My hand pauses on the zipper. "Reggie just kinda walked in when Sasha and I were talking about it."

"So, Reggie knows that you and I have never had sex?"

I scrunch my brows. "I mean, *yeah.*"

"Mo, he shouldn't know something like that about you. I don't like that he's helping you with this. That's crossing the line."

"But look," I say, trying to steer the conversation away from Reggie. I unzip my purse and pull out the box of dilators with an automatic smile on my face. I still can't believe we got them. I'm so excited to be done with all this.

"What's that?" he asks, taking a step closer.

"Dilators. These are going to cure me."

His face relaxes and his eyes open a little wider. "Really?" I nod, then after a hesitant glance at my closed bedroom door, I slide the box under my bed alongside the lingerie Dom bought me and the bra Reggie accidentally stole. "How soon will you be . . . ready?"

I try to ignore how that sounds, like I'm an engine that needs a tune-up or something. "I'm not sure. One girl was able to work her way through all the sizes in a month."

"A month?" he asks in the same way I had when Sasha told me—like a month is too long. Like he can't wait for me that long. He twists his mouth. "Well, maybe you can do it even faster, if you try hard enough."

My stomach falls, and so does my smile.

He steps closer and sits on the bed next to me. "Coach always said that records are meant to be broken." Then he grabs my hand out of my lap. "I believe in you, Mo. You can do it."

"But what if I can't?"

"You *can*. Just do it for me." Then he gives me a pleading smile that sinks my stomach even further. That's what I've *been* doing. That's why I've been running all over the world, looking for dilators, asking Sasha to risk her future for me—for *him*. To get him back. To please him. But hearing him actually ask me to makes me want to run away from him and not do anything about my condition.

Because my mind keeps doing this awful thing where it compares him to Reggie, and Dom keeps coming up short.

The first thing Dom asked me when he found out about my condition is if I'll ever be able to have sex. Reggie asked me if I was okay, if I needed to be rushed to the hospital for a possible collapsing vagina. Reggie makes me forget that I have this condition, but Dom lets it define me. Dom makes me feel broken.

He stands up. "I love you, Mo-Mo, and I can't wait for us to get back together." He reaches his hand down for mine. I give it to him, and he pulls me up. He starts to lean in and my heart stops. *No.* I kissed Reggie with these lips just a little while ago. I can't kiss Dom. Not like this. Not with my lips like this. Not with my *mind* like this.

I turn my head and his lips catch my cheek. He pulls back, eyebrows scrunched. "What's up? I can't kiss you now?"

"I just . . . I had onions for dinner."

He smiles. "You know I don't care about that." Then he tries to lean in again.

I lean back. "I care."

"You never have before."

"Dom, stop." I pull out of his arms, looking down at his black socks on my carpet. "I don't want you to kiss me right now."

"Why not?" he asks, stunned.

"I don't want to kiss until we're back together." Then I peek back up at him, timid.

He looks like he feels rejected. He nods, not making eye contact. "Okay, fine."

"It's just, I want to do this the right way. Let me figure out my condition first."

238

"That's it? This doesn't have anything to do with Reggie, right?"

"No," I say with a flabbergasted laugh. *Yes. Yes, it does.* And I can't help but notice the distinction between the way Reggie handled rejection and the way Dom is taking it.

"Okay." He takes a step backward. "Keep me updated, okay? Let me know how far you get tonight."

"Oh," I say, surprised. "You want me to work on it tonight?"

"Might as well, right? You went through all this trouble to get those . . . what are they called?"

"Dilators."

"And since you have the dilators now, that means you won't need to hang out with Reggie and that Bible-thumper anymore . . . right?"

My face droops. I remember the last night Dom and I were together, how we talked about Sasha so ruthlessly—that thing I said about her grandma—but now I know what her relationship with church is. Now I know so much about both of them.

"Right, Mo?"

"But they're my friends," I say weakly.

"Reggie is not your friend. The only reason he was involved with this whole thing is so he could have sex with you. Whatever about Sasha, but I don't want you hanging out with him. Okay?"

I nod. I don't know why I nod. I just want him to leave. I would like to be alone now.

He walks back over to me, kisses my forehead. "Text me tonight after you're done with the dilators."

I nod again. Then he's gone. And I'm left wondering when he got to be so controlling and selfish and *ugly*. I realize after I hear the front door shut that he isn't different. Not at all. In the past, he scared off any and every boy who's ever tried getting close to me, and he always insisted that I give up my time with Donyae and Brittaniya for him. He hasn't changed one bit. But I have.

The person I am now can't go back to how things were.

I don't pull the dilators out from under my bed. And I don't text him.

26

It's been three days. I haven't talked to Dom since that night. The Sunday after, I drove myself to church, just so I could jump in my car right after service and drive home—avoid any chances of conversation with him. He's been texting me, asking me how my training is going. I've been ignoring his texts.

And I haven't touched the dilators either. Mostly because I haven't felt ready. And a little because it feels like Dom is watching me, waiting for me to succeed, so he can claim me again.

Instead, yesterday, I went with Mom to get our hair and nails done. I've been doing a lot of yoga stretches and thinking. I realized what Mom meant about doing things—not for men, but for ourselves. And to exemplify that point, she paid for it herself and not with Daddy's credit card.

I've been doing a lot of thinking about Sasha's question too. *What makes me a catch? Who am I, if not Dom's girlfriend?*

Aunt Dee made me remember that I'm careful and deliberate, that I take my time with every decision, so I don't fall and break my face. I smile, remembering how I used to be such a good tree climber. How high up I used to get. How it always scared my parents. But I never fell.

I pull my legs to my chest, sitting on the yoga mat Sasha lent me. Then I stand up, put my shoes on, and run with a big smile on my face all the way to the sliding back door. When I get outside, I find my daddy and Reggie working on the deck. My steps falter, but I don't let them stop me.

"Hey, Mo, what's the rush?"

"I'm gonna climb that tree!" I shout, running to the biggest tree in our backyard.

"You're gonna what?" Daddy asks, confused and a little concerned.

I step my foot in the lowest groove and hug the trunk like it's all I have. Then I pull myself up, taking a deep breath. The next groove is a little high up. I hold on to both sides of the splitting trunk, then hoist myself up, releasing my breath as I stand one foot on top of the other.

"Mo-Mo, I don't want to have to take you to the hospital if you fall."

"I won't fall!" I shout, confident, because I'm not rushing. I'm enjoying every step, considering every option, testing my weight, before committing to any one branch.

This is an elm tree—I'm pretty sure of it. I look up through the leaves at the clear blue sky and smell the purple wisteria flowering by the back fence. The next step is pretty steep. Too steep. And I'm not as limber as I used to be, so maybe another day, but right now, this is high enough. I lean against the trunk and look down as Reggie comes walking over, hands on his hips. "Having fun?" he asks, looking up at me, squinting against the sun.

I can't help but smile. "A blast."

"This is a bit random, okay? So don't judge me."

"I would never." I grin.

"Can I take a picture of you up there? I would love to sketch this later." He makes a picture frame out of his hands and puts me at the center.

I shrug. "Okay. Sure. Should I smile?"

He pulls out his phone. "If you want to."

I do want to. He takes a picture of me way up in the tree, then he squints up into the sunlight. "Do you need help getting down?"

"No, I'm okay."

He smiles, biting his bottom lip. And my eyes fall to his mouth, and my mind falls back into our kiss. I feel a sudden surge of desire that takes my breath away, so I hug the trunk tighter and hold on to all the decisions I haven't made yet—all the decisions he's making it easier to land on.

"Reggie, can you come hold this?" my daddy calls.

"Sure thing." Reggie pulls his head up with a smirk, then walks back over to my father. I let out my breath and watch him walk away, glance down at the band of his underwear peeking out from beneath his semi-lifted T-shirt. Then I start making my descent, and with every step down, I commit to a new piece of myself.

After my daddy and Reggie are done for the day, I stumble upon something weird in the kitchen. Reggie's sitting at the table, while Mom is unloading the dishwasher. He says, "You know, Miss T—"

"Mrs. Tinsley," she corrects him.

"You know, I was thinking about something the other day."

"What's that?" she asks, struggling to put the bowls in the cabinet above her head.

He stands up and nonchalantly takes the bowls out of her hands, easily placing them in the cabinet that's eye level for him. "You know how the *virgin* Mary was with Joseph, or whatever, and then she had this magical baby that she claims was God's baby?"

I stand straight as a needle on the threshold between the kitchen and the living room.

Mom stops what she's doing and turns to face him. "Uh-huh."

Reggie grabs a few plates out of the dishwasher and places them in that high cabinet above her head. "Wouldn't it be easier to believe that she actually had premarital sex with Joseph, and in order to not be killed, she lied about Jesus being God's baby?"

"Of course," Mom says, surprisingly non-argumentatively. "That's definitely easier to believe, and a lot of people did believe that. It's easier to believe that nothing matters than it is to believe in something you can't see. It's called faith," she says. "What makes the most sense isn't always the answer."

Reggie nods. "I guess I get that. What do you think, Mo?" he asks, turning his head to look at me. I feel caught. I didn't think he knew I was standing here.

"What do I think about what?"

"Do you tend to go with what makes the most sense? Or do you depend on faith?"

"Um . . ."

Mom finishes up the dishes as he takes a seat back at the table. I sit down across from him. "I think a little bit of both. I like to take my time and weigh my options before committing to anything. I like to be sure that I'm comfortable with my decision. Otherwise . . ."

"Otherwise?" he asks, staring intently at my face.

"Otherwise, I might get hurt."

Mom glances over her shoulder at us, and I think I see her smile. Which is weird. I didn't think she could smile in Reggie's presence. I didn't think the two of them could even have a civil conversation like that.

Then Daddy comes into the kitchen, jingling his keys. "All right, Reggie, you ready?"

"Yes, sir." Reggie stands, keeping his eyes on me. And I keep my eyes on him and the brown curls falling over his forehead.

Then as they pass, Daddy says to me, "By the way, Mo-Mo, Dom wants you to call him."

I stare at his back, not sure what to say to that. I have no intentions of calling Dom, but saying that to Daddy feels useless. He doesn't let me get off with silence, though. He pauses with Reggie right behind him. "Are you gonna call him?"

I shift my eyes and shrug.

He lowers his chin. "I thought you wanted to get back together with him." He sighs. "I invited him over Saturday night to give you a chance to talk, and now you're ignoring him? What happened?"

"Wait . . . you invited him?"

"I'm trying to help you, baby." He shakes his head at me. "You can bring a horse to water, but you can't make him drink."

"I'm not a horse," I say, disgusted.

"It's a metaphor."

"A *bad* one."

Daddy stares me down, frustrated at how difficult I'm making this. He was so close to getting Dom back as his future son, but here I am messing it all up. He looks at Reggie. "Why don't you go wait in the car?"

"Actually," Mom says, shutting the dishwasher, "Mo, why don't you take Reggie home? I need to talk to your father."

"You need to talk to *me*?" he asks, confused. "About what?"

"Go on," she says to me.

I stand and snatch my keys out of the bowl on the counter, then hurry past my father with Reggie right behind me. "Why are you pushing her to talk to Dom?" I hear my mother ask before I make it outside.

"Hey," Reggie calls after me, as I'm trekking down the driveway to my car. "Wait up."

But I don't wait. I'm trying to get away from these feelings stacking up inside of me. I'm trying to outrun the rain pouring on my parade. I don't want to think about Dom and all his missed calls. I don't want to have to deal with him right now.

"Mo, please wait!" Reggie shouts.

I stop and spin around. When I look at him, the concern on his face burns my eyes and they start to water. "Who I am and what I want doesn't matter to him. He doesn't care. All he wants is for me to go to college, probably become a teacher and marry . . . a church boy." The realization hits me hard. "Wow, I sound just like Myracle." I nod, slowly understanding exactly what she was going through.

"Who's Myracle?" Reggie asks.

"My older sister."

He tilts his head. "I don't think I knew you had an older sister."

"Yeah, she—" I shake my head. "We don't really talk." I wipe my hand over my forehead, dismissing the subject. "All he cares about is if I get back together with Dom, and I can't get back together with Dom until I . . ." I look at Reggie, not wanting to finish that sentence, not needing to. He already knows Dom's conditions. Then I watch through glassy eyes as he steps close to me, in the middle of my daddy's driveway, and reaches up to wipe my cheek. "Do you know how that makes me feel?" I whisper.

"Like you're not good enough," he answers quickly and correctly. It stuns me, because it looks like he can relate. "Come on," he says, nudging his head to my car. "I wanna show you something."

His mom's car is in the driveway when we pull in. "Is it okay that I'm here?" I ask as I pull my keys out of the ignition.

"Of course. She kept asking last night, 'When is Monique coming back?' It was"—he rolls his eyes, his cheeks suddenly flushed—"embarrassing."

I grin, getting out and following him up the rocky driveway. He leads me inside, where we find his mom sitting on the couch. "Oh, hey, Monique. Good to see you again," she says, turning back to the action movie on the television.

"You too. Thank you," I say politely.

"Come on." Reggie nudges his head, then I'm following him down the dark hallway, back to his room. My first thought is of our kiss. The thought keeps breaking in, flooding me with sudden desire, a rush of want, a burst of lip-biting need.

Reggie goes over to his *RAS* box and invites me to sit with him. I cross the room, looking at his big open window and the pine trees standing tall along his driveway. When I sit down, he pulls out a white envelope, opens it, and shakes out a wallet-sized photo. Then he hands it to me. It's a photo of a random white family. One dad, a mom, and two young girls—all blond, all very pretty.

I look up at Reggie, confused.

His face is expressionless. "That's my dad and his new family."

Oh. My eyes widen as I look back down at it, spending extra time on his dad. Okay, I can sort of see the resemblance—mostly in his face structure—that clean-cut jawline and long chin.

"He sent me that photo for my thirteenth birthday." I look up with a scrunched face, and he laughs. "Yeah, it's a bit tone deaf, right? Like, not a picture of me and him when I was baby, but a picture of his new family."

"Wow, that's . . . stupid."

He nods, licking his lips. "It's hard to look at that and not feel like a disappointment. You know?"

"Yeah."

"But I don't care what that man has to say about me and my life. Nothing he does will change my future, so fuck it. Fuck him." Then he lowers his chin, leveling with me. "What I'm trying to say is, I don't think you should feel this much pressure about your boyfriend. Not when it comes to your future, and definitely not when it comes to sex. You should be happy," he says with a sunny smile. A cute, naive little smile.

I smile back, dropping my eyes down to his shirt. "Yeah, I guess."

He studies me like he wants to tell me to be more certain, but he doesn't.

"I'm sorry your dad's stupid," I say.

"I'm sorry your boyfriend's an idiot. And I'm sorry your dad loves him so much."

"Ex," I correct him.

He flicks his eyebrows up, then nods, like he's pleased with that distinction.

"Reggie! Babe, come here," his mom shouts from the living room. "You too, Monique."

"Are we in trouble?" I ask.

He shakes his head and rolls his eyes. "Nah. She's just overly dramatic about everything." He stands up and offers me a hand. When I take it, he pulls me up, but he doesn't let me go. He squeezes my hand and pulls me behind him out of his room and into the living room.

"Hey," his mom says, taking quick notice of our joined hands. "Wanna watch this movie with me?" She points to a Netflix horror movie on the big screen.

Reggie looks at me with question-mark eyebrows. I shrug and nod. "I'll have to ask my parents if I can stay."

"Only if you want to," she says with a smile. "Do you like stuff like this?"

"I used to, but my parents don't really let me watch it."

"Oh," she says, deflated.

"I can just tell them we're watching a Disney movie. It's fine."

She looks at me blankly for a while, then she suddenly starts laughing. Reggie laughs too, waffling his fingers with mine. I look down at our hands, smiling. So I guess we're really doing this. We're really holding hands.

I step away for a moment to call my mom (not my daddy), and when she answers, she sounds like she's still in the middle of arguing with him, so she barely even listens long enough before she says, "Yeah, sure. Be back by ten."

Reggie's mom sends us out to pick up pizza. As soon as we get in my car, he looks at me and says, "See? She likes you." Then he rolls his eyes. "For whatever reason."

"Shut up!" I push his shoulder, laughing.

"I'm just kidding," he sings as I start the car. Then he says, "For obvious reasons."

At Pizza Hut, we walk across the parking lot together, joking about the movie and who will end up jumping first. And as I'm opening the door, he squeezes my hips and whispers "Boo!" in my ear. I spin around, slapping at his chest, laughing, when his hands find my hips again and my hands find his shoulders. I'm walking backward inside the building. He's matching my steps, looking down into my eyes.

"Hi, what can I get for you?" the guy behind the counter says.

Then I remember that I'm in public.

Somehow Reggie makes it so easy to forget where I am and how I'm supposed to behave and everything that's going wrong in the other parts of my life.

I wait by the door as he pays and picks up the two boxes of

pizza his mom ordered. "Ready, Freddie?" he asks, walking past and holding the door for me.

It makes me smile, all the cute little things he does. It makes me laugh. He looks over his shoulder with his eyebrows cocked, which just makes me laugh harder.

"What are you laughing at?"

"You," I say, unlocking my car doors.

"Why? You think I'm funny looking?"

We get inside and my laughter shuts off, but my smile doesn't. "Of course not."

"Then what's so funny?" He narrows his eyes. "You laughing at the way I walk? My mom says I lope."

"You don't lope," I say, still smiling.

"Then what is it?"

I bite the corner of my lip, start the car, then turn back to him. He's still waiting with the pizza boxes sitting in his lap. "Nothing. You're just . . . cute."

"Oh." His face falls a bit. "Cute. Like a teddy bear."

I smirk at his disappointment. "No. Cute like a cute boy."

"And what do you do with cute boys? Pinch their cheeks."

"Sometimes," I say, doing just that, but then I smooth my fingers along his hard jawline. "But I also kiss them . . . if they let me."

His lips part at that admission. Well, it's not really an admission, what with the fact that we kissed only a few days ago. It's more like a commitment. A realization that I want to do it again.

And again, and again.

I watch his plump lips as they say, "You can kiss me anytime, cute girl. Have at it." Then he leans over the console, peering down at my lips.

My hand slides past his ear and into the back of his hair—feeling the soft prickles of his shaved head until I'm pulling at his curls on top. They spring back when I release them, and I smile. I lean over the console, getting closer to his breath, and watch his eyes flit from one of my deep, dark eyes to the other. "Only if you're sure it won't be a mistake," he whispers.

"I'm sure," I say. I've already taken the time I needed to step fully and wholly on this branch with him. I'm sure this is exactly where I want to be. So I lean closer, brush my lips across his, gentle at first, testing the waters, then I press harder, his mouth softer and warmer than I remember from our Magic 8 Ball kiss. It feels like all my organs are made of Pop Rocks. Especially my skin. Everything is crackling, turning on.

He takes a shaky breath, parting his lips. I slip my bottom lip between his, my fingers clutching his curls, until he pulls away suddenly. "Wait," he says breathlessly, then he hurries to slide the boxes of pizza atop my dash. When he turns back to me, I can see in his eyes that he's waiting for me to lead again. He has a dark freckle at the bottom of his cheek, about two inches away from his lips. I stare at it, wondering how many of my kisses it'd take to get back to his pillowy lips—one and a half.

When he opens his mouth and our tongues meet in the middle, my Pop Rocks organs explode. He's pulling on my arms. He's trying to pull me into his lap. And I'm trying to find my way across the console when suddenly there's a deafening, gut-dropping *bang, bang* on my car window.

Our lips rips apart, and our heads whip over to the left. I fall back against my seat and into Dom's horrified gaze.

27

"Mo-Mo!" he shouts. "What are you doing?"

He reaches for the handle and opens my door. Now there's
nothing separating me from him and his rage. I instinctively
lean away from him, and Reggie throws his arm out across my
body. "Hey, man, take it easy!"

"Nah, *you* better be glad I'm not on your side of the car. Get
your fucking hand out my face. I'm trying to talk to my girl."
Then he bends at the knees, one hand on the edge of my seat
and the other on my door. "So, this is why you've been too busy
to return my calls? You've been busy making out with lames."
He laughs furiously and shakes his head. "I'm over here worried
about you, and you're making out with this screwup, wannabe
bad boy."

I don't know what to say to him. My tongue is tied and my
mind—my mind is still trying to catch up. Dom is here? And
he just caught me and Reggie kissing.

Dom ducks his head to find my eyes because they've veered down to the asphalt beneath his feet. "Baby, look at me." He places a hand on my knee, making me jerk upright. I give him my eyes, and he says, "We were so good together. We were perfect. Your parents love me. My dad loves you. *I* love you. Mo, I was gonna make you my *wife*."

"All right. We don't have time for this," Reggie says, opening his door abruptly.

"Stop." I grab his arm. It's the first word I've spoken since Dom showed up. I look at Reggie, eyes red hot. And he looks back at me, desperate. He looks so scared that he's about to lose me. I turn away from him, though, and back to Dom, because I don't need a stupid fight breaking out right now. Besides . . . I have something to say.

"Dom." I tilt my head, looking in his deep-set eyes. "*You* broke up with *me*. Remember?"

He looks stunned. "We talked Saturday. I thought we agreed that once you fixed your condition, we would get back together."

"*You* talked." I look down at his shoes and the mud on the toe. He must have been working in the pasture before coming here.

"Okay, so what then, Mo? You're gonna go fuck this nigga?"

I furrow my brow.

"I waited two years for you," he says. "I tried so many things with you, and the only reason *you* started trying is because I broke up with you. So then, this broke bastard comes along, helps you get dilators, and now *he's* the hero? I waited two years, and he's been around for what? A week? That's some bullshit, Mo!"

"First of all," I say, heat rising in my chest, "Reggie isn't my hero. He didn't do anything to help get the dilators. He was basically useless in the operation."

"Hey," Reggie says, laughing.

"Getting the dilators was all Sasha. Second of all, you talk as if you *deserve* my body more than Reggie does, just because we were together for two years."

"I *do*," he says, not seeing the issue.

"My body isn't a prize—some trophy you get after a certain amount of time. You don't deserve my body, and neither does Reggie—it doesn't work like that. My body is mine to give whenever I want to whoever I want. My choice to have sex is just that—my choice. And at this point, I'm not interested in having sex with you." I brush his hand off my knee. "It has nothing to do with heroes. It has nothing to do with Reggie. It has everything to do with the fact that I just can't do this with you anymore."

"So you're gonna fuck Reggie?" he asks with a furious smile. I *hate* how he smiles when he's pissed. It makes my stomach turn.

I shrug. "That's none of your business."

"It kind of is," he says confidently.

And I'm not sure why he's so confident. I'm not sure what claim he thinks he has on me, where he thinks it's his business who I see and who I kiss and who I (eventually) have sex with. But I feel it, sitting heavy on my collarbone. The necklace. His claim that his love for me was only getting deeper and stronger. The idea that so long as I wear it, I belong to him. So I reach around and unclasp it. His eyes zero in on the silver heart dangling from the loose chain. "It absolutely isn't your business," I say, thrusting it in his hand.

He looks down at it, breathless. "Wow. Okay." Then he stands up tall and takes a few steps back, clutching it in his palm. "I hope you're sure about this, Mo-Mo, 'cause the second people find out I'm single, it's over."

"I'm fine with that."

He laughs, shaking his head, looking down at the ground. But his laugh turns into a sort of whimper. He stops and stares at me, pain trembling across his lips. The cocky arrogance fades all of a sudden, and his disbelief squeezes my heart. "Mo, what am I supposed to do without you? You're my best friend. Your family is closer to me than my own family. Your dad . . ."

My eyes heat up. I know that my daddy is even more like a father to him than his own dad. Pops is great. He's sweet and supportive, but he's not as open with his feelings as my daddy. My daddy is like Dom's counselor. All I know how to do is hold Dom when he cries, but my daddy knows just what to say.

"I'm . . . sorry," I say, biting down on my own trembling lip.

He tilts his head, disappointed. It's not what he wanted me to say. He wanted me to say, *You're right—let's get back together.*

But I can't. No matter if his relationship with my daddy is on the line, no matter if he won't have anyone else to cry with, I can't sacrifice myself for his happiness. Not anymore.

He places his hands on the top of his head, narrowing his eyes so no tears will fall. Then he spins around, gets in his truck, and slams the door.

I close my door too. Reggie and I both watch as Dom speeds out of the parking lot, then we turn to each other.

"That was intense," Reggie says. "Are you okay?"

"Um." I take a deep breath. "I feel . . . sad? And like I might want to cry."

"Yeah. You basically broke up, for real this time."

I search his gentle eyes. "That doesn't make you mad? That I want to cry over Dom?"

"No. That was really messy," he says, motioning to the parking lot. "And I get it. You two were together for a really long time. Of course you're gonna feel something after that." He reaches over and wipes a fallen tear off my cheek. "How about this? I'll drive. We'll go back to my house, eat some pizza, watch a terrible horror movie, and have fun. Okay?"

I smile, despite everything. "Do you even have your license?"

"No, but it's fine."

So we trade places. I climb in the passenger seat, put on my seat belt, and slide the warm pizza onto my lap. I don't know what I feel. Closure? It's like a door has shut, and even though I didn't want to walk through it, it feels like an opportunity missed. Being with Dom had been my future for so long. I was gonna be his wife. And my daddy was so excited to have him as his son. And everything was gonna be perfect, even though none of it ever felt perfect.

We were trying to have premarital sex while our parents thought we were at the movies or having dinner. My body was steadily pushing him away, rejecting him, testing us until we broke. And when I was with him I always felt pressured to make him happy and do whatever he wanted, because there was this whole sector of our relationship where I knew I was constantly disappointing him.

We weren't perfect. We were never perfect. We were liars and broken and unbalanced. Nothing about us was ever perfect.

When the lights are out, Reggie's living room almost feels like a movie theater. The U-shaped sectional sofa is plushy and instantly swallows me whole. It makes me want to pull my feet in tight, but my parents would murder me if they knew I put my feet in someone else's couch. They already have a hard enough time getting me to stop at home.

The pepperoni pizza box lies open on the coffee table. The shades are drawn, making the room so dark, I can barely see my hands in front of me. And they have surround sound, so it almost makes this awful movie seem good. *Almost.*

"Can someone explain to me why these people think it's appropriate to have sex right now? They just found their friend murdered in cold blood!"

I snicker, covering my mouth. Reggie making fun of the sex scene almost makes it easy to watch. *Almost.*

"Shut up, Reggie," his mom grumbles. She's not as amused by his teasing as I am.

Reggie sits back with a sigh as the murderer kills the idiots in the middle of having sex. I lean into his arm, and his knee bumps into mine. Then he lowers his lips to my ear. "You scared yet?"

I turn to look at him, and only get glimpses of his face from the flashes of television light. I shake my head, then lean into his ear. "Are you?"

When I pull away, he's looking down at my lips. He doesn't answer my question. I already knew the answer anyway. Instead, he starts leaning in. The television is like a strobe light, making his approach appear glitchy, like I can't keep up with him, and suddenly, he's on my lips.

Something horrific is happening on the TV screen—someone is screaming, someone is dying—but something beautiful is happening on the couch. He pecks my top lip and then my bottom, then twists his head and parts his lips. We inhale at the same time, his exhale flowing from his nostrils and bumping against my cheek.

"Son," his mom says, and we pull away. "I'm *in the room,*" she reminds us.

"Oops, sorry, Mom. I must have forgotten."

And he's teasing, but I seriously let myself forget that she was in the room. A few weeks ago, I would have never let myself kiss a boy in the presence of an adult, let alone his parent. Who am I and what has Reggie done to me? Is he even the one to blame?

"I'm so sorry, Miss Jackie," I say softly.

"It's just Jackie. Drop the 'miss,'" she says with a laugh.

"Oh, sorry."

Reggie puts his arm around my shoulders, pulling me against his side. I start to settle in again, but then my phone vibrates. *Daddy.* I decline the call, glance at Reggie with a smile, then turn back to the television.

It vibrates again. *Daddy.* Oh my God, I really don't want to talk to him right now. But after I decline again, *Mom* starts calling. Okay, this might actually be serious. "I need to take this." I stand and hurry past the screen.

"Do you want me to pause it?" Jackie asks.

"No, ma'am, it's fine. I'll just be a second." I tiptoe down the dark hallway and close myself in Reggie's bathroom. "Hey, Mom. What's up?"

"Monique," a deep voice booms. It's Daddy using Mom's phone. I should have known.

"Yes, sir?"

"Where are you?"

"I'm at Reggie's house. Mom said it was okay."

"She said it was okay for you to have dinner at Reggie's house, not to hang out in the parking lot of Pizza Hut!"

My stomach plummets. Oh God, Dom told my *father* about that? I cannot believe him!

"We were picking up pizza for dinner."

"I want you home *now.*"

"Daddy, you can't tell me who to date. I don't want—"

"This isn't about that!" he yells. Daddy never yells. He's never more angry than he is desperate to understand. But he's *pissed.* And why? Because I kissed Reggie? Because I don't want to date Dom? He says, "Get home this second, Monique. Don't make me come get you."

"Okay, geez. I'm on my way."

Then he hangs up without saying goodbye. We never hang up without saying goodbye.

I stagger out of the bathroom, suddenly scared. I don't think Daddy has ever been this mad at me. At Myracle, sure. But never me.

"I have to go," I announce when I get back to the living room.

Reggie looks over the couch suddenly. "What? Why? Is everything okay?"

I twist my mouth, holding down my fear of facing my father and my anger at Dom for bringing this upon me. "My father is upset because Dom told him that he saw us together."

"Are you serious? That little snitch-ass bitch!"

"Reggie! I'm *in* the *room!*" his mom reminds him again.

"I'm sorry, but he is, Mom! I can't believe he ran and told. What a punk."

"Yep, and my daddy is unreasonably mad. So, I have to go deal with that," I say.

"Do you want me to come with you?"

"No, I'm sure that'll make it worse. I'm fine. I can handle it."

He stands up anyway. "Mom, I'm gonna walk Mo out."

"Should I pause the movie?" she asks.

He sighs. "This movie is terrible. You just . . . enjoy that." He makes his way around the couch, grabs my hand, and leads me to the door.

"Thank you for the pizza and the movie. Good night, Miss Jackie. I mean Jackie!"

She laughs. "Good night, Monique."

Outside, the sun is gone, but there's still a little light out. Crickets chirp, cicadas sing, mosquitos swarm. I swat them away from my face, barely even feeling anything but rage. "I can't believe Dom told my daddy about us. What a . . ."

"Snitch-ass bitch?" he asks with a smile.

I laugh. "Yeah. That."

When we get to the driver's-side door, he spins around and stops in front of me. His eyes fall to my tennis shoes. "I'm sorry your dad knows about us."

"It's not that he knows. It's how he found out." When he looks up, I lose myself in the space between his lips and mine. I get lost thinking about the one-and-a-half kisses it takes to get from his lips to that cute freckle beside his mouth. I say, while staring at his lips, "Besides, I barely know what we are." My eyes flicker up to his.

His eyebrows arch. "Is this the part where we *define the relationship?*"

"I don't know. Is it?"

He smirks. "You should do it. Go ahead, define us."

"Why me?"

"Because." He slides his fingers through mine. "Whatever you want to do, I'm willing to make it work."

My brows pinch at how light that makes me feel. Everything he does, everything he says makes me feel lighter, like a weight, a pressure, an expectation is lifted off my shoulders. I don't have to *do* anything to make him want to be near me. I can just be.

"Okay." I shrug, rubbing my cheek with my shoulder. "We're dating. We're . . . seeing each other. Feeling each other out."

"Feeling each other." He steps up real close, wraps his free hand around my low back.

I smile. "That too."

He leans down and kisses me. And I *would* let him kiss me all night—I really would—but my phone vibrates in my pocket. I sigh, pulling away. Daddy: **Are you on your way?** It's like he knows I'm not.

"I really have to go," I say.

"Okay. Text me if you need me."

I steal one last kiss before climbing in my Kia. He watches me turn around in his driveway, then waves as I drive away. My heart is a mess—fluttering and deflating and inflating over and over again. I feel okay when I'm with Reggie, but the farther I get away from him, the more reality starts to set in. Daddy knows about us, and he's pissed. *Really* pissed. But this is it. I can't deal with the pressure of pleasing him and the pressure of pleasing Dom. Now that I've experienced what it feels like to be free, I can't go back. I won't.

When I pull in, the porch light is on. But I can't see anything in the sky watching over me—not the moon, not the stars.

I climb the porch steps, taking a deep breath. Here goes. I have to stand up for myself. I have to stand up for me and Reggie. I'm seventeen years old. I'm old enough to decide who I want to date, and there's nothing Daddy can do about it.

Except . . . when I walk through the front door, I bump into bags lining the wall—*my* bags packed and ready to go. My heart stops. *Wait, what?*

I stumble past my stuff, eyes wide and already watering. Mom and Daddy are waiting for me in the living room. Before I've even realized it, I've turned into Myracle. They're kicking me out? Over preferring Reggie over Dom? "Mom, Dad, are you serious right now?" I whimper. This makes absolutely no sense!

Then they stand up, and my eyes settle on the box of dilators in my father's hands.

Oh . . . oh no.

28

I've never had my life flash before my eyes. But in the last second—that second when my stomach plummeted and my ears were ringing—I saw the past week with Sasha and Reggie flash by vividly. I saw myself on the front porch after Dom broke up with me, saw myself stopped in my tracks when I ran into Sasha at the Women's Clinic, us discussing vaginismus in my bedroom and Reggie walking in. Reggie and me dancing at Shenanigans, Reggie and me kissing on his bedroom floor, Dom catching us a few hours ago, then telling my father.

And now here I stand among all my belongings packed at the door, staring at my dilators in my father's hands. His eyes are fiery hot. Mom, on the other hand, looks confused. And typically their expressions would be swapped. Typically, Daddy would be eager to understand, while Mom would be unreasonably angry. I'm never scared when Mom is angry, because

Daddy always gets the last word, but when Daddy is angry, the whole world stops.

"Wanna explain yourself?" he asks, jaw clenched.

"I . . . how did you—"

"Dom showed me where you keep your sex toys," he says, slamming them down on the coffee table.

I flinch. Sasha, Reggie, and I went through so much trouble to finally get those. I didn't even get to use them, and now I definitely won't.

"They're not . . . sex toys."

"Oh, they're not?" He looks at the box. "Vaginal dilators. So they aren't for your . . ." He nods his head at my body.

"They are, but it's not for *that*."

"So you aren't using these for sex?" he asks.

"I mean," I say, brows pinched, "I can't have sex—I mean, they're for—"

"Dom said that you've been having sex with Reggie."

"What?!" I screech.

"He said these help you have sex, and that you've been see-ing Reggie since you and him broke up."

"Are you serious?" A smile breaks out across my lips—one of those furious smiles that Dom's so good at. "*Dom's* the one I was trying to have sex with. Dom's the whole reason I even got those!"

Daddy's face is a stone wall. He doesn't look like he believes me. How can he not believe me? Reggie and I have gotten nowhere near sex. Dom is the only reason I'm even in this situation.

"What—you believe Dom? You think I'm lying?"

"I don't know what to believe. What I do know for sure is that I found these under *your* bed," he says, pointing at the box, "as well as these." Then he pinches the red lingerie that I had hidden under my bed between his fingers.

Oh my God. This just keeps getting worse.

"Dom bought me those for our anniversary! The whole reason he broke up with me that night was because I couldn't have sex with him."

"He said he broke up with you because *you* kept pressuring *him* to have sex."

I laugh in disbelief. My hands fly up to my forehead. "Oh my God, what is happening right now?" It feels like I'm screaming into a void. Like nothing I say matters because he's already made up his mind. He believes Dom, not me.

I stand up straight, dropping my hands by my sides. I wonder if this is how Myracle felt when she decided nothing could make her stay another second in this house. If she felt this disappointed, betrayed, and downright disgusted by our parents. I look at Daddy, hot tears in my eyes. "I can't even have sex. I was with Dom for *two years*. We tried to have sex twenty-nine times, but it hurt too bad. Then Dom broke up with me, because *he* got tired of waiting."

Daddy purses his lips, unmoved by my confession. But

Mom . . . she looks contemplative. She looks like she's trying to parse through my words, trying to find every inkling of truth.

"I was desperate to win Dom back. So, I went to the Women's Clinic to see if I could get checked out—"

Mom's face falls.

"Sasha's mom works there. Did you know that? I ran into Sasha and she started helping me. She thinks I have a condition called vaginismus." I point to the box of dilators. "That's what those are supposed to cure. I haven't even opened the box, though, because I'm so scared." My voice shakes. "I'm so scared of hurting myself. I'm still a virgin, Daddy. No matter how much I don't want to be."

"So, you're telling me Dom came in here and lied to my face?"

"Yes!" I say desperately.

"You're telling me he was pressuring you to have sex?" Daddy blinks, jaw clenched, and I finally think he might be starting to believe me.

"Yes. Reggie and I have never gotten anywhere near sex. It was Dom."

Daddy nods with folded arms. "I really don't know what to believe, Mo."

"Believe *me*—your daughter."

"How can I?" he says. "When Dom came in here, he was still wearing the promise ring I gave y'all. But I can't help but notice that yours is gone."

I look down at my bare hands and remember how I threw my promise ring in my glove compartment. How taking it off meant that I decided to break that promise. How taking it off felt so freeing. And now it'll be the reason I'm sent to prison.

But you know what? I don't regret taking it off. Not at all. I don't regret anything I've done in the past week—nothing except trusting Dom.

"I've told you the entire truth," I say. "Dom is the one who lies when he wears that ring. He's not even a virgin, so." I shrug. "Believe what you want to believe."

"Even if Dom is lying to me, you lied too. You're my daughter, and I can't . . . I can't trust you. We're sending you to your granny's house for the rest of the summer. You've been around a lot of bad influences, and I think it's best if you spend a little time away from it all. Give me your phone and your keys . . ."

I don't hear the rest. He's like a judge reading my sentence. I don't hear much past "rest of the summer." No more Reggie. No more Sasha. No dilators. No therapy sessions. Nothing. Nothing but the Bible, daytime television, and the chickens in Granny's backyard.

If you ask me, that's hell. Not some fiery pit beneath our feet. But being cut off from the world, being cut off from the boy I like minutes after DTRing, being cut off from the first friend I've made in years. Yeah, that's hell.

I blink away the tears as I hand over my phone and my keys, but I stare at Mom over Daddy's shoulder. I stare at the unrest in her expression. Because maybe she'll say something. Maybe she'll stop him.

"Go to bed," Daddy says. "We've got an early morning ahead of us."

Mom stands stone still as Daddy grabs the dilators off the table and walks them to the trash can. This is the moment that Myracle decided to run. I can feel it in my bones, ready to burst. And I don't blame her for taking off—not anymore, not one bit.

I would run too if I still had at least two out of three of the following: my phone, my keys, and a place to run to.

29

Somehow, I slept. Despite the fact that sleep would only lead to the morning and the morning would only lead to my life ending, somehow, I found a way to fall.

Now my mother is shaking me awake, with the overhead light shining bright in my eyes. "Get up, Monique. Let's go. Hurry up." She's whispering, like that'll soften the blow of what comes next.

"Why would I want to hurry and go to Granny's?" I grumble, turning on my side.

She goes over to my closet, pulls out a summer dress, and tosses it on my bed. "We're not going to Granny's. Your daddy is still asleep. So, hurry up. Let's go." Then she turns and heads to the door.

Wait, wait, wait. Daddy's still asleep and we're leaving? I sit up with a start. Are we running away? The thought gets me excited, but only for a second. Because as much as I don't want to go to Granny's, I don't want my parents splitting up over it. I would rather spend a year in Granny's chicken pen than watch my parents break up.

"Mom," I say, watching her walk away.

She ignores me.

"*Mom*," I hiss.

She makes it to the door.

"Momma," I say, calling her *momma* for the first time in years. I think I stopped at the same time that Myracle stopped, and Myracle stopped when she turned thirteen—when she and Mom couldn't go five seconds without fighting.

She turns in my doorway.

"Where are we going?" I ask, scared.

She looks at me with intention in her eyes. "The Women's Clinic." Then she closes my door gently and silently, leaving me in a surprised stupor.

My mom is taking me to the doctor? *No way.* A teary smile crosses my lips. I throw the covers off my body and pull my bonnet off my head.

On the drive over, we're silent. There are so many questions I want to ask, but this whole operation seems extremely fragile. I don't want to do or say anything that'll make her change her mind.

The office opens at eight, and we're the only car parked in the lot at seven forty-five. We both stare ahead at the building, like it'll do the talking for us. But then Mom's cell phone starts ringing. We both look at the central touch screen in her dash. *Hubby* is calling. My blood runs cold, but Mom seems much less alarmed.

She answers, "Hey."

He comes crackling over the car speakers. "B, where'd you go? Is Mo with you?"

"Yeah, she's right here."

Then absolute silence. I look at her with rainbow eyebrows.

He says, "Okay, where are y'all?"

"Oh, we're in Huntsville," she says casually. "We'll be back in an hour or so." She is completely calm, cool, and collected, and it's a little scary.

"B, what are you doing in Huntsville?" Daddy asks.

"We're at the doctor's office. Getting Mo checked out."

I start sweating like the AC isn't blasting in my face. He seems stunned by this information because he's silent for a good five seconds. "I'm sorry, you're *where*? B, we talked about this. She's too young! And we need to get her back on track before we start *encouraging* sex. Now, I don't understand how you could do this without talking to me—"

She hangs up on him. . . .

She hangs up on him.

I look at her, eyes round, mouth in the shape of an O.

"Oops. Looks like it's eight," she says, turning off the engine and opening her door.

I stare through the windshield as she makes her way to the double doors of the building. Oh my God, this woman is my hero. What happened to her? Who is she?

I can't believe my *mom*, of all people, is taking me to the gynecologist. I remember the first time I came here, and how I passed that mom and her teenage daughter and how jealous I was, how lucky I thought she was. I guess it turns out I'm lucky too.

I join my mom in front of the building. The doors are still locked, until Sasha's mom unlocks them from the inside. "Hey, Bianca," Mrs. Howser says as soon as the doors are open.

"Leslie, thank you so much for getting us in on such late notice."

Mrs. Howser hugs my mom before we've even gotten all the way in the building. They hug for a really long time, really tightly. And Mrs. Howser hums to my mom, "I know how worried you are. And I know how urgent it is, with the pastor trying to ship her off."

"He thinks he understands my daughter's body, but he doesn't get it," Mom spits. It sounds like she wants to cry.

"When I told Dr. Marion the situation, she agreed to come in right away. She's a fantastic doctor, and she loves what she does." Mrs. Howser pulls away, then she looks at me past my mother's arm. She gives me a weak smile. "You're in good hands."

"Thank you, Les," Mom says.

We follow Mrs. Howser inside. "Sasha, get them the new

patient forms. I have to get the office opened up."

And there she is, sitting behind the front desk, just like the first time I came here. She smiles big at me. "Hey."

I wave, smiling bigger. As she hands my mom a clipboard with a bunch of forms clipped to it and a black ink pen, Mrs. Howser goes over to unlock the door beside the desk. "Usually we don't take appointments until eight thirty, and since there is someone scheduled for that eight thirty slot, we gotta get you squeezed in quickly, sweetie." Then, with one last glance, she disappears in the back.

My mom takes the clipboard and goes to sit in the empty waiting area. I stand by the desk next to Sasha. "I can't believe this is happening," I whisper.

"I know!" she practically squeals. "Your mom called my mom last night. Then my mom asked me about the dilators." Sasha clenches her teeth. "She was pretty pissed when she found out I stole them from here. But then she called Dr. Marion. Oh my God, I can't wait for you to meet her. And, oh my God—" She presses her hands to the counter, leans forward with her eyes rounded. "I can't believe Dom lied like that. I told your mom that he's a total liar. I got your back."

I smile at her frantic excitement. "Thanks, Sasha. Thanks for everything. I'm sorry if you got in trouble for the dilators."

She makes a face. "Yeah, I'm not really allowed in the back for a while, but it's fine. Because you're here! I'm so glad your mom brought you here."

I look over my shoulder at her hunched figure, her hand

scribbling away on the new-patient forms. "Me too," I say with a smile.

The side door opens and Mrs. Howser's head pops out. "Monique, you ready? How about you, Momma?" she asks my mom.

"Not completely finished with the paperwork."

"That's fine. You can finish them up in here." She waves us over. "I'm just gonna get started with Monique's physical." She leads us down the white hallway with the harsh white lights, all the way to Dr. Marion's office.

I'm sitting on the edge of the bed, staring in horror at the metal stirrups. Ew, God, I'll put my feet in those and then some lady is gonna have a full-frontal view of my vagina. Mrs. Howser takes my blood pressure, jots down my height and weight, all the while chatting up my mom.

"Okay, Monique." She stands up from her chair with a smile, hands me a paper gown, and instructs me to strip down. "Dr. Marion will be with you shortly." Then she steps out.

I look over my shoulder at Mom. "I'll close my eyes," she says without me having to ask.

"Thanks," I whisper. Then as I'm taking off my dress, I say, "For everything, Mom. Thanks for bringing me here. Thanks for believing me." I slip the gown on and tell her, "You can open your eyes now."

She does with tears glazing them over. "It doesn't matter if I believe you or not. It's my responsibility as your parent to make sure you're okay."

I nod, grateful, but not exactly satisfied with that answer. But then she says, "I do believe you, though. I *never* for a second thought that Dom was innocent in this."

"If anyone is innocent in this situation, it's Reggie. He knows I have this condition, and he doesn't care."

"How do you know he doesn't care?" she asks. "Are you sure?"

I try closing the gown the best I can, because the draft in this office is relentless. "I think so," I say. "He seems . . . to care about me, as a person."

She studies me meticulously. "I want you to be sure," she says. "I don't want another boy to hurt you."

I bite the corner of my lip, unsure of how to handle this sentiment coming from her. My mother is usually more concerned about my physical well-being than my mental well-being. She's usually more concerned about our image than how I feel. So, this is heavy for me. And at the same time, I lose a little weight off my heart.

"I'll be sure," I say. "I'll make sure."

She nods solemnly. Then there's a knock at the door. "Can I come in?" we hear.

"Yes. Come in," Mom says, after waiting for me to confirm that I'm ready.

Then the office door opens and in floats a middle-aged light-skinned Black woman with straight, kind of fluffy shoulder-length hair, a thick gold-link necklace beneath her white lab coat, and berry-red lipstick. "Hello, hello, hello," she sings. "How are we this morning?"

"Good," Mom answers quickly, then presses her palms together. "Thank you so much for seeing us on such short notice. You don't know how much this means to us."

"I think I do," she says, nodding at my mother. "It means just as much to me. No woman should have to go without care. Especially not because some power-hungry man thinks he knows what's best, when he doesn't know diddly-squat about women's bodies."

I raise my eyebrows at her controlled rage.

She walks over to my mom. "I praise you for bringing your daughter in anyway. You're the hero here. Not me. I'm just doing my job."

Mom's eyes twinkle as she smiles up at Dr. Marion. "I am too."

"And what a fine job you're doing, Momma." Then she grabs her rolly chair and drags it over to my side of the bed, clipboard in hand. "I've heard a lot about you, my dear, from Sasha and her mom," she says.

"Oh?"

"Sasha begged me to see you today. She was adamant about getting you help—I mean, obviously, since she so desperately stole dilators for you."

My jaw drops. "That was all my fault. Please don't blame Sasha."

"I do blame Sasha, just a little bit, because she could have come to me. But as much as I lost a little trust in her, I gained it all back in respect." She looks up from my chart and smiles at me. "You know, I see a little of myself in her. Her passion drives her, and I love that."

"She'd make a fantastic gynecologist."

"That she would," Dr. Marion agrees.

I smile as she drops her eyes back down to the clipboard. "Okay, Monique, may I ask what your pronouns are?"

"Oh . . ." I've never been asked that before. "Um, she/her."

Dr. Marion nods and writes them down. "And you, Momma?"

My mom looks just as surprised as me. "The same."

I twist my mouth, appreciative of the fact that she asked, and a little ashamed that I assumed Dr. Marion's pronouns, so I ask, "What about you?"

Dr. Marion smiles up at me. "She/her as well." Then she rests the clipboard on the bed and leans in with her stethoscope. She checks my heart and my lungs and says that everything sounds great. She leans back in her chair. "I've got quite a few personal questions I need to ask. If you'd like Momma to step out for this portion, that's fine."

I glance back at Mom. "No, no. It's okay." I want her here. Surprisingly, she makes me feel . . . comfortable and safe. She makes me feel like I can share anything with her, because she's more concerned about my health and my safety than what this all says about my image.

"Do you remember at what age you got your first period?"

"Fourteen."

"What do you typically use as a means of collection? Tampons? Pads?"

"Always pads. I can't do tampons."

"Have you ever attempted?"

I shake my head. "No. . . . My mom has never bought me tampons."

She glances back at Mom.

"It's just not something I think a teenage girl *needs*. I, uh, never really considered it."

"And I've never understood how they work," I say. "How does a virgin wear tampons? Won't that break her . . . hymen?"

Dr. Marion's eyes are unbothered, unwavering, dark, and beautiful. She looks like she can see right through me. It's intimidating and comforting at the same time. "No, dear. By the time girls reach your age, the hymen has receded quite a bit. If you're able to have a period, then that means your hymen has an opening. Girls who have never had sex can still wear tampons—*typically*."

She goes on to explain that hymens are not a good representation of whether or not a girl is a virgin, that they can easily tear during physical exercise. That my first time having sex is not guaranteed to bleed—my eyes widen at this. What about the whole "pop the cherry" saying? I thought everyone had to deal with a bloody mess on their first time.

She asks me about my flow, and the intensity of my cramps, and the regularity of my cycle. Then she moves on to my first experience with sex, my relationship with Dom (at which point

Mom butts in to call him an overbearing, possessive control freak), whether we used protection *every time*, and then she asks to describe in detail the type of pain I felt.

"Um, it felt like it was too tight, or like he was hitting a wall that wouldn't give."

"Was it a lasting pain?"

I think to myself. "What do you mean?"

"Did you still feel pain after he stopped?"

"Oh, no, ma'am. After he stopped, it didn't hurt anymore."

She writes some stuff down, and then she asks me about my family history and genetic illnesses, all of which my mom answers.

"Okay, Monique." She stands up from her chair. "Today, I would like to do a breast exam, a pelvic exam—"

"A pelvic exam?" I ask fearfully.

"Don't worry. I won't force you to go through anything too painful. I'll do an external exam, and then see how far we can get with an internal. I don't believe we'll get as far as a pap smear. So don't fret!" She smiles.

The next twenty minutes pass me by in a blur. I'm instructed to put my feet up in the stirrups. That's when I start hyperventilating. It's like every time Dom and I would try to have sex. She and my mom work together to get me to calm down.

She attempts to insert a finger, slowly and gently, but when I groan in pain, she stops. Her face, when I finally open my eyes, doesn't look perplexed, surprised, or disappointed at all.

After taking notes, she gives me a few minutes to get

dressed, then she gives my mother the rundown—she explains the results of my exam, the benefits of birth control, and why I should get tested for STDs . . .

But all I can really concentrate on is my official diagnosis of vaginismus.

30

Mom is crying.

Crying.

I'm sitting in the passenger seat, staring awkwardly out the window with a new box of dilators in my lap.

"I can't believe you went two years. You could have hurt yourself. I—I failed you."

I reach over and pat my mother's shoulder. I don't remember the last time I saw my mom cry. I think it was in church. That's the only place I *ever* see her cry.

"There was so much you didn't know about your body." She looks at me, mascara running beneath her eyes. "I just thought if I kept the information from you, that you'd stay away from it. Well, it worked! In the worst way possible. You developed a disorder!"

"It's not just you. I also didn't learn anything at school."

"Yeah, that's by design. Coach Dale and your father are pretty tight—and don't even get me started on your father." She points at me like I'm the one she's angry at. "That man . . . I love him. I love him so much, but he thinks he's right about everything. And I'm done with it."

Le'Andria Johnson plays in the background all the way home. I want to ask if this means that I don't have to go to Granny's, but I don't want to push my luck. When we pull into the driveway, she turns to me. "When we get in here, you go directly to your room and stay there. Got it?"

I nod vigorously. Then she gets out and I follow. Like a baby duckling, I stick close to her steps. She'll protect me. She'll stick up for me. She won't let him send me away. As soon as we walk through the door, Daddy's in front of us. "Bianca—"

·   Then Mom pushes me toward my room. I hurry away, doing exactly as she said.

"B, are those dilators in her hands? Bianca, what are you doing?"

I shut my bedroom door, lean my back against it, and listen.

"No, Jesse, you listen to me! Our daughter is so afraid of sex that she has a *medical condition*. That's on us! We let this happen to her. And how *dare* you believe Dom over Monique. She's tried having sex with Dom twenty-nine times in the past two years. That boy pressured our daughter, gave her an ultimatum—have sex with me or it's over—then he came in here, lied to your face, manipulated your feelings, and you *believed him*."

286

"So, you didn't believe him?"

"Not for a second. That boy is not as perfect as you paint him to be. He's a jealous, possessive control freak . . . and I think you need to take a hard look at who made him that way."

There's a pause. Then Daddy asks, "Are you saying *I* made him that way?"

"I'm saying that you might have encouraged it. Reggie may not open Mo's door or pull out her chair, but I've seen the way he interacts with her. He listens to her."

"Here's the bottom line," Daddy says. "Even if Dom was wrong, Monique tried having premarital sex. Now is not the time for us to start falling apart, not when her morals are in question. And now is definitely not the time for us to give her the *tools* to have sex."

"I'm giving her tools to have *safe* sex. She's seventeen years old and she didn't know—" Mom pauses. Her incessant crying starts back up. I lean my head against the door, holding back my own tears. "She didn't know so much about her body. Keeping this information from kids is doing more harm than good, Jesse."

"It's not information they need, if they're abstaining from all sexual contact until marriage."

"But clearly they're not waiting!"

"Which is why we need to get our daughter back on track! I'm grabbing her bags and I'm taking her to her granny's."

I move away from the door, trying to think of a place to

hide my new dilators. I won't lose them again. I don't care how deluded my father is. I'm done letting him make decisions about my body.

"I'll tell you this," Mom says. "You're not taking my daughter to your mom's house."

"Bianca!"

Then my bedroom door opens. Mom points at me, tears streaking her cheeks. "Let's go."

This time we might actually be running away, and it scares me, because I've never seen my parents like this . . . or, I guess more accurately, I've never seen my mom like this. Daddy's always gotten the last word, but not today.

I fall in behind her again, holding my dilators tight to my chest. "Bianca, wait. Let's just talk about this."

"What's the point in talking when you won't listen to me?"

And as we pass him in the living room, I look him in the eye, fearfully. I'm afraid he'll try to snatch me up, buckle me in the back seat of his Cadillac, and drive me to Granny's. I'm scared he'll try to take away my dilators, my freedom.

He sees the fear in my eyes and how closely I walk behind Mom. And he softens. "Mo-Mo," he whispers.

I turn away quickly. I don't know who that man is anymore. I used to think he was my hero. Wow, and I thought Mom was the villain. It's crazy how they switched places. I follow behind her, thinking of all the times Daddy bulldozed over Mom, and how many times I rooted for him. I was on his side, because he was always on *my* side, but I guess I didn't realize how maybe

I shouldn't have cheered for my daddy to silence my mom—despite the fact that I didn't usually like what she was saying.

He lets me pass without incident. And he lets us leave without another word. I buckle myself in Mom's car knowing three things for sure: 1. I'm not going to Granny's. 2. These dilators are mine until I don't need them anymore, because I know my mom has my back. 3. Aunt Dee was right about Mom—she *is* too cool for my daddy.

31

The sky is gray and getting darker by the second when we pull into Aunt Dee's driveway. Mom's tears have dried since we left Daddy at the house, but her fury was apparent just by how fast she was driving.

We get out, but before we can knock, the door opens and out pours an Aretha Franklin song. Aunt Dee lets us in, singing along. "You make me feel like a natural woman!" She's wearing a robe and a matching silk headwrap, and she's holding a champagne flute full of orange liquid. "Here you go," she says, shoving it in my mom's hands.

I close the door behind us, as Mom smells the glass. "Is this orange juice?"

"It's a mimosa," Aunt Dee says.

"Dee-Dee, it's barely even eleven." Mom tries handing the glass back.

"Yeah, it's brunch time."

"I don't drink anymore, and you know that."

"Yeah, yeah, yeah. Today you do." She nudges her head at Mom. "Go on."

And I can't believe the contemplation on Mom's brows. Mom and Daddy have never brought a drop of alcohol into the house. I never imagined that Mom has *ever* drunk in her life, but by the way she throws the mimosa back and swallows it all down in less than ten seconds, it's clear that there's a lot I don't know about her.

"And there's more where that came from," Aunt Dee says in a singsongy voice, leading us into the kitchen, swishing her hips to Aretha and spinning in circles. Zula is eating from her bowl in the corner, but when she sees us, she comes scampering over for kisses.

Aunt Dee gets Mom set up at the bar as I rub Zula's belly. "How's that asshole husband of yours?"

"Dee-Dee, don't."

Aunt Dee pours champagne in Mom's glass, then pulls the orange juice out of the fridge. "Hey, li'l bit, you want some juice?" she asks me.

"I'm good." I stand up, leaving Zula's side, and sit at the bar beside my mom.

She pours me a glass anyway, then she reaches for my hand. I shift my eyes and lay my palm in hers. "I hear your vagina is broken."

My eyes widen. Mom chokes out, "Dinah!"

"What? That's what you said."

"That is *not* what I said." Mom glances at me, embarrassed.

Aunt Dee lets go of my hand and paces the floor. "You said that she can't have sex because her vagina snaps shut, yadda yadda yadda. Broken," she concludes.

"It's not broken," I say, my cheeks on fire.

She turns to face me with an amused smile. "No?"

"It's just . . . I'm just scared."

Her eyes soften, as do her cheeks. "What are you so scared of?" she asks. "It's just sex." My eyes instantly shift over to my mother's. She's staring at Aunt Dee's shoes until she feels me watching her. Aunt Dee says, "You should hurry up and get your first time out of the way, because it's going to suck. Bianca knows a little about shitty first times. Don't you, B?"

My mom looks mortified.

"Drink up," Aunt Dee says, and laughs, then she makes her own mimosa. She takes a big gulp, as does my mother, while I sip my orange juice, just watching. Aunt Dee wags her finger at me. "Your mom might be a stuffy pastor's wife now, but before Jesse, she was—"

"Dinah, stop," Mom says. She's serious now. Myracle and I never pushed her past this point, but Aunt Dee . . .

"Tell her about your first time, Bianca." Aunt Dee looks at my mom with her hands on her hips. Mom tilts her head, snarling. "Okay, fine, I get it. I'll go first, then," Aunt Dee says, turning to me. "My first time was in the back seat of Jared

Bastrop's old Honda Accord. I was eighteen. He was seventeen and ugly, his car was nasty, and it took him thirty minutes to finally get it in."

"I really don't like this conversation," Mom says.

"Tell her, B. Tell her about your first time, and how it *wasn't* with Jesse on your wedding night."

Mom's eyes widen. So do mine. Wait, Mom didn't wait until marriage?

"And even though you gave your virginity to that football player when you were sixteen, you're still not going to hell," Aunt Dee says. "Now, are you? God forgives. Right?"

"I don't want my daughter to make the same mistake I made."

"Yeah, because she needs to make her *own* mistakes." Aunt Dee takes a sip of her mimosa. "You've changed, B, ever since you married that preacher."

"I got saved."

"Nah. It's like you—you gave up. You used to be bossy and headstrong, and nobody could tell you shit."

"Watch your mouth."

"But that man's got you so . . . submissive."

"Not anymore," Mom snaps. Her eyes glisten. She looks like she's up against a wall, like she's being attacked and she can't move. Aunt Dee is the only person who can do this to her. Turn her speechless, like she's trying to hold down a part of herself that only her sister knows exists.

I'm sitting on the edge of my stool, at the edge of the

conversation, just watching. Until Mom looks at me. She says, "I was too young. I wasn't ready. And I used . . . sex as a way to get closer to this boy I'd had a crush on for years. I thought if I gave him my body, he'd love me as much as I loved him, but it doesn't work that way."

"Preach," Aunt Dee says.

"I gave him my virginity, and he broke up with me right after, and my God, I felt so empty and worthless." She looks at her sister. "I didn't want my daughter to go through that. Waiting until marriage, until you know for sure that a man is committed to you, can save you a whole lot of heartache."

"But that's a decision you have to let your daughter make," Aunt Dee says. "And being open about your past might have been better than pushing fear."

Mom watches her sister go to the freezer for something a little harder—the vodka she offered me last time. Then Mom's eyes fall to me. And I'm just sitting here, watching my whole life change before my eyes, watching *her* change before my eyes. It used to be easy to write her off as impossible and inhuman. She built so many walls between us. And she had so many expectations for me that, it turns out, *she* couldn't even meet.

Aunt Dee mixes vodka and Sprite in two bar glasses. She pushes one to my mom, then takes a sip of her own. "If we're being honest, Brandon *was* sexy," Aunt Dee says. "Wouldn't have minded losing my virginity to that man. Wonder where his ass ended up." Then she grabs her phone.

"You have a husband," Mom reminds her.

"*A fine-ass husband*—I know. I'm just curious."

"But the thing is," Mom says, changing the subject kind of abruptly, "after losing my virginity to Brandon, I felt so empty and worthless and hurt . . . the night of my wedding, I couldn't do it again."

I look at her with a quick snap of my neck. "What do you mean you couldn't do it again?"

She nibbles the corner of her lip, takes a sip of her drink, then nods at me. "I couldn't have sex. I felt like I wasn't good enough for Jesse—he'd waited until marriage, and I hadn't. I felt like my body already belonged to another man, so . . ."

"You had vaginismus?" I ask, eyes bulging out of my head.

"I looked it up while we were in Dr. Marion's office—whether or not it's possible to develop vaginismus after having sex before. Apparently, there's such a thing as secondary vaginismus."

"Why didn't you talk to Dr. Marion about it?" I ask. I don't even know what I feel right now. I'm kind of mad. If only I'd known she had this problem early on, maybe I would have come to her about my situation.

"Well, I don't have that issue anymore."

"Why didn't you . . . tell me?" I ask, pain stealing my voice.

She looks at me, the same pain creasing her face in folds. "I didn't realize until today that it was something other women went through. I've just now put a name to what I experienced back then." She reaches over and cups my chin. I almost jump away, startled by her sudden affection. "I thought if you waited until marriage, nothing like that could happen to you—look how wrong I was. I'm so glad you have doctors to help you through it."

"How did you get over yours?"

"It took me a few months, but it was really your dad who helped me through it. He never pressured me or rushed me. He wasn't anything like Brandon, and I had to realize that. I also had to forgive myself. I did *a lot* of praying."

"I didn't know about that," Aunt Dee says, squinting her eyes.

"You were thirteen. It's not like I could go to you for advice."

She smirks. "True." Then she leans over the bar and starts talking about when she was sixteen and Mom was twenty-six and Myracle was one. How Aunt Dee would give my daddy hell, as if he was the stepfather she never wanted.

The two sisters walk hand in hand down memory lane, and I listen for a while, smiling at how close they are and how much closer I feel to them right now. Like I'm not staring through a window at "grown folks' business," but instead, I'm included in the conversation. I've never felt so welcome to share.

While they talk about boys from high school and where they ended up, I can't help but think of my own sister. My eyes drift over to Aunt Dee's fridge and the postcard there. Myracle's drawing style hasn't changed much, but her talent has grown immensely. The details are crazy good. It just makes me regret saying what I did that night even more. She's not just as good as everyone else. She's better.

When I turn back to Aunt Dee and my mom, they're both staring at me. I shift my eyes. "What?"

Aunt Dee looks at my mom, and it's like they have a silent conversation between their gazes. My mom nods with her eyes closed, takes a big sip of her drink, then Aunt Dee says to me, "I have to show you something."

"What is it?" I ask, more than a little worried.

"Come here." She stands from the bar, and I follow her out of the kitchen, down the hall. Zula trots behind us, all the way to Aunt Dee's office.

I step in after her and look around. Gosh, I think this is my favorite room in her house. Everything else in the house is dark and warm and cozy, but in here, it's open and light. Her desk is a minimalist pine-colored L-shaped table with a laptop open on top, a desk lamp, and a few succulents in colorful pots. Her bookshelf against the wall is full of Black history books and Black fiction. The walls are painted light gray with her master's degree in communications hanging behind her desk, and posters of Barack Obama and his family on the front wall.

But the best part of this office is the glass sliding door leading to their picturesque backyard and their in-ground pool. The sky is dark, casting a gray ambiance over the light hardwood. A streak of lightning cracks its way across the sky, and thunder booms right after. Zula barks and runs out of the room. I hadn't realized it was raining—not until we got away from all the music and the conversation. It's quiet in here, except for the pitter-patter on the roof.

Aunt Dee goes over to her desk. I wait on the other side as she opens a drawer. "Listen, don't be mad at me for this."

"For what?" I scrunch my brows.

"At the time, your mom and dad thought it would be best to not give you this, but I think now's a good time . . . to be completely honest."

She slides over a small rectangular piece of paper . . . oh, it's a postcard. There's a sketch on the front of an apartment building and a happy Myracle standing outside of it. At the top, she wrote, "My new place!" And at the bottom she wrote her address. She's living in Austin now.

I flip it over and can't believe my eyes. The postcard is addressed to me. And the rest of it is filled with tiny script—a letter.

"When did she send this?" I ask, tears flooding my eyes.

"A month after she left."

"Oh my God." This whole time, for two whole years, I thought she hated my guts. I thought she wanted nothing to do with me. I don't know if I can forgive my parents for keeping this from me. Keeping *her* from me.

As I start to read, Aunt Dee comes around and claps a hand on my shoulder. "I'm so sorry, sweetie. There's paper in the second drawer. Feel free . . ." Then she leaves me be.

Mo-Mo, I miss you already, you big pumpkin head.

I laugh, wiping tears from beneath my eyes.

I'm sorry I took off like that. What you said that night— how I'm good, but so is everyone else—that hurt me more than anything, because it's my biggest fear. Maybe I don't measure up. Maybe I won't make it as an artist. Maybe I made a mistake. But I don't care anymore. This is worth it. Dreams are worth it.

And I know you're just a kid. I don't blame you for being scared for me. I know you love me, and I know how much Mom and Dad treasure you—you're the daughter they got right—but I hope you'll understand one day why I had to leave. Mom and Dad aren't perfect. They aren't right about everything, and I know for sure they're not right about me. Don't let them keep you from living your life the way you want to live it. At the end of the day, it's your life. You have to answer for your decisions—not them.

I don't have much room left to write, haha! I love you. Write me back, pumpkin head!

She wrote this a month after she left?

A month after she left, I was torn up. I was so full of regret. I was trying to call her number, even though I knew her phone had been disconnected. I was desperately trying to find her online, but she'd deleted all of her profiles. I needed to know where she was, and if she was okay, but Mom and Daddy kept saying that she'd made her choice. To let her go. Somehow, that was easy for them, but she was my *sister*. She was my best friend.

I sit at Aunt Dee's desk, full-on crying, tears pouring down my face at the pace of the rain pouring out of the sky. I turn on the desk lamp, hurry to pull a piece of paper out of the second drawer, and find a pen lying beside Aunt Dee's laptop. Then I write a letter to my big sister after two years of no contact. And I tell her *everything*.

32

After I've folded the letter into thirds, I hear the doorbell ring at the front of the house. Then Aunt Dee slurs, "Nope! He thinks he can just show up to my house? I'll beat his fucking ass."

"Dee-Dee, stop! I called him over. Go back in the kitchen!"

I know she doesn't like my father, but I don't think I've ever seen her drunk enough to fight him.

"You better call me if he starts saying some bullshit."

"Watch your mouth," my mom grumbles. Then I hear the front door open and shut.

I turn off the desk lamp and walk back into the kitchen where Aunt Dee is pouring another glass of vodka Sprite.

"Will you mail my letter for me?" I ask, holding it up.

She closes her eyes and nods. "Of course. I'm sure Myracle will be happy to get it. She asks about you all the time."

I sit at the bar across from her. "Where is she? What is she doing now?"

"She's still living in Austin. She's almost done getting her degree in digital art. And you won't believe it!" Aunt Dee smiles. "She just got offered representation by an amazing illustration agency."

My eyes widen. "What does that mean?"

"It means she has an agent! It means she has access to all sorts of illustration gigs—like book covers, ads, all kinds of stuff."

"Wow, that's amazing." The only thing I heard was book covers. She's starting her half of our shared dream. I write the books and she illustrates the covers. That lights a fire in my soul. Why did I ever stop writing? *When* did I stop writing? I don't even have to think about it—I stopped everything after I started dating Dom. I stopped hanging out with friends, I stopped dreaming. He *was* my dream. I would have given up everything for him. I would have thrown away my dreams to become his wife. And he would have let me.

"I miss her so much," I say.

Aunt Dee grins a sad, sideways grin. "She misses you too."

Mom comes back inside after what feels like an hour. "Monique, ride home with your daddy. He's waiting in the car outside."

My stomach drops. Did he convince her to change her mind about all of this? Is he gonna throw away my new dilators, drive me to Granny's, and forbid me from ever seeing Reggie?

She sees the fear in my eyes, so she comes over and presses her lips to my forehead. It feels strange, her affection—distant, but not unfamiliar. We haven't always had walls between us. When I was younger, I was much closer to her. We'd go to gospel concerts together, just me and her, because Daddy used to work nights and Myracle absolutely did not want to go. And on those nights, we'd start off our day by getting our hair and nails done. Little eight-year-old me would sit in one of those big nail salon recliners, right next to my mom, and she'd let me pick out any color that I wanted, except red, because red was for grown women only. Then we'd get all dressed up and go see Mary Mary in concert, or Tye Tribbett.

That all stopped when I started to think gospel music was uncool and started noticing boys and wanted to wear makeup to impress them. She got stricter, and I got resentful.

I close my eyes and melt into her forehead kiss. "It's okay. He only wants to talk to you. He's not taking you to Granny's."

"Yeah, and if he tries to, I'll come get you myself," Aunt Dee says.

"Hush," Mom hisses at Aunt Dee. Then she looks down into my eyes. "Just talk to him. It's okay."

I nod, baby duckling to momma duck. After I hand my letter to Aunt Dee and she gives me a reassuring smile, I walk out of the kitchen and then out of the front door. It's still raining, but Daddy's car is running with the passenger door only a few feet from the steps. I stare at it, hesitant, but I can't see him through the rain or the dark tint on the windows.

Mom said it's okay. And I trust her. So I run down the steps through the pouring rain and jump inside my father's Cadillac. I'm wiping drops of rain out of my eyes and off my arms and down my legs, avoiding his eyes. But I can't avoid him forever. I know that. Especially since I can feel him staring at me. So I peek over at him, timid as a deer.

He looks just as timid, like he wants to pet me but he doesn't want me to run away. He reaches over, and I let him wipe rainwater off my cheek. "I hate how scared you look right now."

I peer down at the console between us, so as not to say the mean things swirling around in my head.

His hand slips off my cheek and plops down on his thigh. "Mo-Mo, I'm so sorry, sweetie."

My eyes focus on the dash. My ears focus on the soft gospel music playing under the pounding rain. But somehow his gentle voice cuts through all of that. No matter how much I don't want it to.

"I was so scared. I thought this was your fall from grace. I was scared about your morals and your soul and what I wanted you to be. I wanted you to be . . ."

I look at him resentfully. "Perfect?"

He shifts his eyes, thinking, like that's not quite the word he was looking for. "The thing is, what I want for you doesn't matter. Your mother told me that. She gave it to me straight. And that's why I love her so much, because she keeps me humble. She keeps me grounded. And so do you."

I wince, because here he goes, doing that thing he does—saying exactly the right thing.

"It's not my job to want for you. It's my job to keep you safe and make sure that you're taken care of, until even that's not my job anymore."

Like Myracle wrote, *At the end of the day, it's your life. You have to answer for your decisions—not them.*

"Baby, I'm ashamed that my first instinct wasn't to take you to the doctor, like your mother's was."

"No, your first instinct was to send me away, just like you tried to send away Myracle. Your first instinct was to believe everything Dom said, because it's easier for you to believe him. You have more to lose with Dom than you ever did with me or Myracle."

I almost slap my hand over my mouth, surprised that I tore into him like that. I guess I'm more upset with him than I realized. More than *he* realized, because he genuinely looks stunned.

He stammers, "I—baby, no . . ." He takes a breath and leans toward me. "You and Myracle are my world."

"Then why is it so easy for you to throw us away?"

"I was never trying to throw you away. I was trying to keep you safe, get you as far away from bad influences as possible and get you closer to God. But look at me, sweetie, please."

I shift my eyes stubbornly, but eventually end up on his face. He looks the same as I remember. The same old Daddy who I thought was my hero, who I thought could never hurt me, who

I thought knew better than Mom and would do anything to understand my feelings. Turns out there are limitations to his understanding.

"After you and your mom left, I invited Dom over."

Everything in my stomach turns solid. All the blood in my veins turns to gas at the mention of his name. Dom's betrayal hasn't quite settled over me because I'm still dealing with the aftermath. I haven't had time to process what he did to me, what with my home life seemingly being ripped apart.

"Your mother said she knew as soon as he started talking that he was lying. And I just couldn't understand how I was so blind. That woman sees so much that I don't." He shakes his head, blinking down to the console, then back up at me. "She said she knew that sex was the reason you two broke up the night you came back late. She knew it right away."

My eyebrows draw together. *Wait, she knew?* "How?" I ask.

"That's what I said," he says with a smile. "She said that *a mother knows.*" He shrugs, while I'm over here rethinking *everything* about that night. That maybe there *was* sympathy in her eyes. And when she said that Dom wasn't worth it, she meant he wasn't worth *my body*, not just my time.

"Anyway, it was a rude awakening for me, hearing that everything Dom told us was a lie. I trusted that boy *so much.* I would have let you two spend the night together in the same room without a care in the world, because I was *so sure* that he'd never lay a lustful hand on you. I would have sworn on my life that he was . . ."

"The perfect gentleman?" I ask.

He nods. "But as soon as I asked him if what he told us was true, he crumbled. I asked why he would do something like that, and his answer was—" Daddy shakes his head. "He wanted to keep you away from Reggie. He said that he'd put in two years of patience with you, and that it wouldn't be fair if Reggie had sex with you after a week. He said he deserved it more."

I wrinkle my nose and so does Daddy.

"I told him that *no one* deserves to have premarital sex with my daughter. That the only person who deserves to have sex with my daughter is the man she chooses to be her husband."

I roll my eyes at that.

"What?" He smiles. "Was that the wrong thing to say?"

"No one *deserves* to have sex with me. Sex isn't some prize at the end of an obstacle course, or a carrot you dangle in front of a horse."

He laughs. "That's not what I meant."

"But that's how y'all are treating it."

"Who is y'all?" he asks, scrunching his face.

"You and Dom. Men. I don't know."

"You don't include Reggie in that?"

I pause, my heart slowing. "No, Reggie is different," I say. "Reggie knew about my vaginismus from the start. He doesn't make me feel like there's anything wrong with me."

"And I do?" Daddy asks, genuinely trying to understand.

"You make me feel like I'll be less of a person if I have sex before marriage. Like I'm worth more *because* I'm a virgin."

He nods slowly, then he presses his back against his seat, facing the windshield and the rain pouring down the glass. "That's . . . wow. You know, your mother wasn't a virgin when we got married, and it didn't matter to me one bit. I didn't think that she was dirty or worthless, but she was so scared that I would. I think that might be one reason she's so angry with me—this is bringing up a lot of old emotions for her. Wow." He nods again, working it out in his head.

Then he looks at me, looks me directly in my eyes. "I am so sorry I ever made you feel that way. You are worth more than anything in my life, regardless of your virginity. Regardless of *everything*."

"Okay, so . . . does that mean you approve?"

"Of you having sex? Absolutely not, Monique! I can't tell you to wait until marriage, but I *can* tell you to wait until you're out of my house. You are definitely not *allowed* to have sex. Who do you think I am?"

I roll my eyes, smiling.

"But my love for you is unconditional, Mo-Mo."

I nibble my bottom lip, letting that fill me up. Trying to believe it with all my heart, but for some reason, I don't think I can. At least, not immediately. Words are one thing, but actions are more.

I ask him, "Is that true for Myracle too?"

His eyes soften. "Yes, of course it is. I miss My-My so much."

I shrug with a twisted mouth. "Then why don't you tell her that?"

After a minute of searching my eyes, searching for a way to answer me, he reaches over and pinches my cheek. "I love learning from you kids—it keeps me humble. Looks like I've still got a lot of growing to do. Huh, Mo-Mo?" He flips on his windshield wipers, puts on his seat belt, and starts to pull out of Aunt Dee's driveway. "I'm glad you were able to talk to me about this, Mo. I'm sorry I made it so difficult."

My heart swells as we leave Aunt Dee's posh neighborhood, heading back to our old country town. I never thought I'd hear those words from him—not about this. My parents know that I've tried having sex. They know I have vaginismus and they know I have dilators. I'm still alive, and I haven't been shipped off to Granny's. No, quite the opposite. I've got an appointment with a therapist this week and the intentions to finally have sex.

33

Dr. Wright, my new therapist, told me I need to feel safe
when I try using the dilators—but how can I? Both my parents
know I have the dilators, and it's doctor's orders for me to be
using them, but it still feels like I'll get in trouble if I get caught.
I've tried using them in the shower after checking the lock
twice, but it's still too scary. I can't make myself hurt myself.

During our last session, Dr. Wright said something really
interesting. She said, first of all, for me to stop calling it "my
vaginismus." To stop taking ownership of it. To stop talking
about it like it will be mine forever. Then she said to not think
of vaginismus as this big, bad disorder. To instead think of it as
a superpower. I gave her a crazy look when she said that, like
she might need a therapist of her own, because in what world is
vaginismus a superpower?

She said, "Hear me out. I'm not saying you should be happy

that you are experiencing vaginismus—absolutely not. But I want you to recognize how truly amazing your body is. Simply because it expects penetration to be harmful, it puts up every shield it can to keep you safe."

I liked the way she said *to keep you safe*. It made me feel warm inside. It is kind of like a superpower, a super shield that my body developed because it thought I was in danger.

Then she asked me if I had ever seen the Spider-Man movie. She said, "The one with Miles Morales: *Into the Spider-Verse?*"

And I was like, "Oh, yeah, I love that movie." Because I really, really do. Is it weird that I think Miles is a straight hottie?

She said, "Do you remember when Miles first discovered his powers? How he couldn't really control them? He had to learn how to make himself stop sticking and how to turn himself invisible on command."

I nodded, a knowing light blossoming in me.

"That's kind of like you, right? You have to learn how to make your vaginal canal stop contracting. And remember what Peter Parker told him to do when he was stuck to the ceiling? To just relax."

I nodded again, this time with a smile. Jesus, she was good.

"So, you, Monique, can think of me as your very own Peter Parker. I'm here to help you control your superpowers."

I laughed, I did. Because she's a super-cute lady, and I couldn't help how good that analogy made me feel. Don't get me wrong, vaginismus is annoying and extremely *unfortunate*, to say the least, but once you understand what your body is trying to do, how it's just trying to keep you safe, the idea of learning how to control it doesn't seem so impossible.

I haven't had my phone in about four days. For no good reason, really. I feel like my parents forgot they had it, and I've been too afraid to ask for it back. It feels like the floor is made of eggshells, and if I crack any of them, I'm falling straight into a pit of lava. So I've been careful. I've been quiet and obedient.

But once Daddy hands my phone back, a lot of that goes straight out the window. I run, feet pounding, directly to my room.

"You're welcome!" Daddy shouts after me.

"Yeah, thanks!" Then I loudly shut my bedroom door behind me. I have a few missed calls from Reggie and Sasha. And a whole bunch of texts from Reggie. One from Dom—I delete it without even reading, then back to Reggie.

Everything okay?

Mo, how's everything going at home?

Do I need to go find Dom and beat his ass?

Sasha just told me what happened . . . so I assume they took away your phone :(

God, I miss you.

I text back, **I've missed you too.**

He sees it instantly and texts back: **You're alive!**

Can we talk? I ask.

He answers my question by FaceTiming me. I fluff my hair about my shoulders and rub my glossy lips together, then I accept the call. He's lounging on his bed, *shirtless*, arm propped up behind his head, (inadvertently) flexing his bicep. At the sight of him, my whole body feels weightless, and I can't stop myself from smiling. "Hi," I squeak, excited.

"Hey," he says sleepily.

"Wait, were you sleeping?" I ask, eyes trained on his collarbone, then back up to his barely open eyes.

"Maybe a little."

"It's one in the afternoon!" I laugh.

"That's early."

"What time do you usually get up?"

He shifts his eyes, thinking, then pulls his gaze back to the camera. "Four, if I'm not interrupted."

"Oh my God," I say, laughing. "I could never."

"What time do you get up?" he asks with a lazy smile.

"Like, eight, every day."

"Jesus! What are you—a morning person?"

I shrug. "Maybe a little."

"Gross. I can't believe I'm dating a morning person."

I bite my lip at that sweet reminder that we are in fact dating. "I can't believe I'm dating someone who wakes up at four in the evening."

"Four is still the afternoon."

I make a face. "It's definitely not."

After a short, breathy laugh, his lips settle and his eyes study me on the screen of his phone. I watch his eyes and his lips, wishing he was right in front of me. "Hey, so, are you okay?" he asks, on a serious note.

I nod. "A lot has happened."

"I know—at least, from what Sasha's told me. Tell me everything. I want to know everything."

I sit on the edge of my bed, then pull my legs into my chest. "Okay, so . . ." I start from when I got home from his house that day, and tell him about all of Dom's lies, and about my mom. I have to keep my voice down, though. I don't want my parents to hear me talking about them. I finish the story with my therapy session. "I actually feel confident about using the dilators."

"That's so good, Mo." He smiles genuinely. "I'm sorry that Dom was able to do that to you, though. I guess I should have gone and beat his ass."

"No. At this point, I don't even care. I realized when I was talking to Dr. Wright how unhealthy my relationship with Dom was. How all I cared about was pleasing him and making him happy—I wasn't at all concerned about whether or not I was happy. And when we'd try to have sex, I basically hadn't asked my body for its consent. So it denied me access. I thought that was a really cool way of thinking about it."

"It is a really cool way to think about it," Reggie agrees. "So when you're using the dilators, you're having to ask your body for permission."

"Exactly." I smile. "The dilators are basically like training my body to trust me."

"Wow." He smiles too. "Your body is strong-willed."

"Right? It has a mind of its own, and I have to win it over."

After a moment of smiling at each other, he sits up and shakes his hand through his curly hair. "When can I see you?"

"I don't know. Hopefully soon."

"Ask your parents if you can come over," he begs. "My mom's going out tonight. We'll have the whole house to ourselves."

"I don't think they'd let me, knowing we'd be unsupervised.'

He groans. "Ask if I can come over, then."

And as if he heard us talking about him, Daddy knocks on my door. "Mo?"

"Yeah?" I call. "Hold on, Reggie," I whisper to the screen.

Then Daddy knocks again, like he didn't hear me.

"Yes? You may enter," I say louder.

The door cracks open. "You decent?" Daddy asks.

"Yes," I say, annoyed. That's been happening a lot. It's like he thinks now that I have dilators that I'm going to be using them all hours of the day. He doesn't understand that I don't want to be caught using them as much as he doesn't want to catch me.

He peeks his head around the door with cautious eyes. I stare at him, straight-faced and annoyed. "Your mother and I are going out tonight."

"Oh?" I nod. "Okay."

"We're going to dinner and a movie, then we'll probably walk around the pavilion or go to Aunt Dee's house. We will be back no sooner than eleven." Then he repeats himself. "No sooner than eleven."

"No sooner than eleven." I nod.

He says it again, dropping his chin. "No sooner than eleven. So . . ."

Okay, I get it. I have a guaranteed five hours alone in the house—I better use them *and the dilators* wisely.

"Great. Thanks for letting me know." I shift my eyes awkwardly.

Then he backs out of my room. "Keep the doors locked. And don't go *anywhere*, unless it's an emergency. I've checked your odometer, so I'll know if you move your car."

I roll my eyes. "I'm not leaving."

"There's pizza in the freezer."

"'Kay. Thanks, Dad."

He shuts my door. I wait for him to walk away before I drop my eyes back down to the screen. Reggie's staring at me. "My parents will be gone until eleven tonight. If you can find a ride, you should come over."

He scrambles out of bed. "I'm on my way."

34

When I open the door, his smile is big and goofy and infec-tious.

"How did you get here?" I say, mirroring his smile.

"My mom's car."

I open the door wider, letting him inside, then peek around his shoulder at her car in my driveway. "I thought she was going out tonight."

"Her friends came to pick her up." He spins around in the walkway and looks me over. Then he rushes back to me, closes the door, and pulls me into his chest. Do you know what it feels like to be hugged by a boy you really like? It's like everything about him is interesting, like the way he dips down so that my chin can rest on his shoulder, and how solid he feels—like I can't believe he's real—and how his hair smells like As I Am hair conditioner.

He pulls away, leaving me with nothing to keep my feet on the ground. Then he's just staring. I blink down to my bare feet, cheeks hot. "Um." I smile, biting my bottom lip. "I don't really have food to offer. All I have is a frozen pizza. . . . It's in the oven right now."

"That's fine." He furrows his brow, continuing to study me. "I didn't really come here to eat your food."

The heat in my cheeks spreads down to my neck and my chest. I don't know why I'm being so awkward right now. I know why he came here. I know why I *wanted* him to come here. Because I missed him . . . and his lips. But I don't want to be too forward. I don't really know how to be, so I step past and lead him into the living room. "We can watch a movie," I offer. "But my parents have a child lock on our Netflix, so I can't really watch anything that's not G or PG."

I peek over my shoulder as I head to the couch. He's watching my body, not my face. Then he says, "Again—I'm not really here to watch a movie."

I plop down on the couch, mostly because his admissions are leaving me weak in the knees. He stalks closer. "Why are you here?" I ask too quietly, because I'm scared of his answer.

"For you," he says, sitting next to me on the couch. "I just want to be near you. We can do whatever you want to do, as long as I can be close to you."

I swallow hard. What if all I want to do is make out?

I don't say that, though. And I don't lean in. Frightened of the intensity in this moment, I reach over and grab the remote off the coffee table. "I think there's a new animated movie out. Does that sound good?" I ask, switching apps on the smart TV.

"Yeah. Love 'em."

"Cool. This one is about aliens, I think," I say nervously.

Then I start the movie, throw the remote down, and lean back against the sofa. Reggie scoots closer to me, where our legs are touching, then he rests his arm behind my head. I'm hyperaware of how open his chest looks and how inviting his lap looks and how every five seconds, his knee presses tighter against mine. I scoot closer, into the crook of his arm and chest, and my hand lands on his blue-jeaned thigh.

Five minutes into the movie, I have no idea what's going on. Let's be honest, the real movie is us on the couch. At least, that's where my attention is. His arm slips off the back of the couch and around my shoulders. Then he pulls me closer into his chest, and his hand slips down my arm to my waist. I'm melting into him, like a chocolate kiss in the sun. I'm slowly turning, and he's slowly turning, until our eyes meet.

I study the freckles on his nose and trail down to his lips. His eyes follow the same trail down to my lips as his hand on my waist slips down to my hip, and his other hand tips my chin up. Then we're kissing. Gentle at first, getting reoriented with each other's taste and each other's heat and each other's pace. He lets me take the lead again, and I always have preferred long, slow, gentle kisses to overbearing, tongue-heavy kisses. But the more he lets me take my time, the less inhibited I feel; the less I'm thinking about whether I'm doing the right thing.

It feels natural—we're giving and receiving and not over-thinking it.

My fingers inch over his T-shirt, past his collarbone, around the back of his neck, until I'm holding on to him and pulling myself up. Until I'm straddling his lap. And he's moaning, the low rumble of his voice melting on my tongue. And I'm moving my hips in a way that I probably shouldn't, because for a normal couple, after a few more minutes of this, we would start to take off clothes, he'd pull a condom out of thin air, and we'd have sex.

If this were Dom, we'd try again, despite the odds. He'd say, "Maybe it'll work this time," because a large part of him thought the problem was how turned on I was. We would fail again. He'd get disappointed. We'd end up at IHOP. And the night would be ruined.

I can't let that happen again. Not with Reggie. Especially not since I know what's happening to my body. I haven't earned her trust yet, and neither has Reggie. I say against his mouth, "I have to tell you that tonight won't end in sex."

He pushes his lips against mine. I think he'll say, *I know it won't* or *Are you sure we can't try?* But he just says, "Okay."

"It may never end in sex, Reggie." I pull away, searching his eyes.

"Okay," he says again.

"Are you sure you're okay with that?"

"I could do this forever. Just this." He leans in gently, kissing me. "Besides, we can be forever virgins together."

He tries leaning in again, but I pull back. "Wait. You're a virgin?"

He raises his eyebrows at me. "Yeah. Is that okay?"

"Of course. I'm just . . . surprised."

He laughs. "Why?"

"Because you're, like . . ."

"I'm like what?" He smiles, running his hands up my back, making me arch my spine from how good it feels.

"Good at this," I say, breathless.

He laughs again. "Thanks. I'm just going with your flow, though." His hands slide back down and squeeze my back pockets.

"You're really good at this." I fall back on his mouth, even more confident than before, because despite the fact that I haven't had sex, I might have more experience than him, which is wild. Me? More experienced?

And I like knowing that he's a virgin. I feel a lot less pressure to hurry through the dilators, and less like I'm keeping him from something he's used to getting from his girlfriends. When we have sex, it'll be the first time for both of us.

We make out while the movie plays behind us. We make out until our lips are swollen and sore. My hands are tangled in his hair. His hands are under my shirt, fingertips pressing into my back.

When suddenly the smoke detector blasts us apart. My heart jumps out of my chest, and I scramble out of Reggie's lap. "Ohmygod, the pizza!" I run into the hazy kitchen, Reggie right behind me. Then I open the oven and a gust of smoke hits me in the face.

"Holy shit!" Reggie says, trying to reach the blaring smoke detector to turn it off. He finally does as I'm pulling the pizza pan out of the oven with an oven mitt. After I drop it on the stovetop, close the oven door, and turn off the heat, I look at Reggie through the smoke. And he looks back at me with his hand covering his mouth.

The pizza is black. Entirely black, and I don't even have to touch it to know that it's hard as a rock. I stare at Reggie in panicky silence. First of all, now I have no dinner. Second of all, the whole house is full of smoke and it stinks really bad.

When I look back at the black Sheetrock on my stovetop, I can't help it; I bust out laughing. Reggie does too, practically at the same time. I have never seen a more burnt pizza. And I can't believe we were so caught up in making out that we hadn't realized that dinner was burning. How will I explain this to my parents?

We laugh and laugh and laugh at how ridiculous it is. Until the fire alarm starts blaring again. Reggie jumps up and turns it off.

"Okay, we gotta do something about this smoke. Can you open the patio door?" I ask. With the door open, the smoke starts to dissipate, but the smell isn't going anywhere. "What should I do with this?" I say, smiling at the pizza. I don't even know if you can call it a pizza anymore.

"What do you mean? You're not gonna eat it?"

I look at him like he's insane.

"Burnt pizza is the best pizza."

"Okay." I put my hands on my hips. "You eat it."

"You want me to . . . ?" He scratches his neck. "I don't want to eat your dinner or anything."

"No, it's fine. I'm offering." I smile. "Go ahead."

"All right. No problem." He shrugs, goes over to it, literally breaks off a piece with an audible crunch, and throws it in his mouth. And it legit sounds like he's eating a chip or a cracker. His face scrunches up and he sticks out his tongue in anguish. "Ahhhh!" he screeches, showing me the black crumbles on his tongue.

"Ewww!" I laugh as he spits it out in the sink.

We throw the "pizza" away, then take the trash out, hoping it'll help the smell—it doesn't. We bleach the floor and the counters, hoping the chemicals will mask the smell—they don't. Now it just smells like bleach and burnt pizza, which is somehow worse.

"Okay, um . . ." I put my hands atop my head and look around. "I don't think this can be helped." I close the patio door and say goodbye to my freedom.

"Just say you got distracted."

"I *did* get distracted." I smile slyly, and he smiles back.

"They don't have to know by what."

"I'm definitely not going to tell them."

It's getting late. My parents will be home in half an hour, so I walk him to the front door. "This has been fun," he says.

"This has been a disaster."

"A fun disaster, though." He turns around and faces me, grabs both of my hands, and pulls me closer.

I stand on the tips of my toes and kiss him goodbye, deep and slow, but when I pull away, I make a face. "Your mouth tastes—"

"Bad," he says.

"Awful, yeah." I cringe at the burnt-pizza taste on my tongue.

"Well, I'm sorry. That's your fault—you dared me."

"Excuse me? You're the one who said burnt pizza is the best pizza."

He laughs, throwing his head back, but then he reaches for me again. "Okay, okay, I gotta go." He tries kissing me again.

"No. Not until you get that figured out," I say, motioning to his mouth.

"Really? Are you serious?" He looks so hurt, then he spins around. "Stingy," he gripes, opening the front door.

"Wait, wait, I'm just kidding." I pull him back to me and kiss his lips gently. Burnt-pizza taste or not, I'd still kiss him all night if I could.

When we pull away, he looks woozy. "Good night, Mo."

"Good night, Reggie."

I watch him through the peephole as he reverses out of my driveway. Then when he's gone, I fall face-first on the couch, swooning hard. Tonight was a disaster. A perfect, *perfect* disaster.

35

Daddy isn't happy about me dating Reggie. Mom is . . . *more* *supportive*? She's very vocal about the fact that she hopes he is only a phase but is otherwise not opposed to us. Aunt Dee *loves* Reggie. She thinks he's so funny. But I think she just likes how unafraid he is to challenge literally everything my daddy says.

One evening at dinner, Reggie dug into his mashed potatoes the second they hit his plate. And my daddy looked at him, horrified. "In this house, we don't eat until after we say grace."

Reggie looked up, mouth full. "Oh, I wasn't . . ." He swallowed. "I was just testing it to make sure it's not poisoned. I haven't died yet, so I think we're safe." Then he bit off a piece of his pork chop and hummed at how good it was. "Yeah. I would be willing to make this sacrifice from here on out, if you'd like."

"That's okay," Daddy said, deadpan. "I'm pretty confident that my wife isn't trying to poison *everyone at this table*."

Reggie shrugged. "You can never be too sure." Then he nodded and looked at Mom. "Right, Mrs. Tinsley?"

She just stared at him with her mouth ajar, speechless.

Aunt Dee coughed out a quick, short laugh, like it caught her by surprise as much as it caught *us* by surprise. She said, "Who is this kid?" That's what she says every time he makes her laugh. *Who is this kid?*

And each time Reggie answers earnestly, "I'm Reggie. We literally met two weeks ago. I've told you my name at least a dozen times." And she keels over laughing.

As much as Aunt Dee loves Reggie, Reggie's mom, Jackie, loves Aunt Dee. I think they're closer to the same age than Jackie is to my mom. But, either way, I think Jackie's warming up to my mom too.

She's here in my kitchen right now, along with Sasha's mom, *not* using their inside voices. Mrs. Howser dared to bring alcohol into my mother's house, and before Mom could chastise her, Jackie pulled out a bottle of her own. It was decided, at that point, that there was no other choice but to drink it. Daddy's outside with Uncle Raven and Pops, getting more ideas for the backyard—now that he and Reggie are finished with the deck—while Reggie and Sasha and I are sitting in the grass under the big elm tree near the fence.

I'm leaning my back against the trunk, sitting between the two of them, bathing in the sun. "I can't believe my mom is drinking with y'all's moms right now."

"I can't believe my mom thinks *your* mom is actually cool," Reggie says.

"I can't believe that strawberries aren't actually a berry," Sasha says.

Reggie and I both look at her. She's staring down at her phone screen, smiling as she types a message. Then she laughs a second later.

"Who are you texting?" Reggie asks.

Then she finally looks up with a stank face, like it's none of our business. "Brandy," we both say at the same time, already knowing the answer.

She laughs again, typing another message.

"So when will we get to officially meet her?" I ask.

"God, you sound like my mom," she says. "Brandy's not exactly out yet, and she's not comfortable meeting the whole family. We're taking it slow. And could you guys not tell anyone about her? I don't want people finding out."

"We don't even know her," Reggie says. "Who are we gonna tell? Each other?" Then he turns to me. "Hey, Mo, did you know that Sasha is seeing a girl named Brandy?"

I say, playing along, "Brandy? Who's that? I've never heard of a Brandy."

"Y'all are so annoying." Then she stands up and walks back inside the house, eyes glued to her phone.

As soon as the door slides shut, Reggie rests his head back against the tree, then gently grabs my hand out of my lap. His touch turns my stomach into a hot-air balloon, floating up and up and up. I look over at the sun shining in his eyes, the tree branches above us casting shadows across his face.

"You're so beautiful," he says, and a spark flashes through me. "I just wish I could draw you, but nothing I do can truly capture . . . you."

I smile, reaching for his curly hair. "My sister used to say the same thing. Well, not the *you're so beautiful* part." He laughs. "But that I'm hard to draw. I think that means I'm not photogenic."

"You're very photogenic," he says, running a hand through the back of my hair. "It's just that photos will never do you justice."

Things with Reggie have been good. I mean, as good as they can be, considering that all our "dates" have been highly supervised. And the only time we get to kiss is in my car when I'm dropping him off at home, or sneaky kisses after church, when my parents are mingling with the congregation.

But the best part about Reggie has been his lack of check-ins. I mean, he asks how my therapy sessions are going, and I've told him all about Dr. Wright and Dr. Marion, but as far as the dilators, he lets me bring it up first. There's no pressure and no rush. He's just happy that I'm happy. Like, the first night I was able to comfortably get the first dilator in, I called him crying out of excitement. And he said, "Oh, sunflower, I'm so happy for you!" Because sometimes he calls me "sunflower" for no reason at all.

"You're sweet, moon pie." I've started calling him "moon pie" just because.

He clutches the back of my head, peering down at my glossy lips, and starts leaning in. But like the pesky mosquitoes they are, my father, Uncle Raven, and Pops swarm us. Daddy claps a hand on Reggie's shoulder. "Reggie, my boy, come hang out with us men."

Reggie lets go of my hair, looking up at the three men with their hands on their hips, then he turns back to me. "But—"

"Come on. It'll be fun," Daddy says, practically ripping him up by the arm.

"Daddy!" I complain, watching them drag my boyfriend away.

"Go hang out with the women, Mo-Mo."

I mean, what is this? Lunchtime in elementary school, back when girls couldn't sit with boys? Did I somehow become five years old again?

They herd Reggie to the far edge of the yard, and I begrudgingly get up and join the moms in the kitchen. I walk into a wall of sound, shrill laughter and screeches. Sasha's sitting at the kitchen table, taking in the scene with a big smile on her face. She waves me over, and I sit beside her, trying to catch up on the conversation. Mom has a glass of brown liquor in her hand, so does Reggie's mom, and so does Sasha's. They're all talking at once, talking over each other.

"No, okay, Lawrence is cute. I'll give you that," Jackie says.

"But if Daniel so much as looked at me, my panties would fly right off."

"Jackie!" My mom screams and laughs.

"That man could plant so many seeds in me," Jackie says.

My eyes widen. Are they really talking about this in front of me and Sasha?

"How long has this been happening?" I hiss at Sasha.

"I don't know. I walked in on it, and nobody told me to leave." We giggle to each other, watching the women talk openly.

"Listen," Mrs. Howser says, setting her glass down on the counter. "There is never an excuse for infidelity. I don't care how fine a man is. Right, Sasha?"

"Right, Mommy," Sasha says.

"I agree with you there," my mom says, taking a sip of her liquor. "There's never an excuse for infidelity, no matter how delicious a man is."

The women laugh.

I raise my eyebrows at Sasha, silently squealing at my mom's use of the word delicious to describe a man. Sasha giggles with me, but then we hear footsteps at the edge of the kitchen. "Why do we always end up arguing about this?" Aunt Dee says, appearing out of nowhere. "I'm not saying Issa handled it the right way. She should have dumped Lawrence the second Daniel kissed her. But there's no competition here. Daniel is the one."

The conversation stops suddenly, though. Not because Aunt

Dee seemingly walked into our house without knocking—that's normal. No—conversation stops because she doesn't walk in alone. I gasp, and so does Sasha, as my big sister enters the room. I have to be dreaming. Tell me I'm dreaming. There's no way Myracle is actually here. I sit staring at her, speechless.

She looks so different than I remember. She looks so different from our old pictures. Her hair is in a big Afro, all fluffed up around her head. She's wearing thick-rimmed glasses and red lipstick. She never used to wear lipstick. And she's so thin. So much thinner than she used to be.

"My-My!" Mom sings, setting down her glass on the counter and running to her with her arms open wide. "My little girl!"

"Hey, Mom," Myracle says with a sheepish laugh. Even her voice sounds different.

I stand up, eyes wide and full of something. I'm not even sure what I'm full of. But I feel like I'm going to explode.

Mom wraps her hands around the back of my sister's head and presses her lips against Myracle's forehead. Myracle closes her eyes, melting into Mom's arms. I haven't seen the two of them so affectionate—not since both of us were kids. My eyes water.

Aunt Dee picks out my sister's Afro with her fingers. "See how long her hair has gotten? And it's so healthy." Then Mom's picking through her hair too and fawning over how beautiful she is.

"Hey, Myracle." Mrs. Howser smiles, lifting her glass.

Sasha greets her too. And Jackie whispers to Mrs. Howser,

asking who Myracle is. As Mrs. Howser explains, I feel like I'm waiting in line—waiting for my turn to hug my sister.

"Do you want a drink?" Aunt Dee asks her, walking over to the counter.

"Oh." Myracle looks uncertain. "I'm not twenty-one yet. My birthday is in a few months."

Aunt Dee blinks at her, silent and still. "Okay. Not what I asked. I asked if you wanted a drink . . . ?"

Jackie laughs, pouring two glasses of brown liquor. She hands one to Aunt Dee.

Mom is still holding Myracle's cheeks hostage. She says, "Go ahead. Fix her a drink." Myracle's eyes widen. "Everything okay with the roommate?" Mom asks.

Myracle nods. "We're like best friends now."

"Good. I thought you would be." Mom pulls Myracle to her chest again. Then they're rocking and murmuring soft words. Some "I'm sorrys" and "I missed yous" and "I love yous."

I'm bouncing on my toes behind Mom. Waiting. Just waiting. I have so many questions, but not nearly enough time to get all the answers. And so many stories to tell her. I don't think there's enough time in the world to possibly catch up on everything we've missed.

And behind me, Jackie continues the conversation, like she's not in the midst of a major life-changing moment. "But here's the question, if the actor that plays Daniel—what's his name?"

"Y'lan Noel," Aunt Dee sings. "His name just rolls off my

tongue. I wonder what else could—"

"Dinah!" Mom shouts, finally releasing my sister. Jackie and Aunt Dee laugh.

And there's finally room for me to greet my big sister. Her eyes fall on me, and they're just as wet as mine. "Hey, pumpkin head," she says.

I smile uncontrollably. "Hey, big head." Then I cling to her middle and press my face tight against her arm. It's a binding kind of a hug. A *just for me* kind of hug. "How are you here right now?"

"Aunt Dee brought me down."

"Yeah, but—" I pull away and look up into her eyes. My question is deeper, because surely that hasn't been the issue for two years. What changed? Why is she here *now*?

She catches the meaning in my eyes. She smiles gently. "You did something to them, Mo." She raises her eyebrows at me. "They apologized first."

I did something? The corners of my lips lift. All I did was fight for my freedom. All I did was try to heal myself from the wounds of my childhood. Mom and Daddy just kind of got in the way of that. I say, "I didn't do anything that you didn't do first."

She smiles at me, but then Aunt Dee comes over and hands her a glass of liquor, inviting her to be one of the adults—officially inviting her into grown folks' business.

"I'm sorry, if that man invites me anywhere, I'm going. I'm

gonna have to tell my baby that we need to take a quick break."

Jackie squeals, as does Aunt Dee. They clasp hands and laugh hysterically while Mrs. Howser and my mom shake their heads. Mom says, "You ought to be ashamed of yourself, Dinah. You've got yourself a good husband out there."

"Oh, calm down, Bianca. I'm just kidding. I love me some Raven McDowell."

"Well, I'm gonna need you to tell me where I can find my own Raven McDowell," Jackie says.

Aunt Dee's eyes light up. "Girl, I got you. Ray's got some fine-ass, boss-ass friends. I will introduce you tomorrow."

"I'm gonna hold you to that," Jackie says.

"I got you, babe."

I'm not sure, but I think I'm watching two women become best friends. It makes me smile so wide, witnessing the chemistry. Myracle watches too, sipping her liquor, and I can't stop glancing over at her, just to make sure she's really here. All the women in the room are going about their business, like none of this is abnormal. And you know what? I really like that. It's like we're not giving ourselves any time to let this be awkward and tense. Myracle is just finding her place in the scene, as if she never left it.

Myracle says, "Are we just gonna *not* talk about that other boy."

"What other boy?" Jackie asks.

"You know—that light-skinned boy who ends up ghosting all of a sudden."

"Oooh," Aunt Dee says. "Nathan. Yeah, that man is fine too, but I'm not feeling the chemistry from him."

"Yeah, me either," Jackie says.

I sit beside Sasha again. Myracle sits across from us. And as the women describe in detail the chemistry between Issa and each of the three men, Myracle hisses at Sasha and me, "Hey! Who's that woman?" She nudges her head over to Jackie.

I grin. "That's Reggie's mom."

She lowers her chin. "*The* Reggie? As in the boyfriend?"

"Yes," Sasha says with a roll of her eyes. "They're so annoyingly cute, oh my God."

"Good," Myracle says, letting out her breath. "I never understood why you were so obsessed with that other eggheaded boy."

I roll my eyes. *That's right.* Myracle was the first to start calling Dom an egghead. Then Aunt Dee picked it up, and now it's like they don't even know his name.

"Speaking of that eggheaded boy," she says, and then her eyes turn into slits. "Has anyone pummeled his face in yet?"

I raise my brows, not sure how to answer that. If I say no, is she gonna make it her business to take care of that?

Sasha answers for me, "No, but there's a line forming. You'll have to get to the back."

Myracle laughs. "Cool, cool, cool. As long as it gets done."

Aunt Dee pulls Jackie aside and starts describing this "boss-ass" friend of Uncle Raven's. Mom and Mrs. Howser start shouting over each other again, moving on to an older generation of "eye candy." Myracle downs her drink and starts throwing out names of random Black men. "Michael Ealy! Idris Elba! Morris Chestnut!" Sasha and I are dying laughing. The whole kitchen is chaotic. I barely know which thread to follow, when suddenly, the doorbell rings.

Mom has her head in the oven, checking on her homemade mac and cheese. She says, "Dee-Dee, can you get that?"

Aunt Dee goes, glass in hand, to answer the door, mumbling to herself, "Who the hell is that? Ain't everybody already here?"

"Now I'm just wondering how we've gone this long without mentioning Blair Underwood," Jackie says.

"Because that man only ever plays evil characters," Mom says, pulling the casserole dish out and turning off the oven. "He's got an evil spirit. I can feel it."

"Speaking of evil spirits," Aunt Dee says, ushering in the guest, "look who's here."

All of our eyes fall on Dom.

Poor boy doesn't know what he walked into.

All is silent for a solid five seconds, while we stare at him and the foil-wrapped tin in his hands, smelling distinctly of his dad's barbecue. He speaks first. "I just came to drop this off. I'm not staying."

"Great. I'll take that," Aunt Dee says, grabbing the tin and walking it over to the stove.

No one else speaks until Sasha says, "Okay. You can leave now. *Bye.*"

"Sasha, be nice," Mrs. Howser says, not taking her stony eyes off Dom.

"I'm sorry, Mommy, you're right." She stares Dom down too. "You *may* leave now. Good day, sir."

"That's better," Mrs. Howser says.

"Now, who is this boy again?" Jackie asks Aunt Dee.

"Oh, that egghead? That's Joe's son."

"Wait, the boy who lied on Monique and *my* son?" Jackie asks, propping her fist under her chin.

"Yeah, the one who gave Mo an ultimatum to have sex with him," Sasha says.

"Probably worsened her condition with all the times he pressured her into having sex," Mrs. Howser says.

"The eggheaded boy whose ass needs to be beat," Myracle says, popping her knuckles. "Remember all those times at daycare, Dumb-Dumb?"

My sister used to be a bully at daycare. She'd pound any kid who got in her way, including Dom.

My mom narrows her eyes at him. "The boy who hurt my daughter physically, mentally, and emotionally, tried to ruin her reputation and destroy her current, *much healthier* relationship with Reggie, manipulated my husband and took advantage of everything we've done for him." She nods, stewing. "Yeah, that's Dom, all right."

"Oh, okay," Jackie says. "That's what I thought."

He looks like he's about to cry. He avoids their eyes, staring down at his shoes, and I feel a little embarrassed for him. But

I mostly feel proud—proud to be surrounded by women who have my back.

Then Dom's eyes meet mine, and my stomach clenches. A swirl of emotions wipes out all sound. I'm angry. I'm sad. I'm distraught. I'm *furious*. He says, "Can I talk to you? Alone?"

Six out of seven of us say, "No," at the very same time.

And then I open my mouth and say, "No," too. I honestly don't want to have a conversation with him. I've been done with him for a long time. I've moved on from the way he used to make me feel—so damaged. And I've moved on from my love for him. I still care. It's hard not to care when I know where he came from. I mean, I was there when his mom died. But I'm done feeling guilty or responsible for his emotions. I shrug. "If you have something to say, go ahead."

Seven out of seven of us cross our arms over our chests.

He takes a noticeable step back. "I just wanted to say that I'm sorry."

"Hell, yeah, you are," Aunt Dee says.

"I never should have lied like that. I was just jealous."

"You were possessive is what you were," my mom says.

"If you can't have her, no one else can, right?" Mrs. Howser says.

Sasha adds, "If she can't have sex with you, then she can't have sex with anyone, right?"

"No, I just—" He clenches his teeth, then begs me with his eyes. "I really want to talk to you alone."

"I'm sorry, but I don't have anything to say to you." I shrug again, dismissively.

"But I have a lot to say."

Myracle rolls her eyes. "Nobody gives a damn about what you have to say. If my sister is done with you, then so are we. You may leave."

Then the patio door opens and in walks my father, Dom's father, Uncle Raven, and Reggie. The four of them take in the scene, and it's a brutal one.

"Dom," Daddy says with a horrified expression. "You were supposed to come around back."

Pops shakes his head and starts to walk his son out.

"You *need* to keep your son in his cage, Joe," Aunt Dee shouts after him.

Reggie comes over to me with a confused expression. "Are you okay? Did that get ugly?"

"Yeah," I say, "for *him*."

Then Sasha laughs. "I think we made him cry. I think he was crying when he turned away."

"No, he definitely was," Reggie says.

I laugh. "He wasn't. But he was about to."

"I don't know what y'all said to him, but whatever it was, I'm sure he deserved it."

I look at Sasha. Then I look at her mom, Aunt Dee, Jackie, my sister, and my mom. And I think of how these women offered me asylum, each in their own way. I'm so lucky to have them in my life. They all start trash-talking Dom when my father notices his oldest daughter sitting at the kitchen table. He rushes over, pulls her out of her chair and into his arms. He swings her around like she doesn't weigh anything. "My-My," he sings. "My little miracle child."

"Daddy, I can't breathe," she says, her voice muffled by his shirt.

When Myracle was born, Mom and Daddy planned to name her Mariah, but on her way out, her neck got tangled in the umbilical cord. She didn't come out screaming or crying or even sleeping. She came out dead. Not breathing. She came out blue. But my daddy prayed. He cried and he prayed, while the doctors pumped air into her lungs. And like a miracle, she came back to life. And she's been giving our parents hell ever since.

Everyone crowds around the dining room table, pulling in chairs from the kitchen. Daddy blesses the food. He thanks God for his family and for bringing Myracle home to him. He says, "My God, I hadn't realized how much I needed to see her face until I saw her. I'm sorry it took us so long to reach out."

I never close my eyes during prayer. It's not an act of rebellion. I just like how it looks when everyone fades into their own head, squeezing the hand of the person next to them. It's an intimacy between family members that you can't really get at any other time—at least, not with my family.

"I'm so sorry I ever doubted her, and that I tried to make it my job to teach her a lesson."

Daddy's eyes are squeezed closed, but his face is pointed up to the ceiling. And with every phrase he shakes Mom's hand on his left and Myracle's on his right. Mom is nodding along, rubbing her lips together to keep from crying.

"Father, you've taught me some tough lessons this summer. You've taught me how to be a better father, how to be a better husband, and how to be a better follower of you, Lord. You taught me that my only job is to love my daughters, and to keep them safe. And I love them both so much, just the way they are."

The rest of the table has their heads bowed and their eyes closed gently. I peek over to my right, and Reggie smiles back at me. I think he understands how monumental this moment is. And how good and filling it is to hear my daddy say he loves me just the way I am, despite everything I've done this summer—everything I was so afraid to tell him. I think Reggie must understand how I feel, knowing that I don't have to hide anymore and that I don't have to be afraid anymore, because he squeezes my hand and leans his head down and presses his forehead against mine.

"I'm so proud of them. And so grateful to have them both here. I'm so sorry to you both. I'm so sorry," he whispers over and over again, each one softer than the last, but each one heavier too.

Myracle's eyes are open too. She's biting down on a sob, her eyes shimmery with tears.

"Amen," Daddy says, opening his eyes. But when he looks at Myracle's face, he stands, and I finally hear her sniffle. He pulls her up into another one of his tight, breathtaking hugs. He murmurs to her, while the rest of us watch with wet eyes. "I've missed you so much, my little girl. You look so, so beautiful and . . . happy."

"I missed you too," she says, her voice muffled against his shirt.

Something's got me blurry-eyed. I'm guessing it's the same thing that's got *everyone* blurry-eyed—this beautiful, beautiful moment.

While we eat and while everyone carries on separate, *loud* conversations, Myracle looks past me to Reggie. "Hey, you! Reggie, is it?"

He looks at her, cheeks filled with mac and cheese. He nods, chewing.

"Listen, I'm not gonna be here for long, so I'm leaving Dom in your hands. Do you have what it takes to beat his ass?"

"Myracle, watch your mouth," Mom hisses, like she would Aunt Dee.

Reggie doesn't hesitate. "I got him. Don't worry."

"No," I say. "No fighting."

Myracle rolls her eyes, then looks past me at Reggie, giving him eyebrow signals. Then they're nodding at each other. "Hey, pumpkin head," she says, distracting me from their eyebrow conversation. "I read your letter," she whispers ominously. "There's so much I have to tell you."

In my letter, I told her about Reggie and Sasha and vaginismus and Dom, but a large part of it was about how sorry I am for what I said to her that night.

She glances around the table, then she leans in and whispers, "Mom acts like a hard-ass, but she's actually much softer than Daddy."

I furrow my brow. "How do you know?" I mean, she's not wrong.

"After I sent you that postcard, she wrote me a letter back. She said Daddy was waiting for me to apologize first, that he was trying to teach me a lesson, but Mom couldn't stand not knowing if I was okay. She also sent me a check for rent. She's been sending me checks every month to help with rent."

"Seriously?" I ask.

Myracle closes her eyes and nods. And when she opens her eyes again, they glisten. "Momma is my hero," she whispers.

My lips twitch. She just called Mom *Momma*. I haven't heard her call Mom that in years, and I realize I'd done the same thing when I was scared. When I didn't know what was happening with my family or with my body. I called her Momma when I needed her and when she was the only person I trusted . . . just like when I was little. I smile and lean into Myracle's ear. "Momma's my hero too."

Then we turn back to our food, and both glance across the table. She's watching us with narrowed, suspicious eyes. "What are you girls whispering about over there?"

"Nothing," we say at the same time.

Girls. I miss being part of *girls* with Myracle.

Then Dad and Aunt Dee start hounding Myracle with questions. How's school going? How's work going? How's life going? Mom is mostly silent, until she opens her mouth and asks, "So, Myracle, any new boyfriend we should know about . . . or girlfriend?"

Girlfriend? I scrunch my face, but Myracle looks like she just saw a ghost. "Yeah, actually . . . her name is Pixie."

Her? Myracle likes girls? How did Mom know that? How am I just finding this out?

I think Myracle is just as confused, because she stammers, "How—how did you know?"

"I know my daughters," Mom says nonchalantly. "Ask your sister."

Myracle looks at me, still stunned. I shrug. "I don't know. She's magic or something."

"Not magic. Creepy," Aunt Dee says. "She used to do the same to me. The night I lost my virginity, she just *knew*. I still don't know how she does it."

Myracle looks at me, then turns back to our parents and laughs. I think it's a laugh of relief, because she kind of haphazardly came out, and the world didn't end. Our pastor father didn't jump up in a rage. On the contrary, he asks, "So when can we meet this Pixie?"

"She's a fun girl. You're gonna love her," Aunt Dee says.

I snarl at her. "You've already *met* her! That's not fair!"

Myracle animatedly tells us about her girlfriend. She goes

to UT. She's a business major. She's artsy and beautiful and the sweetest person Myracle has ever met. I think they're in love, but she doesn't say all that. I can just tell by the shimmer in Myracle's eyes. I wonder if Mom sees that too, with her magic vision.

Our voices rise high and wide, until we finish eating, and then we all naturally drift back into the kitchen. While everyone listens to Aunt Dee talk about her days in college, I grab Myracle's hand and pull her down our hallway—the one that leads to my room and her old room and the bathroom we used to share.

When we walk inside her old room, she stops to stare at everything—everything that's changed since she left. Her footsteps pad the carpet slowly as she runs her hand over the top of her dresser and her old desk, tracing the carvings she made. Then she looks at me regretfully. "I was so fucked up back then."

"You were still trying to figure out what you wanted in life."

"I didn't know who I was." She twists her mouth, looking at the stained carpet. "There's so much pain in here. I'm so glad I left."

As much as it hurt me, I'm glad she left too. I've missed her so much, but I'm glad she was able to figure out who she is and what she wants. "I get why you left," I say. "You couldn't grow in here."

She nods, staring at the walls where she used to hang her drawings.

"But I'm really glad you're back."

She smiles. "Me too. I always thought I'd only ever come back to spit on their graves, or to show off how successful of an artist I am, but . . ." She shrugs. "I stopped being angry once I was too happy to be angry. I've never been good at holding grudges. Neither has Mom. But you and Daddy—y'all are something else."

I laugh. "I don't know what you're talking about."

"Yeah, whatever." She laughs, but then her smile fades, and she leans in really close to me. "I hope they give you more room than they gave me, but if they don't . . . fucking run. Okay? It'll be the best decision you ever make. I promise."

My eyes blink at her, taking in the intensity. "I don't think I'll have to run. I think they'll let me go on my own."

She smiles, studying me. Then she takes one last look around. "I'm happy for you. I'm glad you got help for your vaginismus."

"Me too," I say. "I've made a lot of progress with the dilators, but the only way I'll know if I'm cured is if I actually try to have sex."

She flinches. "Wait, did you just say the word *sex* in our parents' house?"

"It's not a bad word. My therapist says I shouldn't shy away from it."

Myracle nods with an amused smile. "Therapist? Great. No, yeah, Mom and Dad are completely different people now. *Therapist?*" She leads me out of her old room, arm around my shoulder. "Good for you, Mo-Mo."

346

I savor walking in this space again, in the crook of her side. Her body feels tiny beside mine. Too tiny. It feels like there's not enough of her to fill the gap between when she left and now. There's not enough of her to make me feel full, and to stop me from missing her. Even though she's right next to me. I press against her a little tighter.

I hope we can keep doing this forever. I hope we end up like Mom and Aunt Dee, always forgiving, always truthful with each other, and always pushing each other to be better.

"Oh!" I glance up at her as we cross through the living room. "I'm also writing a new story."

Her beautiful eyes widen. "You're writing again? Oh, thank God. I thought I was the only one still on that dream of ours."

I smile inside and out. "You remember that?"

"Of course I do. Did Aunt Dee tell you—"

"About your agent? Yes!" I squeal, squeezing her arm with mine. "Congratulations!"

"Thanks," she says, smiling. "When you get that book published, tell your people to hit me up for an illustration."

My people. I smile and laugh, feeling a path being carved out for me. I have to say, the future looks bright. It looks open and everything feels possible and nothing feels forced. The future finally feels like *mine.*

When we get back to the kitchen, Aunt Dee and Jackie have decided that they are crashing here tonight and they call Myracle over for a round of shots. My mom just shakes her head at them, profusely declining their invitation to join. Sasha's mom has agreed to drop Reggie off at home, and they're waiting for him in the car.

I walk Reggie to the door, but before opening it, I turn and hug him, hopping up on my tippy-toes, knotting my arms around his neck. He leans down, wrapping his arms around my back.

"I had a really good time," he says, spilling a little leftover laughter.

"Me too."

"I'm so happy you got to see your sister, and that I got to meet her."

I smile, biting down on my bottom lip. "Me too."

Then I untie my arms and fall back on my heels. He bends down, kisses my cheek, then dares to taste my mouth. Jesus, I've been missing his soft, full lips like crazy. I let my fingers fall down the front of his shirt.

My mom clears her throat from the living room, sweeping the hardwood with the broom. We pull away, averting our eyes, embarrassed, when my mom says, "Why don't you kids go out to see a movie or something? Your dad and I can hold it down here." Daddy stops behind her, letting her take the lead, because that's what he does now. He's come to learn that she has better judgment than him, and I've come to realize just how observant she is. We can't get away with *anything* when she's around.

But I guess she trusts us now. After weeks of these in-house dates, she trusts us.

"Okay, yeah." I smile. "Thanks, Mom."

Daddy grabs the broom from her and kisses her on the cheek. Then he says to us, "Be back by ten, Monique. No exceptions."

"Yes, sir." After I grab my keys, my purse, and my shoes, Reggie and I run to my car before they can change their minds.

36

His house is empty and dark when we pull into the driveway.

In the car I told him, "I think I want to try with you tonight."

His brows flew up. "Yeah? Are you ready?"

"I'm comfortable with the biggest dilator now. If I can get that monster in, I think I'm ready for anything."

He laughed lightly, then let his face fall back, serious. "Are you sure?"

"Yeah." I nodded, sneaking a taste of his lips. "Super sure."

But now that we're here, my nerves are holding my stomach hostage. I follow him up the porch steps in complete silence. He holds my hand, guiding me in the dark to his bedroom. He turns on the light and lets go of my hand. "You know, my mom is actually thinking about becoming a member of your church."

He paces inside, but I linger in the doorway. "My daddy's church. Not mine."

He spins around and nods at me. "Right." His eyes flick over my body with a smirk as he takes backward steps to his bed. "She's starting to really like your mom, and she obviously loves your aunt Dinah."

I roll my eyes, smiling. "Figures." I look around the room, at the absence of boxes on his floor. He's all unpacked now. His dresser drawers are full of clothes, and his pictures are sitting on top, along with his Magic 8 Ball. I walk over and pick it up, whispering to myself, *Should I have sex with Reggie tonight?* Then I shake it and wait.

Better not tell you now.

I frown. What does that mean?

When I look at Reggie, he's sitting on the edge of his bed, staring at me expectantly. "Well, what did it say?"

I shrug, disappointed. "Nothing."

"Well . . . what do you say?"

I avert my eyes and walk toward him sitting on the bed. "I don't know either." My footsteps are small and uneven.

"We don't have to do this," he reminds me, watching as I sit down next to him.

"I know. I want to. I'm just not sure how to . . . work our way up to that." Surely we can't just start having sex. We should start by kissing and slowly make our way through the bases. But knowing that sex is our destination makes even kissing seem challenging.

He's staring at his hands in his lap, a mile of mattress between us. "I don't think *I'm* ready for this, Mo."

"Oh?" I ask, surprised. It catches me off guard. I hadn't even considered that maybe he wasn't ready to have sex.

"I know you're excited," he says with a smile. "Excited to try out your new powers."

I smile, happy to know that he actually listens when I detail my visits with Dr. Wright.

"But I really want our first time to be a good experience. Maybe we should wait until we're more comfortable with each other's bodies. I mean, you still haven't even seen my . . ."

"Penis," I say. Dr. Wright always makes me say it. At this point, she's effectively removed the weirdness from the words *penis*, *vagina*, and *sex*.

Reggie smiles. "Yeah. That." He grabs my hand out of my lap. "Maybe we should wait until we don't have to question how to work our way up to it."

"I get that."

"Is that okay?" he asks.

"Of course." And maybe I'm a little relieved too. When I was in the car, and I said that I wanted to try with him, I really did want to. But once I got here, I didn't feel ready anymore, but I didn't want to go back on my word. I didn't want to disappoint him. . . .

I have to stop thinking like that! I have the right to say no at any point, I tell myself.

"So what do you want to do, then?" I ask.

He shrugs with a smile. "You wanna actually watch a movie?"

I smile, then laugh. To do what our parents think we're doing—why does that sound so fantastic? I guess because I've been doing enough sneaking around and lying for a lifetime. I like that my parents trust me, and I like that they're starting to trust Reggie. I don't want to break that trust so soon. And I like that he doesn't either.

As we're getting up to leave, I notice his sketch pad sitting on the floor among a bunch of colored pencils. "Any new sketches?" I ask, glancing at him over my shoulder.

"Why don't you go see?" He grins.

I kneel down and open the sketchbook, past the portrait of his mom, all the way to the back. My lips curl up and my eyes glisten. It's me, up in the tree in my backyard, looking down at him with the most honest smile I've ever seen on my face. I look over at him, biting down on a smile that's just as honest.

"I tried," he says, "but like I told you, your beauty is hard to capture."

"I think you did great." I stand up, holding the sketch in my hand. "Can I have it?"

"You want it?" he asks, surprised.

"More than anything."

Because look at how far I've come since then. And even when I was up in the tree, I'd come a long way. I took my time and made some tough decisions. I've been discovering who I am and what I want—and why I'm a catch.

Like Aunt Dee said, I'm a good tree climber. Like Reggie said, I'm full of surprises and I've got guts. Like Sasha said, I am more than what my body can do for other people. I'm open to new ideas and new definitions of what it means to have fun and what it means to be happy. I'm a writer, and maybe one day I'll be an actress-slash-model.

Whatever I decide, I'll decide because it's what I want for myself.

I stand up with his sketch in my hands. Then I follow him out of his bedroom to watch a movie—putting sex on the back burner. Sex can wait until Reggie's ready—until we're *both* sure that we're ready.

37

At home, I park behind Jackie's old Ford Taurus, and beside Aunt Dee's white BMW. The porch light is on, and when I get inside at ten p.m. on the dot, I flip it off.

"Mo, is that you?" my mom calls from the kitchen.

"Yes, ma'am."

"Come in here."

I cross through the living room, still floating on a cloud from Reggie's good-night kiss, but as I'm passing the couch, I spot a body laid out across the cushions. Then I see the short purple hair and I hear her snoring. *Wow.* She passed out early. Usually Aunt Dee can go all night.

In the kitchen, Mom's putting the leftover food into Tupperware. She looks at me over her shoulder. "Jackie is in your bed. Just sleep with your sister tonight."

"Oh, okay." I get so excited hearing *sleep with your sister tonight.* We used to sleep together all the time when we were kids, but when we got to be teens, it was much more rare. For good reason too, because Myracle and I would stay up way too late talking about absolutely nothing.

I'm turning away when Mom calls me back. She's standing behind the island, holding a stack of Tupperware. "Yeah?" I ask.

She tilts her head and smiles, light as a feather. "I'm really glad you and Reggie are taking it slow."

I freeze and stare at her like the witch she is. I mean, me and Reggie *just* decided to take it slow. What, does she have cameras following me around or something?

When I don't say anything, she grabs the Tupperware and walks it over to the fridge. "Reggie's a pretty good boy, huh?"

I smile at that. Finally, someone sees it. Finally, someone sees past his goofiness and his reputation and all the rumors to how genuinely good of a person he is. "Yeah," I say. "He's pretty great." I turn on my heel then. "Good night, Mom."

"Night, sweetie. I love you."

My footsteps falter and my lips twitch up into a smile. Usually we save "I love you" for when we're hanging up the phone or if we're in church. But right now, she says I love you so that I know no matter what, no matter if Reggie and I decide that taking it slow is too slow, or when we're finally thinking we're ready to give sex a try, she'll still love me. It's all I ever wanted to know. It's all I've ever needed. "I love you too," I say, flashing a smile over my shoulder, before heading to Myracle's old room.

Her door is open and the light is on. When I walk in, she's sitting on her bed with her sketch pad in her lap. Her pencil is scratching away when she looks up and smiles.

"Hey," I say. "Mom said I should crash with you tonight."

"Yeah, come on." She waves me inside, then pats her mattress. "Tell me about your date." I watch as she flips the page in her sketchbook, landing on a blank page just for me. Oh, how I remember ending so many of my nights like this. How I would tell her my stories, release my wild emotions, and she'd channel them into her pencil and let them fall splat on the page. How I've needed that. How I've needed to be able to unapologetically tell the truth, without fear of judgment or shame.

Myracle knew how to make me feel human.

I don't know how I've gone this long without her, but I don't think I can ever do another two years without having her in my life. I'm not sure about a lot yet. I haven't taken the time to weigh all my options. But I know one thing for sure: I will never let Myracle slip out of my life again. Nothing and no one can keep me from my sister.

I drop my purse on her bedroom floor and shut the door, so Mom can't accidentally overhear. As I make my way over to her mattress, I say, "Okay, so, we didn't even go to the movies. We went back to his house."

I lie on my back, stare up at her ceiling, and settle into the familiar sound of her pencil scratching against paper. I let it lull me into contentment—let it lull me back into believing that we'll always be together—*close* together. Because I know for sure that she's not going anywhere. Not if I can help it.

"Okay," Myracle says when I pause. "And then what happened?"

ACKNOWLEDGMENTS

Through all I've experienced while writing the daunting Book 2 (everything people say about Book 2 is entirely true), I have so many people to thank for helping me get here.

First, my superstar agent, Brianne Johnson: you help me stay sane. When I began this book, I was suffering heavily from imposter syndrome, but after one phone call from you, I felt invincible. Thank you for being my agent, my cheerleader, my fan, my *friend*. I'd follow you anywhere, no hesitation.

Thank you to my lovely editor, Alyson Day, and Aly's amazing assistant editor, Eva Lynch-Comer. I am so grateful for everything you two do for me and my brand within Harper, and I'm so lucky to have you on my team. You have fantastic instincts. Your ideas and suggestions always push me to be a better writer—I am forever grateful.

Thank you so much to everyone at HarperCollins—everyone who touched this book and everyone who cheered me on.

I am so grateful for your love and continued support. Thank you so much to Molly Fehr for always being on point with the designs, and to Mimi Moffie for this dreamy book cover. I fell in love the second I saw it, and I might have ugly cried just a smidge. It. Is. Everything.

Thank you to everyone at Hot Key Books. I am, once again, so grateful for all your support and all your fantastic ideas. Thank you, Tia Albert, for keeping me up to date with everything going on with *Confessions*. Thank you, Sophie, for another terrific design, and Rebecca Hope for a beautiful illustration— you two are so talented. I can't get enough of this cover! And to my lovely UK editor, Carla Hutchinson: I am your biggest fan, I swear. Everything you do is perfection. I am so proud of the moves you've made and so grateful for every second we got to work together. I miss you and your emails so much! Thank you, thank you, thank you!

Thank you to everyone at Writers House! Thank you to Alexandra Levick—so happy for you and everything you've got going on. Thank you to everyone at HG Literary for being so welcoming!

Now, I have to *thoroughly* thank my accounting work family. I miss you ladies so much! You all have taught me about myself and about life in very different, very specific ways. Honestly, my life changed after becoming a part of y'all's dynamic, and I'm so grateful for every second of it. A big thank you for your support of my writing career and the fact that you all would practically force any office visitors to buy my book.

Alexandria, Alexis, Alex, you were right—it *was* nice to meet you lol. Beautiful inside and out, your character is one I wish I could bottle and sprinkle throughout all my books. My dearest Annabelle, I totally get why children and animals always gravitate to you. They could sense your kind, loving, and *pure* spirit. Bethany, I learned so much about childbirth and motherhood (a lot of stuff that I didn't *want* to know) while being in the office, but watching you experience it firsthand was a pleasure. Cathy, thank you so much for joining me on the struggle bus every morning and for always being down for Jim's breakfast. Connie, thank you for always having answers to my I'm-barely-an-adult type questions. And thank you for helping me gear up to go hiking in Washington, even though I clearly wasn't cut out for it. Rebekah, my partner in crime. Your impressions were always spot-on (Tram, I'm sorry for laughing) and you've always got the perfect movie references for every situation, even though I'm always the one who has never seen it. Tram Coco, you were no doubt the Posh Spice of the group. You were quiet (like me), so strangers thought you were nice, but you were probably the most savage of us all (I'm still trying to get on your level). Our fearless leader, Viki: it makes sense that you were our leader because you would *literally* fight for any one of us. Get you and Cathy together, and it was over. Periodt. Thank you, ladies, for texting me through my first gynecologist visit. I love you guys!

Thank you, Jami and Kelsey, for giving me detailed descriptions of your first time at the gynecologist during that period when I was too terrified to go. Thank you, Mom, for answering my random questions about church and church songs. Thank you, Forrest Red (Fred), for my debut author photos. Thank you, Sir Horace Saulsberry, for my dream witchy photo shoot. Thank you to my big sister and my best friend, Taylor, for being pillars in my life.

Kelsey: you're one of the kindest people I know. You completely changed my life when you opened up about the struggles you were having with sex. You introduced me to the term *vaginismus* and to dilators and, within a month, I was able to control the physical aspect of vaginismus. I am forever grateful for you.

Finally, Blake Clark: I love you so much. We have gone through so much together—some of that being vaginismus—and I'm so very proud of where we've ended up in our relationship. Thank you so much for all the times you've effortlessly helped me figure out plot issues and brainstormed solutions with me. You're such a key component of my writing, and I'm so grateful to have you on my team and in my life.